ANGELA CRAY
GETS REAL

DARA CARR

MARVELOUS MAYHEM BOOKS

ANGELA CRAY GETS REAL

Cover design by Design for Writers

ISBN: 978-0-9995267-0-5
eISBN: 978-0-9995267-1-2

This book is dedicated to my father, Don Carr, and the memory of my mother, Millie Carr

I SAY, BEWARE OF ALL ENTERPRISES THAT REQUIRE NEW CLOTHES, AND NOT RATHER A NEW WEARER OF CLOTHES.
—Henry David Thoreau, *Walden*

1

***

Monday morning

My new boss is a lawyer, and that is not on my mother's list of acceptable professions, most lawyers being spawn from Satan's anus. My mother, Moorea, and I tend to agree on this point but I'm inclined to be flexible for a paycheck.

So it's my first day of work for Monalisa Walker. I haven't even started yet and it's already promising to be one of the weirdest jobs I've ever held. And being unskilled, under-educated, and an all-star underperformer, I've had some truly exceptional employment experiences.

In the rude early light of morning, at an hour I try to avoid as it does nothing for my natural beauty and charm, my mother is asking me some pointed questions. Moorea is a master at this sort of thing. Nothing escapes her notice. She is an emergency room nurse, which is like the Navy SEALS of the nursing profession. She has an ironclad grip on reality.

Me, I could take or leave reality, mostly leave it, particularly first thing in the blazing light of a fine spring morning in Phoenix. This has been especially the case since I dropped out of a nursing program, then got fired from a job and hit the skids, losing my apartment and car, and, horror of all horrors, moved back in with my mother.

Technically, my current occupation is disgraced former medical day spa professional. Since there aren't too many openings for people with my unusual mix of skills and experience I've had to get creative. Creative being another word for desperate.

As Moorea interrogates the suspect, moi, it is becoming clear I haven't done basic due diligence with my new employer. I hate when Moorea is right. And of course she's almost always right.

Moorea asks, "How much money is that woman going to pay you?"

That would be a good question, especially since I don't know the answer. I didn't even ask. When Monalisa said she could use my help finding a missing fiancé with cold feet, she pretty much had me right there.

I pour some coffee and try a diversionary tactic. "Uncle Hiro called yesterday. He may need to borrow some more money."

Moorea frowns. Her stepbrother, the subject of hours of tedious family Skype conversations, works in a tuna cannery. Sometimes the family worries about him keeping the job. Other times, if Hiro seems to be enjoying a stretch of sobriety, they wonder if he will ever secure better employment. He's one of Moorea's few remaining relatives in American Samoa, which is where she was born. He never got off the "rock," not having a talent for football or inclination for the military, the two main avenues for men.

You'd think she'd have some mellow Pacific Islander genes in her. A flexible attitude toward time. An amused tolerance toward failure. No such luck. Plus, she doesn't have any of the tender-hearted, mush-brained leniency of mainland American parents either. She has a steely immigrant mentality when it comes to jobs. Acceptable professions: doctor, nurse, teacher, accountant, engineer.

I suppose those are perfectly fine professions if they happen to suit you.

I put a lot of sugar into my coffee. In two and a half years, when I turn thirty, I will probably have to give up this habit. Type 2 diabetes runs in my DNA.

Moorea has no answer for my Uncle Hiro comment. She parries with an indirect query: "How did you find out about this job anyway?"

I drink some of my coffee. It needs more sugar. I know where my mother is heading with these questions. She thinks Monalisa is selling drugs or running a pornography ring. After all, why else would Monalisa want to hire me?

I could try to defend Monalisa and mention the accounting degree she has along with the law degree but, instead, I spoon more sugar into my coffee.

Moorea's hands are on her hips. "Angela? Ann-gel-laaaaa, are you listening to me?"

"I ran into Monalisa and told her I was sorry about the passing of her grandma," I replied. "She said her grandma always spoke so highly of me. I think her exact words were 'sang my praises.' Anyway, Monalisa said she could use some help."

Moorea's head angles dangerously. "Just what kind of help does that woman need?"

I tell her what I know, which has to do with tracking down a groom-to-be who has ghosted a month before the big date.

"You've got to admit," I say, "I have a talent for finding this type of man."

"Do you find them or do they find you?" Moorea asks.

This is an awfully deep question for first thing in the morning.

"It seems like a good opportunity," I reply.

Moorea makes a low humming noise, the sound of an Apache helicopter looming over the horizon. "You're no longer a child. You've got to be realistic."

She says "realistic" as if it's a good thing. What's real: dust bowl breath, early mornings, raw kale. Being realistic for a moment, I would have to conclude that I'm a pity hire. Monalisa feels sorry for me and knows that I was close to her grandma, closer than she ever was.

"Aren't you happy I'm finally going to be working again?"

Well into the dark side of my twenties, my job history is not impressive. Truth is, I don't know and I don't care why Monalisa wants to hire me. I'd do anything to get my repossessed red Honda Coupe back. It's calling to me: *Take me back home, Angela. I miss you.* Unlike so many of my experiences with men, the feelings between the Coupe and me were totally mutual.

Moorea, not to be ignored, stomps on my Honda Coupe love buzz. Naturally, being a devout Christian, her thoughts drift toward vice. "It's something illegal isn't it? Are you going to have to take off your clothes?"

"Of course not."

Sadly, my last job has left my mother to fear the worst. My former boss is in Camp Fed, a cosmetic dermatologist busted for using bootleg Botox, among other things.

Moorea changes course. She goes for the heartstrings, not realizing I have no heart left, let alone any strings.

"Honey," she says, her voice dusted with medicated baby powder, "Why don't you come back with me to church?"

I gaze at her, puzzled. Although I've turned up for the occasional barbecue at the Samoan Christian church, unable to resist a good suckling pig and papaya pudding, it has been six years since I attended services. Moorea usually doesn't mention church except at my lowest, most desperate points. I did not think I was that low.

Have I lost my compass? I give myself a thorough once-over.

Cream blazer, black bi-stretch crop pants, patent leather sling-backs. Long, dark hair perfectly ironed. This morning I even managed my makeup brushes like a true artist, with nary a smear or a do-over as I gave my round face some subtle contour and made my hazel eyes pop with a wing flick of plum liner. I may be a lost soul but, thankfully, I do not look like one. I am dressed for success; this is one of my talents.

Moorea levels her blazing spotlight eyes on me, waiting for an answer. Church. To think how many years I spent praying she would come with a dimmer switch.

"Great goddess of the sun, moon, and sea," I say, training my eyes upward, invoking the deities of our distant ancestors, those deities predating that pushy nouveau Christian religion. "Please give me strength against so many questions. Goddess of mirages, Kuku Lau, keep me clear-eyed and grounded—"

"You're heading down the wrong path."

"Lesa, god of plenty, thank you for this new job I am about to receive."

"We prayed for you at church."

"Even more reason to stay away."

Of course I love my dad who art in heaven but that's a different story altogether.

I finish my sugar coffee. Moorea follows me to the door, rubbing her strong, calloused hands. "Don't you do anything illegal. I don't care how much she pays you."

I walk out the door then pause and flash her my medical day spa smile, a smile that says, welcome to paradise, will you be using Visa or Mastercard?

"Why must your mind always be in the gutter?"

Moorea slowly shakes her head. "I hate to see you make so many mistakes. This so-called job has no security. No future."

Thinking about the future gives me a hangover: nausea, headache, the works.

"It's a paycheck."

As I step onto the walk, she tosses one last grenade. "I hear she bites."

Bites? I pause. "Boo bites?"

Boo is Monalisa's pit bull, who has always been the picture of amiability with me. If Boo bites, that would be important to know, especially in a home office environment.

Moorea gives me a look. "No, I'm not talking about Boo, who is male. I'm talking about Monalisa. She bites."

Before I can get another word out, Moorea, satisfied she has my attention, swings the door shut. *Thanks, Mom.* We love each other, we really do. Sometimes I'd even go as far as to say we like each other.

THE BEST THING so far about my new job with Monalisa is that I can walk to the office. Time will tell if it offers other important perks, such as sufficient earnings to bankroll my re-entry into the wonderful world of Milano gimlets and one-bedroom apartments. How I'd love to drink my favorite breakfast beverages of sugar coffee and strawberry lemonade Pedialyte in peace, without Moorea circling, assaulting me with perfectly reasonable questions about my future.

Monalisa works out of a house that she inherited from her grandma Iona. I could walk the three blocks to the house blindfolded. Iona and I were tight.

I let myself through the front gate and nod to the eyeless stone lions flanking either side of the porch steps. *Greetings dear Archie and Humboldt, good to see you're still at your posts.* They don't respond, being strong, silent types and consummate security professionals. Still, I know they're pleased to see me. I maintain excellent relationships with nearly all the major inanimate objects in my life.

At the door, Monalisa stares for a moment, as if she's trying to place me: *How do I know this person? She looks awfully familiar. Could it be I just hired her?*

"Angela," I say, offering a hopeful smile as my bubble bursts. Monalisa seems to have forgotten that it's my first day of work. She stares at me without making eye contact. It's not exactly an unfriendly gaze. It's as though she's gathering data. On another planet, I imagine advanced beings might greet each other by sensor rather than smiles and eye contact and meaningless chitchat. They read each other's stress hormone levels and adjust accordingly. Monalisa isn't odd; she's merely from somewhere galaxies and light years away.

She is, sadly, nothing like Iona, whose idea of a greeting was a bear hug.

On the other hand, Monalisa's white pit bull, Boo, is enormously welcoming, maybe even a little too excited to see me. Behind Monalisa, he is practically doing somersaults. As Monalisa peers out at me, gathering data, she also blocks Boo from giving me a proper pit bull welcome, part hug and part tackle.

"Hi Boo," I say, inspiring an even more fevered frenzy. If Boo desires my company, maybe Monalisa will decide it's a good idea to have me inside.

Seconds later, Monalisa finally invites me to come into the house. I wait in the hallway while she stows Boo somewhere in the back, then I follow her into what used to be Iona's TV and knitting room, which Monalisa now uses as an office. Although Monalisa swapped out Iona's aqua velvet loveseat for some sleek black furniture, the temperature still registers old lady sauna. I slip off my blazer as Monalisa offers me some stuff called Krakus to drink. She says it's fresh and healthy, two qualities that aren't major attractions for me in a beverage. But needing all the help I can get and morbidly curious about whether Krakus tastes as nasty as it sounds I say yes.

One sip later and the words *intestinal cleanse* pop into my head, completely unbidden. Could it really be that bad? I take another drink. Yes, it could.

I am searching for a nice houseplant that might need some Krakus when my eye snags on a tall wooden sword casually propped against the back wall. This is a new addition to Iona's knitting and TV room. Made from a honey-colored wood, with a snub tip, it looks more useful as a club than an impaling device. Home security? Hobby?

Boo, freshly escaped from wherever Monalisa stowed him, slinks into the room and noses around my feet. Might Boo like a little taste of Krakus? It's healthy! He gazes up at me, one eye blue and the other eye brown. I decide that, no, Krakus is not fit for dog consumption. Besides, I need all the friends I can make.

Monalisa glances at Boo, sighs, and hands me an iPad. "Before we begin, I need you to sign some documents. Basically, you need to agree that everything that happens on this job is confidential. This means no telling anyone, not your mom or your friends or Facebook, Instagram, Snapchat or Twitter. The only exception is if I give you permission and that would need to be in print and signed by me."

She blathers on: blah protect confidentiality, blah, confidentiality, blah. I start to click through pages on the iPad, tapping the screen where the line is highlighted.

Monalisa holds up a hand. "You need to read the pages before you sign them. I want you to understand what you're signing."

I look at her. Seriously? If Monalisa, a lawyer and an accountant, wants me to sign crap, I'll sign it. If she thinks I can afford a lawyer to review these for me, she's nuts.

Monalisa frowns. "You should always read legal documents before you sign them."

I pretend to read. "Do you have any of these documents in English?"

Her lips press inward. Her alien sensor eyes sweep my head and body, searching for signs of intelligent life.

"Sorry, joke," I say.

After I finish signing the screens, I fill out a formal employment application and some tax forms. A few minutes later, I am done. I leave out most of my employment experiences. So sue me. I'm protecting my own confidentiality. I also don't see fit to mention nursing school. Sick people and me: not a good combination.

Monalisa sits behind her desk, staring at a Mac laptop. My gaze strays to the right, where some shelves hold Iona's collection of salt-and-pepper shakers. This is the first time I've been in the house since Iona's death, and I'm relieved to see her collection still intact. The shakers I gave her, a pair of professional wrestlers grappling with each other, are front and center. Iona and I used to watch professional wrestling together. She loved the masked Lucha Libre fighters. On wrestling nights, she'd pour 7-Up and set out some maraschino cherries, and we'd cheer as Psicosis battled Blue Demoncito Jr.

Below the shelves sits a cabinet that used to hold Iona's postcard collection, which she kept in grey acid-free binders. Iona proudly called herself a deltiologist, a postcard collector. Deltiology may have seemed an odd choice of hobby for someone who never traveled, who never experienced the slightest bit of wanderlust, but she was an exceptionally easy-to-please collector, delighted even at the most basic postcard of a Saguaro. I glance at Monalisa, wondering if I should ask about the postcards.

She looks up at me. "Done?"

I nod, handing her back the iPad. I decide not to ask about Iona's postcards, fearful that I won't be able to say Iona's name out loud without crumpling.

Monalisa says, "I specialize in forensic accounting. Do you know what that means?"

Something about numbers and death? I don't dare answer and potentially expose my ignorance, so I shake my head, failing the first big question of my new job.

Monalisa nods, as if expecting this answer, and glances at her watch. "I'll have to explain later. There's not enough time today."

How stupid does she think I am? It's Monday morning. We've got hours and hours of blazing, desert daylight ahead to discuss forensic accounting.

And then I hit on the right answer. "I can research it on the internet."

"That's okay," Monalisa says, flicking her hand. "You won't be working with me on those cases. I need your help in another area. Since I've gone into business, I've been getting other types of requests. I'll be frank. It's like someone wrote my name and number on the wall of a lunatic asylum."

I am beginning to see where I come into the picture. "Really?"

"No. But sometimes I wonder. I don't know where people get their ideas about me."

I have some thoughts on this matter but keep my mouth shut. My mother is a shameless gossip even though she pretends to be above such frivolity.

Monalisa continues, "Right now, I have one matter I need your help with."

"Great," I say. "That's why I'm here."

Boo wags his tail. I would be wagging my tail if I had one.

"Normally it's not the sort of thing I would handle. As I told you before, it seems to be some sort of civil dispute. But I agreed to look into it as a favor to a friend, who practically begged me to help her niece." Monalisa's expression turns almost apologetic. "She's my only friend so I have little choice but to assist. I've never even met the niece."

Only friend? Good goddess. Maybe there's a good reason she works solo. Maybe the two of us deserve each other, the employer and employee of last resort.

"Yes," I say, trying to look encouraging.

"It seems like it should be a straightforward matter, a small job, and Iona told me you were so enterprising and bright—"

The doorbell rings. Boo barks and runs toward the door then back to the office.

Monalisa says, "Here she is now."

Monalisa gazes at me then toward the front door. That would be my cue.

"I'll get it."

As I enter the front hallway, I wonder whether this is it: I'm the door answerer. A step down from day spa employee, but a job is a job is a job.

I open the door, smiling like a good house girl, serious first day game on. On the doorstep stands this sourpuss about my age, with electrocuted hair and warpath eyes. Even as she emanates negativity, her skin is a marvel, an even medium brown with caramel undertones. She hit the Afro-Caribbean jackpot with this skin. Although impressed, I sweep aside these day spa observations and greet her in a conventional, businesslike manner. She tells me her name is Ms. Edmonds and that she's got an appointment with Ms. Walker.

I tell her I'm Angela Fareani Cray, and I'll be taking her in to see Ms. Walker.

Boo's legs seem to have turned into springs as he prances around us.

"Boo sweetie, chill," I say as I lead Ms. Edmonds into the office, where she shakes hands with Monalisa and sits down. Ms. Edmonds stares at Boo.

Through her eyes, it may not appear obvious that Boo is a lover and not a fighter. He is a stout white pit bull with a warrior's low center of gravity and a muscled jaw that could tenderize a live steer.

"Don't worry," I say. "He's very gentle with people."

Monalisa shakes her head. "Only when I'm around."

I give Monalisa a look: *Thanks for making our client feel at home.* She gazes back at me, her expression bland, apparently unaware that pit bulls scare the bejesus out of most people.

"Boo," I say, pointing to Monalisa. "Go."

With a high, sorrowful whine, Boo drags himself away from his new friend Ms. Edmonds and returns to Monalisa's side.

I ask, "Would you like some water, Ms. Edmonds?" Krakus isn't on offer until we know her a lot better.

"Yes thank you," she says. "Please call me Charise."

I decide Charise is okay, especially now that we're on a first-name basis.

When I return with the water, Monalisa has a notebook and pen waiting for me on the edge of her desk. I pull up another chair and grab the notebook. Door answerer and note-taker. Better and better. *Look Mom: all my clothes are still on!*

Charise drinks some water and gazes around the room, pausing at the built-in shelves housing Iona's collectibles.

"Love the purple unicorn salt-and-pepper shakers," she says.

"This was my grandmother's house," Monalisa says, perhaps by way of explanation. "I moved in a few weeks ago but there's a lot of her still here. How can we help you?"

We! We. I write this down. So far so good. I am going to ace this gig. It's going to be different than my other jobs.

"First, thanks for seeing me. My aunt said you're the smartest person she knows."

Monalisa gives the slightest of nods to acknowledge the compliment.

"I'm here because my fiancé is missing," Charise says. "He's been gone since Thursday night. He's not answering calls or texts or e-mails."

I can't help but think, missing or run off?

Monalisa asks, "How do you know he's missing?"

Bam! This is one of those innocent questions that's all sugar plums on the surface then grows hairy spikes the more you think about it. My mother also excels at those.

Charise studies a chipped nail, and I can't help but notice she is overdue for a mani.

"I've talked to his friends and colleagues. They haven't seen or heard from him, either. And..."

Her voice trails off. I stare at Charise. Her mouth is doing funny things. Her shoulders are lifting up, getting ready for take-off. Hairball? Something is caught inside there, something she doesn't want to come out.

On impulse, I ask, "Who saw him last?"

Charise's cheeks puff. "On Thursday night, he was seen leaving American Egg with these two Lady Gaga types."

I write, "Hmmm."

American Egg is an all-night diner where many a young woman's heart has been crushed.

"Gaga types?" Monalisa asks, her expression blank.

"Two women," Charise says. "Dressed like Lady Gaga. Someone put the whole thing on YouTube."

Monalisa's mouth is ajar. I suspect she's never even heard of Lady Gaga.

I lean forward. "The pop singer, Lady Gaga."

Charise pipes up. "They were wearing these Marie Antoinette wigs and spiked heels. You know, showing everything the store has for sale."

Monalisa gives me a helpless look, struggling to find a life preserver in this sea of nonsense. "Is this Gaga look a fashion?"

I perk up, knowing the answer to this one. That's me: door answerer, note-taker, youth expert!

"No, it's not a fashion choice like punk or goth. No one goes out dressed like Lady Gaga. Exceptions are Halloween and maybe celebrity lookalike night at Roxxs, where you get free entry and half-price drinks in costume."

Monalisa's eyes drift away. All that brainpower, trying to process some seriously empty calories. When she returns from her mini-retreat, she asks, "What time did the encounter between your fiancé and these two women take place?"

"Around eight at night," Charise says. "With his schedule, we rarely eat at the same time. He'd just gotten off his shift."

Oh, Charise. From my vantage point, it is easy to see that the goddess has given Charise a wonderful gift. This would be the gift of knowledge, of knowing this man is no good before she marries him. Charise may not be ready, however, to accept this gift.

There's a place for girls in this condition. It is not here, making our acquaintance, telling her tale of woe to two paid listeners. No. Charise needs to be checking into the reality hotel and paying a visit to the move-on lounge, where Bloody Marys are on special 24:7.

I know this because I have so been there myself. Luckily, I now live with my mom, one of the biggest buzz kills on the planet.

"Do you have reason to believe he's still with these women?" Monalisa asks.

Charise shakes her head slowly. "I know this sounds crazy, but I believe he's been abducted. The women were decoys that lured him outside. I can't think of any other explanation."

Oh, goddess, please help Charise. I'll bet no one else has any difficulty coming up with a perfectly reasonable explanation for her fiancé's disappearance.

"Why would anyone abduct your fiancé?" Monalisa asks.

"I don't know." Charise rubs her temples. "None of this makes any sense. Kevin is responsible and trustworthy. He's not a womanizer. What's the opposite of a player?"

I think for a moment. Dead? Monalisa shakes her head. She doesn't know, either.

Charise continues, "Anyway, he's the opposite of a player. The worst thing I can say about him is that he washes his hands too often."

"He hasn't been back at work?" Monalisa asks.

Charise shakes her head again. "He's finished with his residency in anesthesiology. Last Thursday, he was stepping in for someone else. He doesn't start his new position for two months. During his break, we're supposed to get married and go to Italy for our honeymoon."

Monalisa's moon rock eyes betray no emotion. Meanwhile, my toes curl. I gaze at the floor, at the Beech hardwoods Monalisa has installed in place of Iona's peeling linoleum, and an ember of sympathy sparks from the ashes in the cavity where my heart used to reside.

Charise presses ahead: "He's never been in any trouble his entire life. Seriously."

No trouble his entire life? I would say that's a big problem right there.

Monalisa sits back in her chair. "What does his family think?"

"That he's taking a timeout. To me, this is a little more than a timeout. He was last seen leaving a restaurant with two women. He hasn't been home in almost four days. He hasn't been in touch." She bites her lower lip. "We've been living together about six weeks. Honestly, it's been an adjustment for both of us. That's normal, right?"

Monalisa probably would not be the best judge of normal. I nod, trying to be encouraging.

"My dad thinks Kevin has cold feet about the wedding, which is next month." Charise holds up her left hand. A monster rock glitters on the ring finger. "Does this look to you like cold feet?"

It looks to me like a ticket to Italy and then some. *Take that big diamond and run!* My texting finger is itchy. I am dying to tell my friends. *Run, Charise, run!*

Monalisa ignores the dazzling hardware and asks, "Do you have access to his bank account and credit cards?"

"I handle our finances. There haven't been any credit card charges since Thursday night. He's made no ATM withdrawals."

"Is it possible he has a credit card or account you don't know about?"

Charise's lips fold inward. Her eyes lift to heaven. Oh no. Tears. I get up and grab a tissue box from a side table and offer it to her. She clutches the box in her lap.

After the waterworks, she blots her face and says, "I suppose anything's possible. After buying the engagement ring, it's not like he has buckets of money around."

"What about his car?" I ask. "Is it still at American Egg?"

Charise shakes her head. "It's gone too."

I nod and glance at Monalisa, who wears a pensive expression. I'm thinking that it's time we stop this charade. Finding that fiancé is not going to help Charise. Pretending he's been abducted could make things worse. I would not be in the business of parting fools from their money, particularly this kind of fool from her money. I know full well what it is like to be this kind of fool.

Charise hunches over and sniffles.

Then again, she looks like she could use some help. In fact, she looks miserable, with mascara smeared across her cheeks. She doesn't even know how to cry pretty. If she wants to know where this loser is, who am I to stop her? I can't presume to know what is best for her. Some people go to therapists; others go to forensic accountants.

No one speaks for a moment. Monalisa looks like she'd rather be reading a spreadsheet. Boo has snuck away from Monalisa's side, and is gently nosing around Charise's ankles.

"I assume you've contacted the police?" Monalisa asks.

This gets a harsh laugh and an eye roll. "They're stopping at nothing to find him. SWAT teams, detectives at the airport, road blockades. In case none of this works, I've come to you."

"We're flattered," Monalisa says, with a ghost of a smile.

The attempt at humor scoots right past Charise, who blows her nose and says, "I'm going to kill him. Seriously."

I write: "Kill that cheater!" *Yes, Charise, that's the spirit. I can almost hear the proud blast of a conch shell horn through the air. Hark, Charise is rising from the ashes of misery!*

"It's going to take Jesus Christ and all the apostles to bring him back after I finish with him."

Go, Charise, go!

Monalisa steeples her hands on her desk. Her alien eyes are at it again, gazing at Charise as if they're trying to determine the iron level in her blood.

"Now it sounds like you think he's run off with these women," she says.

Charise sniffles. "No. He didn't run off."

I sigh. Charise seemed to be rallying for a few beats. But, in her lovesick state, she's no match for the siren song of denial.

Charise's gaze shifts from Monalisa to me then back again. "I've known Kevin for almost ten years. I know him. Something bad has happened. It must have."

Monalisa leans forward. "If you hire us, we have to look into all possible explanations for his disappearance."

Charise blows her nose. "He's been lured away and abducted."

"Yet you can't think of any apparent motive for someone to abduct your fiancé."

This strikes me as a perfectly reasonable yet devastating comment, which should hit Charise like a slap in the face. I glance at Charise, who is shaking her head, eyes trained on her lap. I watch for signs the question is penetrating her lovesick, delusional state: head up, eyes wide, mouth hanging open as realization hits.

Doesn't happen.

"He wouldn't just leave without a word," she says.

"He may come back on his own in a few days. You're certain you want to pay us to track his whereabouts?" Monalisa asks.

"I have to know," Charise says. "Have you ever loved someone so much it hurt?"

Monalisa's face is a polite mask.

Charise turns to me. I nod. Oh yes. I'm thinking: the cosmetic dermatologist. The jailbird. My former boss. I loved that man.

Charise looks back at Monalisa. "The kind of love that tears right through you?"

Yes! Yes, Charise! But this is the kind of love that probably shouldn't be spoken of in the righteous House of Iona.

"The kind of love, a love so—" Charise makes a low, throaty noise. Boo barks.

"No, I can't say I have," Monalisa says.

Boo wags his tail, a full body shimmy that jangles his collar. He spins around in a circle, then races out of the room and returns with a red ball in his mouth.

Monalisa stares into space, giving this some serious thought. A moment later, she says, "I love Boo."

Boo rushes to her side, ready to catch all that love. Monalisa extracts the ball from his massive jaw. He places his paws on her lap. They rub noses.

Charise's eyes narrow. "You love your pit?"

"He's like a family member to me."

Charise and I exchange a look, both of us probably figuring that, big picture, Monalisa is going to be the happiest girl of all. You could do way worse than Boo. I know this for a fact.

Charise shrugs. "Maybe it's better you don't understand. I need someone with a cool head, someone who can bring their brain to this party."

Monalisa gives Boo another pat. "We'll find out what happened to Kevin. Angela will look into this under my close supervision. She'll document everything."

Did she just say my name? Angela. I look up and smile. Wait, I'm going to be investigating this? I sit up straighter. And then I think, document everything?

I look at my notes. No. This can't be! No.

I have documented squat.

I take a deep breath. Luckily, I have a fine memory for juicy details. And I may have found the one gig where juicy details count for something.

2

*A*fter talking business, Monalisa hands Charise the iPad to review and sign documents. The hourly rate sets my mind whirring. Fingers working, Charise signs away.

Monalisa sighs, giving her a pained look. "Are you reading what you're signing?"

"I don't have a mind for anything right now," Charise says, gazing at us through hundred-year-old eyes.

Monalisa's mouth droops. Her alien sensors have failed to detect intelligent life on this strange planet we call earth.

After Charise hands her back the iPad, Monalisa says, "Before you go, could you give us a list of Kevin's family and friends and their contact details?"

Family and friends? I have been planning to hunt down the two Lady Gaga lookalikes, who would seem to be ground zero in this hot mess. They shouldn't be too difficult to locate in Phoenix, standing out amid the golfers, palm trees and retirees.

"I've already talked to Kevin's friends and his colleagues at the hospital," Charise says. "They say they haven't heard from him. His buddy, Temple, offered to help search. Those two are tighter than white on rice. If Temple doesn't know where he is, no one does."

"You've been thorough." Monalisa rubs her chin.

"I also called around to see if he was hospitalized or arrested."

Monalisa looks slightly puzzled. "Who's left? His family?"

"I also talked to his family but I think they know something they're not saying."

I stifle a comment. Of course his family does. They know he's a faithless loser.

"You want to see if we get further with his family than you did," Monalisa says.

Charise shrugs. "They're not super excited about Kevin marrying me."

"Why not?" I ask.

"I've never asked them directly." She manages a tight little smile. "But I suspect they'd prefer a blue-eyed blond for Kevin."

Immediately I understand that Kevin's family is white. Sadly, their attitudes toward Charise don't surprise me. I've tasted more than my fair share from the undercooked part of the American melting pot.

To me, I've always just been Angela, a person like any other. In grade school, I still remember how confused I was the first time I was asked about my native costume and teased about being a cannibal. By twelfth grade, I'd heard this sort of thing for years. As an adult, it hasn't entirely gone away. I'm always being asked where I'm from. I swear I'm watched more closely in stores, no matter how impeccable I keep my hair and nails. The crazy thing is that I've never even been to American Samoa, and Moorea left when she was a teenager.

Monalisa clears her throat. "How many family members of his do we need to engage with?"

"Three," Charise says in a soft voice, looking a little embarrassed.

"Three?" Monalisa asks.

"His mom, his brother, and his uncle," she says. "His dad passed a few years ago."

"No cousins or grandparents?"

"No. His uncle doesn't have any children. His father was an only child. His grandparents are gone."

Monalisa glances at me. "Very doable."

Charise pulls an iPhone from her Coach bag. It's a nice bag, lavender Napa leather. Even if she doesn't know how to cry pretty, she does have some fashion sense.

As she works her iPhone, I sip some Krakus out of boredom. Boo finds his way over to me and starts panting.

"Boo," Monalisa says, "we'll go out in a few minutes. How about that?"

Boo bounds over to her but still gazes at me, mouth open. I take a long drink of Krakus, pretending to savor it. *Yum. This is what you're missing, Boo!*

A few minutes later, Charise e-mails us contact information for Kevin's close family. She gives me an apologetic look. "I've got to warn you about Kevin's mom. She's got a personality that could take the rust off a pipe."

Monalisa glances at me. "Don't worry. Angela is great with people."

Me? Truthfully, my best relationships are with dead people and inanimate objects. I wonder when I should disclose this to my new employer.

I admit I am good with some people. Out of necessity, I learned to handle seriously pissed off women who paid good money for Botox and got a fake that gave them no results or, worse, gnarly infections at the injection site. Mostly, these were members of the day spa's frequent frowners club, who, after five Botox appointments, got the sixth visit for free. Hell hath no fury like a frequent frowner. In any other setting, say, a battlefield, I would have won medals for my performance. Unfortunately, as I eventually learned, I was defending the wrong side.

After I walk Charise to the door, I return to the office and sit down. Boo rushes to greet me, excited to reunite after an absence of approximately thirty seconds.

Monalisa rests her forearms on her desk. "What do you think?"

I pick my jaw off the floor. Think? No one pays me to do that. I am strictly ornamental.

She gazes at me, waiting. This wasn't a rhetorical question. She actually wants me to think. Well, let's see. I start up the rusty machine, blowing some cobwebs out of the engine.

"I think Charise is in a sorry place."

"You think Kevin is still with the two women?"

I catch the doubt in Monalisa's use of the word "still."

"Maybe he's still with one of them." In my professional opinion, a threesome wouldn't have much lasting power over the course of a few days.

"How about the response of his family?"

"His mom doesn't like Charise. She's probably relieved he's taken off."

Monalisa lets the silence grow between us.

I brace myself before saying, "Shall I go over to the American Egg and ask some questions about the so-called abduction?"

I do not want to go to the American Egg, where I have some history. But I am the consummate professional.

"Yes, that could be helpful."

I sense she has more to say. Her gaze drifts out the front window. I crane my neck around, tracing her gaze.

Iona's Mister Lincoln roses are in bloom, the deep red petals fiery in the sun. Nearby, a plastic all-weather doe noses the base of a Palo Blanco tree. I'm surprised Monalisa hasn't yet ditched Iona's lawn decor for river rocks or something more Zen. Personally, I would leave everything alone, both as a memorial to Iona and as a burglar deterrent. Those lawn ornaments tell even the dumbest criminals that an ancient person lives inside with yellowing newspapers and heavy, analog-era electronics.

A moment later, Monalisa says, "You can begin with the American Egg and see if you learn anything. But I think the family knows Kevin's whereabouts. In that respect, this is a straightforward case. A really good starter case." She massages her knuckles. "The trick is going to be getting this information out of them."

"I'll get it from them," I say. "Whatever it takes."

Boo wags his tail.

Monalisa smiles. Finally. "Welcome aboard, Angela."

BEFORE I LEAVE THE OFFICE, Monalisa tells me to make sure I record my hours. Turns out, I work off-site and only need to check-in at the office as necessary. But I tell her I will check-in often with her. This is my first assignment, I explain. She agrees. I do not tell her that I am not to be trusted with too much freedom.

She reminds me not to forget to document my mileage as well. Mileage. I manage a weak smile, feeling a dull ache from deep in my pelvic cradle, the pain of losing my Honda Coupe.

On the walk home, I check out the YouTube video starring Kevin, which is posted as, "Two Lady Gaga Lookalikes Grab Guy." Charise thoughtfully included a video link in her e-mailed contact list for Kevin's family.

The screen is tough to see in the desert sun. At the end of the block, I find some shade under a palm tree. The video has received forty-six reviews, mostly from heavy mouth-breathers. To wit:

"Grease me up! One for each end."

"Give me more eggs, baby, yeah."

"Poindexter gets lucky! Dawg."

"I'll take what he's having."

The video shows two Lady Gaga impersonators strutting into the main dining area of American Egg, wearing mile-high wigs and black stiletto heel booties. The heels must be five inches on those suckers. These outfits are not for amateurs.

Not surprisingly, there's jeering and pointing. Some people clink their forks against glass, like they're at a wedding and want someone to give a toast. Little do they know this scene probably marks the end of someone's dreams of marital bliss.

One of the Gaga impersonators pulls a plastic gun out of a lace garter and points it at Kevin. The gun is obviously fake, and there's laughter from other patrons. Kevin doesn't look shocked or happy or scared. I think I can detect the slightest hint of an amused smile on his face but I wouldn't swear to it. Mostly, he gazes at them like he sees Gaga lookalikes all the time. Maybe his work at the hospital is a lot more colorful than I imagine. It seems to take a lot to impress this man.

In the end he gets up and goes with the Gagas. They don't grab him by the arms and drag him out of there. One of the Gagas loops an arm around his shoulder, which is awfully friendly as far as abductions go. The other struts behind them, waving the toy gun in the air and grinning. This appears to be fun and games among consenting adults.

For the moment, I think I've seen enough. But I'll double check later. I owe it to Charise to make sure I'm on every last detail.

Some great catch Kevin turned out to be. An anesthesiologist. In the grand fishery of the dating world, he'd be a blue marlin. Smart, good earner, family hours.

Moorea would have a contrary opinion on this matter. She told me never to date a doctor, that there's something seriously wrong with every single one of them. This aligns with my experience with the cosmetic dermatologist. Of course I had to find out for myself. As Moorea is fond of saying, I always opt for the hard way.

This video should answer Charise's questions about Kevin. He wasn't abducted by force. She doesn't need to pay us to tell her it's over. My guess is that she wants face-to-face combat with him. She probably has a scene playing out in her head, a scene on continuous loop, where she reams him out, blasting him into a quivering ball of sorry before turning up the heat to create a gelatinous reduction. In this diminished state, Kevin begs for her forgiveness.

Based on personal experience, I could tell Charise that seeing Kevin in person, pitching a big gotcha scene, probably won't be especially satisfying. Even so, I'll keep my mouth shut. If she wants me to track down a badly behaving man, I will do that. I have a real talent for finding badly behaved men.

OF ALL THE FOOD JOINTS, in all the towns, why did Charise's fiancé have to get abducted at the American Egg? I am stalling for time in my bedroom, trying to decide what to wear for the bike ride to American Egg. My inner infant is acting up, squalling, *I don't wanna go.*

But I am a professional. I am great with people. I will find Kevin, and Charise will move on, maybe land upon another doctor to live with happily ever after. Me? I'll take off into the sunset in my red Honda Coupe. First, though, I've got to get a few paychecks. Before that, I have to go to American Egg and ask some questions.

After much dawdling, I pull on a black stretch t-shirt and black stretchy capris. I go out to the garage, where Moorea's bike spends all of its time. The garage is a shrine to good intentions. The bike keeps company with other lonely, practically brand new items, including a rowing machine, treadmill and rack of free weights.

My guess is that Moorea has ridden the bike, a Christmas

present from her boyfriend Roy, maybe once. The U-lock is mounted to the frame, thanks Roy, with the key taped to it. There's an adorable black backpack looped around one of the front handlebars. A netted side compartment yields a spanking brand new BPA free water bottle.

I stuff some essentials into the backpack and loop it over my shoulders. After donning a helmet, I blast off. Fifteen minutes later, thighs burning, I lock the bike to a no parking sign and enter bacon and egg nirvana.

The hostess, a scrawny pork grease enabler, gives me a sweet smile. "I haven't seen you in a while," she says. "Is it just you today or will—"

"Just me," I say. "And I'm not really here to eat."

"Coffee at the counter?"

"Sure," I say. "I have some questions about the Lady Gaga impersonators who were here the other night. They grabbed my friend's fiancé."

She laughs, maybe thinking I'm joking about the fiancé part.

"That was my day off," she says. "I'll tell our manager Zoltan to find you. He'll give you the scoop."

I sit at the counter and put my bike helmet on the seat next to me. Near a napkin dispenser is a short stack of post cards advertising the American Egg. I take a postcard.

The counter guy approaches, grinning at the postcard in my hand. "You want something to write home about? The blueberry stack is a customer favorite."

"Just some coffee."

He takes a step backward in mock horror. "That's some exciting postcard. Wish you were here, having some diner coffee."

"Luckily, I have other things to write about." I don't tell him I'm writing the postcard to a dead person.

He glances at my bike helmet. "You training for something?"

I nod. Sure I'm in training, training for the Tour de France. I am most definitely not a broke adult back living in my mom's house and riding my mom's bike.

In a flash, I get my coffee.

A minute later, Zoltan is standing next to me. He is blond, which throws me. In my mind, the name Zoltan conjures up a tall, dark-haired guy, Zoltan the Magician, or a wide, dark-haired guy, Zoltan the Mob henchman. But Zoltan the American Egg manager is blond with wide cheekbones and hooded blue eyes. He has the exquisite pore-less skin of a baby's bum. I fight the impulse to ask him about his skin care secret. Could it be exposure to lots of fat and salt? That would rock my world.

"You're the first woman to ask about our famous visitors," he says.

"I know the fiancée of the guy who went with them."

He gives me a smiling grimace. "You know what they say, the better the bachelor party, the happier the husband."

I have to laugh at that one. It would probably even get a cackle out of Moorea. And then I back up a thought. Bachelor party. Upstairs, the little engine that could turns over. I ask myself, if I were Charise's fiancé, would I tell her about a badass bachelor party, the mother of all bachelor parties?

Absolutely not.

"You're sure it was a bachelor's party?"

He laughs. "No, I think two Lady Gaga lookalikes abducted some guy in scrubs for laughs. Of course it was a bachelor's party. What else could it be?"

I drink some coffee. "Did you see where they went?"

"My guess would be a black limo with some fine adult refreshments chilling in a bucket."

"But you didn't see them after they walked out the door."

His mouth opens and shuts. He tilts his head back. And then slowly, his voice full of awe, he says, "That dude is still with the ladies?"

I stare into my coffee. "He hasn't come back. He hasn't called or answered his phone or responded to e-mails."

Zoltan rubs his hairless chin. "Better for the fiancée to know now, before the wedding."

Better not to be engaged to a loser in the first place. There is always a bright side to every disaster, but I am sick of hearing about it. Personally, I've had it with learning experiences. I've had it with men who use the "L" word then dump you for an evening with two Gaga lookalikes or toss you under the bus when facing a little spell of prison time.

"His fiancée wants to know what happened to him," I say.

Zoltan makes a sour face, and I get an inkling of what he looked like as a child, scrunching his mouth against a spoonful of peas. "Some people just need to feel the ice water running down their neck."

"It will make it real for her, easier to get over."

"My guess is he's in Vegas, nice suite at the Bellagio."

A grey-haired man wearing red suspenders and baggy jeans walks by us. Zoltan waves at him. The man winks at me as he heads to the door.

Zoltan leans toward me. "He heard about the impersonators. He's been ordering the Gaga special ever since."

"Gaga special?"

"Four eggs, over easy," he says. "A lot of guys are coming in, ordering that. Business has been great."

"How wonderful," I say, with more than a little touch of sarcasm.

Zoltan's mouth becomes a large gaping circle. "Hey, I hope your friend doesn't blame us. We don't want to lose a customer over it."

"I'll tell her," I say, keeping it dry with a twist of disapproval. It may as well be Moorea speaking.

Zoltan laps it up. "Really, next time the fiancée comes in, tell her to ask for me. Her meal will be on the house."

I nod, unimpressed. A meal in exchange for her fiancé?

"I'll toss in an introduction to Dwayne, one of my line cooks," Zoltan continues. "Poor guy just got divorced. He really needs—"

"A freshly divorced guy," I say, unable to help myself. "What a catch."

Zoltan smiles. "He's a little raw. But all he needs..."

"What?" If Zoltan says all Dwayne needs is an understanding woman I am going to barf up my coffee.

Zoltan's expression changes as his eyes search my face. "I've seen you before," he says. "I've been racking my brain."

"Weather girl," I say. "Channel 5."

His stare penetrates the dermis layer of my skin. A moment later, he realizes I am joking and laughs.

I smile, trying to cover up my dread.

He waves a finger in the air. "You used to come in here with that doctor, we called him Dr. Fantastic because—"

"Because when you ask him how he is he always says fantastic."

"Yes," he says, beaming. "What's he up to these days?"

I refrain from telling him about my Last Supper with my cosmetic dermatologist, which took place at this very eating establishment. A fix-up with Dwayne is the last thing I need.

"Dr. Fantastic is in prison."

Zoltan takes a step backward. "Seriously? Wow. What bad luck."

"It wasn't bad luck. He deserved to go to prison."

"I mean it was bad luck for you."

"No, it wasn't bad luck. I was stupid." I manage a smile, thinking of Dr. Fantastic.

Zoltan says, "Love sucks, doesn't it?"

3

*B*ack at Moorea's house, I make myself a peanut butter and rice cake sandwich. Rice cake is not my first choice but there is not so much as a crumb of bread in the place. I take a bite. The mouth feel is not good.

I glance at the Arizona Highways calendar on the wall. It is indeed March, and bread should be back in stock by now. Moorea is taking things way too far this year. Bread is typically the first sign of a break in the harsh New Year's resolution diet, like crocuses poking out of cold, barren ground in the North. By late March, the kale slowly, leaf by wretched leaf, disappears from the crisper, replaced by leftover meatloaf. In April, bacon starts to make its glistening comeback, first in its low-sodium incarnation then in its thick center cut glory.

For a moment, I consider a radical step: going back out on the bike and purchasing my own food. Alas, I am still two weeks away from my first paycheck. I stare at the rice cake sandwich, determined to practice gratitude. *Thank you, kind goddess, for sustenance.*

As I crunch away, straining to hear myself think, I consider calling Charise. The problem is, I don't want to have a conversation with her about whether Kevin was abducted as part of some bachelor's party extravaganza she knew nothing about. This kind of message calls for a text. I love modern technology for its avoidance potential.

I text Charise. "Kevin on bachelor's party trip?"

While awaiting an answer, I login to Facebook and send a friend request to Charise. Kevin, who is in her friends list, also gets a request. Brilliant detective move, there. I figure it never hurts to try the obvious.

Charise accepts my friend request and texts me back, "No bachelor's party. He didn't want one."

"Victim of someone else's plan?"

She responds, "No way."

Those last two words? Radioactive. I leave them alone for the time being.

I go through Charise's friend list looking for Kevin's brother and uncle. His brother, Tate, is in Charise's friend list. He lives in San Diego. In his profile picture, he wears shorts and sunglasses and stands on a lovely old wooden sailboat. I study the photo. He has the most delicious gap in his teeth. Oh, what a smile!

I send him a friend request. This is all strictly professional. Eventually I tear myself away from Tate to review the rest of Charise's friends. I am surprised to find Kevin's mom, Sandra Sherman, on the list. Mrs. Sherman is a short, skinny blond woman with a blazing smile. Her face is adorable, with round blue eyes and a narrow, slightly turned-up nose. She has the kind of looks men worship with offerings of gold, McMansions, and trips to Paris. Within a minute, women probably size her up as a pain in the butt.

As it turns out, I do not need to friend Mrs. Sherman. An amateur, she has not set any security for her pages. I take a gander at her friend list and find Kevin's uncle, Dave Newman. He is a grey-haired man wearing a pale yellow golf shirt and a pained smile. I send him a friend request.

After this intense round of socializing, I return to Mrs. Sherman's timeline, determined to get to know her better. She hasn't written anything about the disappearance of her son. No apparent worries on that front.

Her primary concerns appear to center around her exercise regimen. Her timeline is dotted with announcements about her jogging achievements. The most recent entry, from two days ago: "Jogged six and a half miles, walked two today. Getting better!" This is a high point. A month before she was jogging three miles and walking one. Still earlier, she seemed to think Facebook was Google. She wrote: "Low-fat taco salad recipe." She wrote it again: "Low-fat taco salad recipe." Kevin, taking pity on his mother, interjected: "Try Google!"

I click on the comments from the week before, where she wrote: "Finally cracked the six mile mark! Beginning to feel like a real runner."

She received many likes and four comments on this post. One of the comments is from Kevin.

He wrote: "Go Mom! I'm so proud of you."

Her response: "Join me!"

"Maybe next week."

"See you on the canal trail!!!"

Based on the dates of these comments, I realize Kevin is suggesting he might join his mom on the trail this week.

I wonder if I can find out what part of the trail she uses. I scroll down her timeline and examine a photo of Mrs. Sherman with three other women, arm in arm, smiling from somewhere on the canal trail. They bedazzle in full makeup, gold jewelry, and black lycra, looking like some overage tribe of ninja sorority members. Scanning Mrs. Sherman's timeline, I see other photos, mostly with these women or ones that look like them. All of them are white and most of them are blond.

I enlarge the photo, peering more closely at their faces. Luckily, I don't recognize any of them from the frequent frowner's club. Luckily, I spot a sign in the background for Olive & Ivy restaurant. When I look closely, I also see a sliver of brown water and bougainvillea and red railing from a canal overpass. Beyond the overpass is a bronze sculpture of two pony express messengers, racing into eternity.

I know exactly where this photo was taken. Beyond the restaurant is Nordstrom. Nordstrom! They are on the section of the canal trail conveniently located near Scottsdale's Fashion Square mall.

The mall is a place I now generally avoid as it evokes painful memories of losing all my money. Even so, I am willing to put my personal issues aside as running into Mrs. Sherman on the trail beats knocking on her door or engaging in an awkward phone call with her.

I text Charise and ask when Mrs. Sherman goes running. A few minutes later, my iPhone chirps.

"Listen Angela," Charise says. "Maybe this is a mistake. Kevin's mom isn't going to be helpful. Maybe the people who abducted Kevin have threatened her. She can't talk. I should never have gone to you and Monalisa. Let's cancel this job. I'll go to the police again and see if they'll take it more seriously."

No. This job can't be over before it's even begun. The rice cakes in my gut reconstitute into a bowling ball. *Don't panic*, I tell myself. Remember the pissed off frequent frowners? Stay calm and empathize.

"I hear what you're saying Charise," I say. "I share your concerns about Kevin's mom. My hope is that she might lead us to Kevin."

There's a pause. "Why would she do that?" Charise asks.

"On Facebook, Mrs. Sherman asked Kevin to join her on the jogging trail. He said okay and suggested this week."

"He did?"

"Yes."

She doesn't say anything right away. I wait it out.

Eventually, she says, "You don't believe he was abducted."

"Charise," I say. "You hired us to look into all the possibilities."

She sighs again. "Mrs. Sherman volunteers at the botanical garden until three p.m. My guess is she's on the trail by four p.m."

"Perfect," I say. "Most likely he won't show up, but we need to make sure."

Charise makes a soft clicking noise. "You're right. Kevin may be in touch with his mom. And, for whatever reason, he doesn't want to contact me. I still believe he's been abducted. Let's rule out any other possibility so that, when I go back to the police I'll have a better case for action."

"I'll text you from the trail."

I hear her inhale deeply. "Thank you, Angela. You're wonderful."

Wonderful. I like the sound of that. I wish it were true. But it is not true. I'm going to end up being the dream killer, the dreaded bearer of bad news, the destroyer of all things good and happy in Charise's life.

Hey, not everyone can be an emergency room nurse.

AROUND THREE THIRTY P.M. I take off in my best ninja sorority finery and ride to the canal trail. When I spot Olive & Ivy restaurant, I stop and look for a small, blond woman with steam coming out of her ears. No such luck.

An older couple wearing matching floppy hats and thick beige walking shoes pad by me. Two men cycle down the trail, a blur of black lycra and Gatorade yellow. A few minutes crawl by, and no Mrs. Sherman.

I check my phone. Kevin's uncle, Dave Newman, has accepted my Friend invitation and written me a message: "Nice to hear from you. Did you quit the Ninth Hole? I haven't seen you lately.

Maybe you're working different shifts. Lunch won't be the same without you serving it!"

At least he didn't mistake me for his cleaning lady.

I quickly look at his profile. Dave Newman works for the Department of Transportation and has seventy-seven friends. His timeline is mostly blank except the year before, in December, he took a trip to that glorious spa destination, Thailand. He posted a number of photos from the vacation. He makes no mention of his nephew disappearing.

I write him back. "Not at Ninth Hole. Am looking for your nephew Kevin. Have U seen him?"

His uncle responds, "Try his fiancée."

Great suggestion, Uncle Dave. "She doesn't know."

"Wherever he is, I'm sure he'll be back soon."

Odd answer. He doesn't claim to know where Kevin is, but seems to know Kevin will be back soon.

I write back: "Any guess where Kevin has gone?"

A minute passes, and there's no response. Perhaps he's had to turn to some citywide emergency, like dialing back the air pollution or dust storms.

A lone female jogger comes to a slow, dramatic halt a few feet from me. Her long dark hair is swept up in a high ponytail. Panting, the woman folds in half. I do not understand running except as an emergency response to an immediate threat. Soon the woman is upright, back among the living, stretching her hamstrings.

I get back on my bike and ride north along the canal, moving at a leisurely pace. Many women I see on the trail seem to be blond and wearing black lycra so I can't move too quickly.

The trail is surprisingly friendly. Two male joggers say hello as they pass. A woman biking toward me flashes a friendly palm. I am feeling the love. I pedal faster, enjoying the breeze, enjoying the cool, fresh air of spring. Yellow buds are showing on the Palo

Verde trees. I ride faster and faster, fast enough to forget about myself for a while.

About fifteen minutes later, my thighs feel heavy. My tush has started to chafe. As I turn the bike around, I think about the ugly padded bike shorts I've seen other bike riders wearing. Those hideous shorts are making more sense.

A few minutes into my return ride, I spot a sole ninja sorority jogger. She is small and blond and fierce, all but spitting tacks, huge sunglasses guarding her movie star privacy. Is she Kevin's mother, aka the Shermanator?

When we are a few feet apart, she gives me a distracted nod. Yes, it's her. Same adorable face.

"Mrs. Sherman?"

She waves. I turn the bike around and ride alongside her. Her chest is heaving. She turns to me, not slowing down.

"Do I know you?" she gasps.

"I'm a friend of Kevin's and—"

"Not now," she says, speeding up.

Trail etiquette suggests I should leave her alone. But my mission, waving the flag of the wronged fiancée, goes beyond trail etiquette. I ride alongside her, feet pushing against the ground to propel the bike forward.

"Is Kevin around? I've been trying to reach him."

She stops and puts her hands on her hips. She can't speak right away. Her head juts backward and her mouth gapes open, which allows for more oxygen down her gullet. It's as though she's giving herself breath-to-breath resuscitation.

Eventually, she says, "Tell Charise that Kevin will contact her when he's ready."

Busted. Some secret agent I would make. Do I bike away, ninja tail between my legs?

Absolutely not. This woman is not going to stand between me and success. "Where is he?"

Mrs. Sherman, still breathing heavily, motors forward. Her face is a saturated pink color. I wonder if she should rest a little longer. As a non-runner, I decide not to provide some advice on this matter.

Mrs. Sherman, feet thumping against the grit of the trail, stares straight ahead, ignoring me even as I stick to her side, on my bike but continuing with a slow, hybrid bike-walking motion.

"Why isn't Kevin contacting his fiancée? The wedding is next month," I say, lathering up my indignation on Charise's behalf. "This is so wrong."

Chin up, Mrs. Sherman continues to ignore me. I can't help but smile. Pretending I don't exist won't make it so.

"Mrs. Sherman," I say. "I'll leave you alone if you answer my questions. It's as simple as that."

No response. She pushes forward, showing admirable sticking power. At the same time, she's lost all form, her shoulders slumping, legs dragging. I would have quit eons ago, heading for a nice bath with a restorative eucalyptus shower gel.

"I'm not leaving until you tell me where he is."

Several minutes later, she slows down and hobbles to the side of the trail. With her hands on her hips, she folds slightly, her chin bobbing against her neck. Her breathing is jagged, chest rising and lowering. I pause, waiting for the inevitable hamstring stretch. But it doesn't come. Instead, she seems to be sinking.

"Mrs. Sherman, are you okay?" She doesn't answer right away. I get off my bike and prop it against a shrub. "Mrs. Sherman?"

Still heaving, she slowly pivots her head and says, "You don't look well."

Moi? Pardon, but I'm not the one who is beet red and oozing sweat. In the interests of client relations, I say, "I'm fine."

She shakes her head. "Your color is off. You look odd."

I do feel winded and my tush is expressing a lot of hostility at the moment. This is only natural, the expected outcome of bike riding for a sedentary person. Nothing is seriously wrong with me.

I study Mrs. Sherman's magenta face, her adorable lap dog features. She's probably trying to psyche me out, make me ill by the power of suggestion.

"I'm just dandy," I say.

She doesn't respond. She doesn't even seem to hear me. She looks around, her expression pained, then lowers herself onto the strip of gravel next to the trail.

I extend my water bottle to her. "Water?"

I expect her to refuse but to my surprise she grabs the bottle and takes some long, sloppy gulps, spilling water down the front of her black tank top. A wave of concern rises up in me.

"I'm dizzy," she says. "I feel faint."

"I'll call for help."

"No," she says. "I'm fine." She drinks more water and carefully sets my bottle onto the ground. "You can go now."

I kneel down and take the water bottle. Meanwhile, Mrs. Sherman presses into the ground with her palms, trying to maneuver her way upright. Partway up, she groans and sits back down with a thud. Her head bobs downward.

My heart thumps, and I feel tachycardia. "Mrs. Sherman?"

She groans.

My hand shakes as I call for help. I do my best to describe our location. Luckily, the emergency operator seems to know the trail well, as if people pass out on it regularly.

When I finish the call, Mrs. Sherman is still sitting on the ground. She is drawing deep breaths, her back rising with each gulp of air. The back of her neck is glistening.

I stare at her, willing her to continue breathing. "Help is coming," I say, offering her the water bottle again. "More?"

She shakes her head.

"You're going to be fine," I say.

"I know," she replies. "I'm fine. And I'll feel even better when you leave."

A jogger, a man with thick salt and pepper hair and sporty sunglasses, stops a few feet from us. "Everything okay?" he asks.

"She feels faint," I say. "I called for help."

He kneels beside her, resting a hand on her back. "Are you okay?"

She gazes up at him. "I'm dizzy," she says. "I can't stand up."

He pats her shoulder. "Help is coming. Hang in there."

She looks at me. "You can go."

"I'm not going to leave you alone," I say.

The man smiles and sits next to Mrs. Sherman. "I'll stay with her."

In a small, sweet voice, Mrs. Sherman says, "Thank you. You're a lifesaver."

The jogger waves me off, mouthing the word, "Go."

I cycle back to Fashion Mall, moving quickly, so quickly my thighs and tush don't have time to complain. About ten minutes later, I am panting. My palms are slick, and I rub them against my thighs. Me and sick people: not a good combination.

I locate my cell-phone and text Charise about Mrs. Sherman falling ill on the trail. Even though it may end the case, I tell her, "Before she collapsed, she said Kevin will contact you when he's ready."

When he's ready! How could Charise even think of marrying into this family?

Sirens ring in the distance. Soon the sirens jangle loudly, sounding much closer. I get back on my bike and pedal forward, trying to escape. The sirens stop abruptly. A few minutes later, I pull my bike off the trail and stop.

Another set of sirens run through my head. I squeeze my eyes shut, trying to block the voice. But I hear it anyway.

"Angie, honey." Iona waves at me from her garden, amid her turnips and beets and peppers. I peer at her over the fence.

"How's it going, Iona?

She shakes her head, like she can't hear me properly.

I smile and speak louder.

Iona stares off, looking lost in thought. I track her gaze. She seems to be sizing up the tomato cages from the previous year, which she'd stacked against the fence.

"Iona?"

She doesn't answer.

"Hello?" says a man's voice.

My eyes flick open, and I hear myself inhale sharply. It's the jogger who was helping Mrs. Sherman, now standing a few feet from me.

"How is Mrs. Sherman?"

He says, "The ambulance picked her up. They're taking her to Scottsdale General. She's in good hands now."

"Thanks so much for staying with her."

His head does a bashful dip, and he gives me an awkward smile. "It was the least I could do. Such a sweet woman. Hates to be a bother to anyone." He shifts his weight from one leg to the other. "Her name is Mrs. Sherman?"

I notice he wears no wedding band. "Yes," I say, "and she's a widow."

"Maybe I should stop by Scottsdale General, see how she's doing."

"I'm sure she'd appreciate that," I say, hoping that this good deed, which I absolutely didn't have to do, would be appreciated by the universe, which would, in turn, smooth my path toward finding Kevin.

Then again, as some people believe, no good deed goes unpunished.

∾

BACK AT HOME, I sit in my office chair—also known as my bed—and drink lemonade Vitamin Water Zero. Moorea and Roy, the lovebirds, are in the kitchen, cooking up another heart-healthy dinner. The swampy stench of steamed broccoli has oozed from the stovetop across the living room, down the hallway, and under the door of my bedroom. This is the smell of love. Moorea met Roy when he was rushed to the hospital with an acute coronary. When cupid strikes under these circumstances, I think broccoli probably takes on aphrodisiacal qualities.

I pull out the postcard from the American Egg and write, "Dear Iona." What do I want to tell her? There's the old standby "wish you were here," but I've already written that on other cards. "The coffee here isn't as good as yours." I can almost hear her pleased cackle. She took pride in her coffee-chicory blend. "Today, I started working for Monalisa." What do I say about this? "A woman hired us to locate her fiancé, who seems to be missing. He was last seen with two half-naked women. I know what you're thinking: good riddance! Don't be a stranger. Love, Angela."

Under the bed, I grab a shoebox that once held my gold strappy sandals. Inside, under some white tissue paper, I deposit the postcard. I close the box and slide it back under the bed, hearing the *whoosh* of postcards sliding around inside.

A moment later, my cell dings.

Charise's text says: "Spoke to Mrs. Sherman. Out of hospital now. Tests say she's fine. She sez leave Kev alone. I sez over my dead body. Find him, Angela, even if you have to look under every rock on Camelback Mountain."

The thought of rocks on Camelback Mountain makes me realize I am hungry. At the same time, I have no desire to witness Moorea and Roy nuzzling together as they cook grim, heart-healthy meals. Waiting for the broccoli stink to dissipate and the couple to migrate into the living room, I rerun the YouTube video starring Kevin and the Gagas.

Kevin walks out of the restaurant like his underwear is too tight. I spot what appears to be a blood splatter on his blue scrubs. That is disgusting. Couldn't he have changed before going out to eat?

I sit back in bed, pondering my brilliant observations. Would you believe I'm a distant relative of Sherlock Holmes? No? I wouldn't either.

I watch the video again. The ladies march into the restaurant, heading straight for Kevin. I click on pause.

This strikes me as odd. My stomach pipes up and says it is hungry. I tell it to shut up.

The two women already seem to know what Kevin looks like. I squint at the screen. No one appears to be accompanying the two women, pointing out Kevin. On the other hand, he seems easily identifiable in his scrubs. My guess is he's the only one in the restaurant wearing scrubs.

The two women arrive at Kevin's table. He looks up at them, his expression cool. Other men in the restaurant appear way more excited by the vision of Les Gagas.

I pause the video. Only an orange rind remains on Kevin's plate. The Gagas arrive right when he's finished eating. Smooth. If he were mid-meal, he might not have wanted to leave. After a long shift at the hospital, I suspect he'd be ravenous.

The timing could have been lucky. But I doubt it. They must have watched him go in and estimated when he'd be finished.

Alternatively, maybe someone was watching Kevin from another table. I peer at the faces of people sitting nearby. There's a four-top of men gawping at the Gagas. An elderly man squinting at them with a mix of disbelief and wonder. Two women looking around, apparently searching in vain for an explanation. No one leaps out as a conspirator.

I tap play, continuing the video. One of the Gagas pulls out the plastic gun and gestures for Kevin to get up. He waits a beat. The other Gaga tosses a twenty on the table, then leans over and says something to Kevin. He wears a hint of a smile but that's it. My guess is she said something sassy to him. A man at an adjoining table bursts into laughter around the same time as the Gaga lookalike is speaking.

The video is about two minutes long. That's all it took to get Kevin out of the restaurant. Slick. The planning and timing don't exactly scream wild and crazy bachelor's party. On the other hand, wouldn't kidnappers want to be more discreet? Sending two Lady Gaga lookalikes into a restaurant guarantees an audience. The video has had 1,196 views so far. It's an audience that thinks Kevin went on the ride of his life.

For Charise's sake, I strain to consider other possibilities. Why would anyone have a reason to abduct Kevin? Medical residents don't make big money. Drugs? At gunpoint, he could probably write some prescriptions. Similarly threatened, he might be able to help someone steal medicines from the hospital.

I can't see either scenario working. For starters, per Charise, Kevin is a straight arrow. If compelled, he could probably draft a fake prescription. I can't see the typical drug dealer having the patience for this sort of scheme. The hassle and risk would be high while the payoff would be relatively low. Plus, according to Charise, Kevin hasn't been seen at the hospital since Thursday.

Still, Kevin should have been in touch with Charise by now. In this day and age, any cowardly lion can end a relationship with a few keystrokes. He could take a minute to draft a text saying, "Hey, Babe, sorry this isn't working. It's me, not you. Have a wonderful life."

"Angela, you want some grilled chicken and broccoli?" Moorea calls.

Before I can formulate words to respond, my aching legs leap off the bed, taking me to the kitchen.

4

*I*f I let nature take its course, first thing in the morning for me would mean around eleven. Unfortunately, a defining characteristic of adult life, even as a starter adult, is that nature must not be allowed to take her course. Given that it is my second day on the job, I drag myself to the office around ten a.m. for a check-in with Monalisa. I am a figment of makeup and sugar coffee.

Cracking open the door a sliver, Monalisa gives me her usual warm greeting. She peers out at me, her alien sensors sweeping me for hostile bacteria. She doesn't seem to recognize me. Behind her, I catch flashes of white fur as Boo jumps out of his skin with excitement. He's rocketing from one side of Monalisa to the other, trying to reach moi, his true love.

"Angela," she says, as though she is guessing.

"Present," I say.

The door opens, and I enter, receiving a proper greeting from Boo, who attempts to lick my entire face and neck.

"Boo sweetheart!" I say, taking him in my arms.

"Boo, stop," Monalisa says, as if I'm not also a guilty party. "Leave Angela alone."

After giving Boo one last hug, I pry myself away and follow Monalisa into her office. Boo is having none of it. He dances around me. I can't help but give him a little shimmy in response. He ducks and springs into the air, tongue out, a kissing machine.

"Boo, sit," Monalisa says.

I pull a chair in front of Monalisa's desk. Boo races from side to side, perhaps thinking I'm playing a game. Monalisa stands and sits, as if demonstrating for Boo.

"Boo," she says, pointing to her side. "Come here."

Boo gazes up at me. I gaze back, wondering why humans can't be more like dogs.

"Boo," Monalisa calls, her voice rising.

Boo slinks off behind the desk and belts out a high-pitched whine.

I notice that the wooden sword that had been against the far wall is now by the cupboard. It has moved up in the world. I decide not to ask how Monalisa puts it to use. Maybe when we know each other better, after I've passed my probationary period, I'll inquire.

Monalisa offers me Krakus, which I decline. She takes a long draw from her mug of Krakus. She manages not to gag or barf it up. I am impressed.

"Where are we in tracking down Kevin?" she asks.

We are nowhere. Correction: I am nowhere. I tell Monalisa that Kevin's mom and uncle don't appear to be worried about Kevin's whereabouts.

"Facebook?" Monalisa asks.

I smile. "I've searched the timelines of his uncle and mom. I'm still waiting for Kevin's brother to accept my friend request."

Kevin's exceedingly *hot* brother. I do not share my enthusiasm with Monalisa.

She tilts her head back like she smells something rotten. "Facebook. I can't believe how people can be so cavalier and contemptuous of their privacy."

I recount how, thanks to Facebook, I found Mrs. Sherman on the canal trail.

Monalisa sips her Krakus, rolling the stuff around in her mouth a little, as though tasting a fine Burgundy. *Fuzzy on the palate. Remnants of tree bark with traces of beetle larvae. A long, composty finish.*

"Mrs. Sherman said Kevin would be in touch with Charise when he's ready," Monalisa repeats, her green eyes gazing thoughtfully into space. "She didn't say anything else?"

I explain that we weren't able to speak for long because Mrs. Sherman became faint and needed to sit down. Monalisa's eyes practically glow when I mention that I'd called an ambulance, which took Mrs. Sherman to the hospital.

"Do you think your questions triggered this fainting spell?" Monalisa asks.

"She looked like she'd pushed herself too hard on the trail."

Monalisa doesn't speak for a moment. This makes me uneasy. Eventually, she says, "Mrs. Sherman was taken to the hospital."

I feel a prickle of trouble. Why is Monalisa repeating what we both already know? Boo peeks around the desk at me. At this point I am not sure what I've done wrong, but I realize something is amiss. I don a preventive apologetic expression on my face. Dogs do this all the time and it seems to work for them.

Monalisa angles her head at me. "You didn't see Kevin at the hospital?"

A small cough issues from my mouth, which now feels like it is lined with sandpaper. The words I don't want to say are springing around my mind. Eventually I corral them and force them out of my mouth. They stumble uneasily into the air.

"I didn't go to the hospital with her."

"Interesting," she says, studying her thumbnails. "Help me understand your thinking."

I don't know what to say but that doesn't stop me from talking. "While we were on the trail, she insisted I leave. Told me to go. A man said he'd stay with her and—"

"She asked you to go away so you did?"

Yes. I can't bear to say the word out loud. I give a small, sorrowful nod.

Monalisa gazes over my shoulder into the front yard, where orange-red blooms on an ocotillo are igniting in the sun.

It's only day two. Usually it takes me a little longer to disappoint. Boo comes to me. I pat his head. He runs to the door and back. Playtime?

"Boo." Monalisa says, with exasperated hoarseness in her voice. Boo runs out of the room. She trains her eyes back on me.

"I'm sorry." I am about to explain that I didn't think to follow Mrs. Sherman. My throat constricts, and I hear myself saying, "I got scared. I kept thinking Mrs. Sherman might die. It reminded me of—"

"Angela."

"I kept thinking, if I could have done CPR or something. But I panicked. If I hadn't failed nursing school, I could have—"

"Angela." Monalisa is shaking her head.

"I could have saved Iona."

My mouth hangs open. I can't believe I just said that. This was not at all the destination I'd planned when I began my pathetic excuse making.

"Angela." Monalisa leans forward over her desk. "There is nothing more you could have done for my grandmother. She had a massive stroke. You called for help."

"Not in time." I shudder, my mind flashing back to Iona's frozen face, her lips moving but nothing coming out. And me, wasting precious seconds, hands fluttering in the air, voice cracking as I called to her, asking if she was okay over and over when it was clear she was not okay. Any idiot could see that.

"You know what I'm grateful to you for?" Monalisa asks.

I shake my head.

"That Iona didn't die alone. She passed away with one of her favorite people holding her hand. How many of us will be that lucky?"

The pressure builds behind my eye sockets. I will not cry. I refuse to cry. I only cry in places and at times of my own choosing.

The moment passes. My eyes sting; thankfully, they are not wet. But I could use a stiff shot of Krakus.

Monalisa says, "Is Mrs. Sherman out of the hospital?"

"Yes," I say, knowing clearly what I need to do. "I'll stake out her house and see if Kevin turns up."

IN MY UNDERSTANDING, gleaned from TV and movies, the typical stakeout is conducted in a white van, maybe tricked up with a fake plumber's logo plastered on an exterior panel. Inside, two detectives exchange quips and drink convenience store coffee, which they chase down with donuts. Typically, they are mismatched in some important ways, such as age, race, marital status, risk tolerance, musical taste. They may have music on, giving them a chance to bicker about the virtues of the Justin Beiber versus Usher.

How a stakeout is supposed to work on a bicycle I do not know. I'm breaking new ground here. I wear soft grey instead of ninja black, hoping I won't stick out as much. Unfortunately, just the fact of being on a bicycle is enough to make me stick out. Recreational cyclists on the mean streets of Phoenix are few and far between on a weekday. The serious road bikers tend to hit the streets on weekend mornings, packs of them streaming by in motion blurs of orange and chartreuse.

My only hope is that Mrs. Sherman is not going to be gazing out her front window. It takes me forty minutes to ride over to her address, which I obtained from Charise's contact list. The house is a sprawling brick ranch with a cluster of lemon trees in the front yard. A white Lexus SUV and a blue Ford Focus are parked in a circular drive in front of the house.

I slow my pedaling and pull onto the sidewalk across the street. Inside my backpack, I grab my phone. As I pretend to take a call, I tilt the phone upward and take a quick photo of the cars in front of the house. I e-mail the photos to Charise.

With any luck, the Focus belongs to Kevin. Somehow, though, I don't see him driving that car. I also don't see him in the pearl white Lexus, which says ninja sorority girl all over it.

After a long draw of lukewarm water, I pedal to the end of the block. The house on the corner has a tall side fence made of slatted wood that abuts the sidewalk. A mesquite tree near the curb provides me with additional cover. I lean my bike against the fence.

From this vantage point, I have an angled view of Mrs. Sherman's driveway. I can see if anyone goes in or out of the house. The distance may be a little too far for me to recognize Kevin, especially since I've only seen him in photographs and video. Too late, I realize I should have taken Moorea's bird-watching binoculars with me.

I stand with arms crossed for a few minutes.

"Nice bike," a man says.

I nearly jump out of my spandex. A white-haired man wearing pastel clothes is smiling at me. He is walking a pug. The pug wears a plaid bowtie collar, quite the dandy.

I smile and mumble something. He waves and continues down the street toward a small park. The pug waddles beside him, breathing like an asthmatic. With the lack of anything better to do, I ponder another swig of water. I am struck by a terrible thought: *where would I urinate?* My thoughts naturally return to TV and movies, where I try and fail to recall a single scene that provides some guidance on toileting on location.

In the park down the street, I watch the pug circle a shrub

before taking a quick pee. I inform my bladder that there will be no urination until further notice.

For sixty minutes, nothing happens. No one pulls onto or off of the street. Then, just when I start to lose hope, a marvelous vision appears, a consolation prize for the lack of civilized restroom facilities. A zippy brown UPS truck turns onto the block and stops a few houses away from me. A man with a truly spectacular set of tanned legs walks to the door of the house. He rings a bell. Moments later, pale arms reach out of the door for the package. The legs trot back to the truck and disappear. The truck drives off.

My iPhone dings. This is almost too much excitement all at once. It's Charise.

She has texted: "Lexus belongs to Mrs. S. DK about Focus."

I write back: "What does K drive?"

She responds: "Camry."

I have an aha moment. A Camry driver is not in Vegas with two Gaga lookalikes. I know this the same way I know I will never be president of the U.S. or an emergency room nurse.

Camry. A workhorse. Some people heed the call of their heart; others hear the call of reason. I imagine it is a silver Camry, the ultimate practical neutral.

I write Charise: "Is Kevin's car silver?"

"OMG. Is he there?"

"No. Sorry. Just guessing about his car."

"How did you know?"

We all have our superpowers. I have no gift for physiology, anatomy or organic chemistry. I have no gift to heal people. My genius is in judging a man by his car.

Charise instructs me to let her know if I see Kevin, and I return to waiting and watching.

An hour later I get back on my bike and cycle a half block up, then zip back down to my spot near the fence. The water bottle calls to me. I take out my phone and start deleting old e-mails.

After another tedious stretch of time, I get on my bike and do a screaming fast cycle past the Sherman's house, then loop around the block until I'm back at my post. Nothing seems to have changed. My legs and tush are tired of bike riding.

Several minutes later, a man in jeans and a blue t-shirt emerges from Mrs. Sherman's house. He strolls down the driveway toward the street. I grab my water bottle for moral support. He continues past the two vehicles. He gazes in my direction.

Is it Kevin? I squint through my sunglasses. No, the hair is longer, wavier. He's got the air of a sailor about him. I recognize this man. It's Tate, Kevin's brother. Be still my heart! It's the vision from Facebook in the actual flesh.

I slowly return my water bottle back to its holder. Pretending not to notice he is walking my direction, I adjust the backpack straps. It's time for me to get on my bike and jet.

I wheel the bike onto the street.

"Wait," he calls.

Behind me, I hear ominous sounds. Tate is running after me in flip flops. My feet start to pedal. My tail is firmly tucked between my legs.

"You on the bike, stop."

I sigh. I plant my feet on the ground and slowly turn. "Yes?" I ask.

Tate is magnificent. He's not exactly smiling, but I catch a glimpse of that gap in his front teeth. I can't quite look him in the face. The voltage from direct eye contact might fry me to a crisp.

"You're upsetting my mom," he says.

Busted. I have some choices here: to lie or not to lie.

"I'm sorry," I say.

I might have tried lying if I could have come up with a reasonable explanation for loitering on the block. Sadly, my imagination is not up to the task.

"Why are you following her?"

"I'm not," I say.

He flashes an annoyed smile. That gap in his teeth. That gap destroys me. It is Kryptonite, able to penetrate my otherwise fool-proof defenses.

"It only *seems* like you're stalking her?"

"I'm looking for Kevin."

He pauses, lifting his head in surprise. "Why?"

"Charise hasn't heard from him since Thursday night. She's worried."

"My mom says Kevin is in Europe, at some medical conference."

"Europe." Pray tell, do Lady Gaga lookalikes go on European tours? "Why didn't Kevin tell Charise he was going to Europe? Why hasn't he sent her a message or returned any calls?"

"I don't know." He looks sincerely puzzled. "That's not like Kevin at all."

"Charise last heard from Kevin on Thursday. That night, he was last seen leaving a restaurant with two Lady Gaga lookalikes."

Tate's head turtles out at me. He blinks several times. "Is this some sort of joke?"

I shake my head. "It's on YouTube. Him leaving with the two women."

"Then it must be real," he says, with more than a touch of sarcasm. "Look, whatever craziness going on with Charise and Kevin is between them. They fight all the time. You know that, right?"

I nod, trying to appear knowledgeable. Funny how Charise didn't mention the constant fighting.

He continues, "Leave my mother alone. You know she was in the hospital yesterday?"

"I called the ambulance for her."

I thought that might warm things up between us, soften his hostility, convince him that we could live happily ever after.

"What did you do to her?" he says.

"I asked her where Kevin was. While we were chatting, she said she felt dizzy and needed to sit down."

"Did you threaten her in any way?"

Our future together is starting to look doubtful. I cancel the reservations for happily ever after.

"Of course not," I say. "Do I look threatening?"

He stares at me. "Yes, actually."

His eyes are blue. His lashes are long. I wait for him to tell me he's joking. He doesn't.

"I'm leaving."

"That's a start," he replies. "If I see you around here again, I'll call the police."

Much as I would have liked to stay and chat with Tate, it is clear I need to jet. The faster the better to outrun my shame at stalking and being caught out.

I fly for seven blocks, my feet pumping the pedals, my angry thighs giving it their all. As I approach the eighth block, I realize this is not sustainable. I take a left at the next intersection, then propel the bike to the midway point of the block and stop.

Stop is an elegant word for collapse. I prop the bike against a tree trunk and lie flat on my back on someone's front lawn. My thighs and tush scream so loud for mercy, even my dad who art in heaven can hear their cries. Soon the cries are drowned out by the racket of my panting.

After several minutes, I turn onto my side. My eyes are wet. I dry them with the sleeve of my moisture wicking t-shirt. They sting. I shut them. I open them. I prop myself up.

I am able to think again. They are not pretty thoughts, and Tate is the least of my problems. I've been yelled at plenty of times in my sorry career. But Monalisa's simple statement of fact was especially painful. *She told you to leave so you did.*

There was nothing in that sentence I could hide behind.

Worse, I can hear Monalisa's saying it again. *Kevin's brother told you to leave so you did.*

Those alien eyes of hers probing me for intelligence and coming up empty.

I sit up and grab my water bottle. I take a quick sip. Like every other part of my body, my bladder is starting to send warning signals.

As I maneuver the bike upright, I realize Kevin is not going to be visiting his mother. Elementary, my dear Angela. By claiming Kevin is in Europe, Mrs. Sherman is explaining his absence.

Could it be true? If it's true, Charise is going to come undone. If it's true, it would explain why Kevin's mom and uncle aren't more concerned about his absence. Then again, if it's true, why didn't Mrs. Sherman tell Charise this from the get go?

I get out my iPhone and text Charise: "Could K be at medical conference in Europe? This is what Mrs. S told Tate."

I wait for an answer. An eruption. A meltdown. After several minutes, I hear nothing. I get on my bike and pedal the general direction of home, moving like a tin woman.

About ten minutes later, my phone chirps. I stop pedaling and pick up the call.

"A medical conference?" Charise asks, each syllable bubbling up from a steaming caldron. "You have got to be joking."

"There's no conference in Europe?"

"There better not be."

On the other side of the line, I hear some jangly music. An espresso machine hisses and spits.

Charise presses on, "If he's in Europe, he's dead. Tell me where he is and I'll finish this job. I'll track that bastard down—"

"Charise."

"I'll fly there and I'll get him. Europe? We're supposed to be in Italy next month. We've got plans. We've got non-refundable deposits. He wouldn't do this to me."

I ask, "Where are you right now?"

"Europe?" she says, her voice starting to crack.

She is moving at warp speed through the stages of betrayal: anger, denial, vengeance, depression.

"Are you at a coffee shop?"

A few seconds later, she says, "I'm at Grove."

"Hold tight," I say.

Grove Coffee is about ten minutes from me by bike. I start pedaling that direction, promising myself that I will purchase an ugly pair of padded bike shorts. Soon.

Fifteen painful minutes later, I wheel up to Grove, an industrial chic coffee shop with large plate glass windows. The scent of freshly roasted coffee beans is dizzying. At this time of the afternoon, the windows are darkened, the sunscreens pulled down. I lock my bike to a rack and hurry inside.

Charise is sitting at a two-top near a display of bagged coffee beans. To her left, on a lizard green wall, is a black and white photograph of an electrical substation. She looks like a storm has recently passed through her. Her eyes are rimmed pink, shiny but dry. Her shoulders are slumped. Three trashed napkins sit on the table. She still holds a napkin balled in one hand. Her cappuccino is barely touched.

I wave at her and quickly detour to the restroom. A few minutes later, with a much happier bladder, I sit across from her.

She says, "He's not at a medical conference. I called two of the other residents at the hospital. The department administrator keeps a list of conference presentations given by staff and residents. Kevin isn't on that list."

"We'll figure this out." I try not to stare at her cappuccino.

"We'll figure this out? My fiancé has disappeared a month before our wedding."

"I'm so sorry."

Charise and I are quiet for several minutes. She stares into the milky foam of her drink. Eventually, she gazes up at me and says, "Have you ever been married?"

I smile, which surprises me. This question does not ordinarily call for a smile. "No," I say. "My last boyfriend tried to implicate me in a felony."

"Seriously?" Charise's eyes widen.

A small laugh comes from my mouth. What is wrong with me? This is not funny. Give it twenty more years, and maybe it will be good for a chuckle.

"Seriously," I say. "He's in prison."

Charise is staring at me. Her shoulders start to shake. A second later, a peel of laughter rips from her. I am laughing as well. I feel like we've been drinking. Drunk on misery!

When we finish laughing, I get back to business, consummate professional that I am. "If Kevin's not at a medical conference, then Mrs. Sherman lied to Tate."

"Yup. By the way, Theodore is his real name."

"He uses Tate on Facebook."

"On Facebook, no one knows you're actually a Theodore. Anyway, back to Mrs. Sherman. There's no getting around it, she's not quite right in the head."

"She's a compulsive liar?"

"No." Charise gazes up at the silver encased pipes overhead.

"She's obsessive?" *Anorexic*, I mentally add. "An exercise addict?"

Charise says, "In psych class, the term was personal delusional system. It's been three years since Mr. Sherman died of a heart attack. She acts like he's still alive. His slippers are still under his side of the bed. The closet is still full of his clothes. His papers are still piled on his desk."

I feel a pang for Mrs. Sherman, who looks so put together. "Does she somehow think he's coming back?"

Charise shrugs. "She knows he's gone. She chooses not to move forward."

I don't bring up the post cards I write to Iona. I tell myself that's perfectly normal, which is why I hide the cards in a shoebox under the bed.

Whatever. Death sucks. No getting around it.

"I never would have guessed," I say. "Mrs. Sherman really keeps up appearances."

Charise glances at her glittering engagement ring and gives me a lopsided smile.

"Angela," she says. "Appearances are the last to go."

BACK AT HOME, I am determined to write notes on the day's events. First, though, I have to put my abused body under the shower. Next I must try to repair the lacerations, otherwise known as chafing, to my thighs and tush. This takes all manner of lotions and potions. Then I get into bed with my laptop and search the Internet for padded biking shorts. After much research, I find an acceptable pair. They cost thirty-five dollars. Seriously! To add insult to injury, you are forking out that kind of cash to make your tush look bigger.

As a general rule, after taking my involuntary vow of poverty, I have no room in my budget for items that are both ugly and costly. My thighs and tush register an objection. *Your honor, we are in terrible pain!* The pea-sized part of my brain governing logic and budgetary decision-making considers the options. Padding for my bum or dollars for the Honda Coupe? My heart cries out for the Honda Coupe. The padded shorts lose.

I pop an Ibuprofen and decide to get tougher. This is easier when wrapped in my fluffy white comforter, my power cocoon, slicked up with perfumed lotion. My power cocoon is where I go to retreat from the world and replenish myself. Sure, being a former spa professional, I would prefer a Hinoki bath scented with cypress or an Abhyanga massage, but you can't beat the power cocoon for price and convenience.

After a half-hour treatment in the power cocoon, I unwrap myself and get to work. I open my laptop and summarize the day's findings. When my fingers tire of tapping at the keyboard, I decide the report is finished. Before closing the file, I review my jottings. As I re-read the report, my feelings of disquiet grow. Will Monalisa can me for not having conducted a successful surveillance? When I was out there, the logic for leaving seemed tight. Now that I see things in cold, hard print, I notice a few moth holes.

Tate could have told me Kevin was in Europe to get rid of me. Mrs. Sherman could have told him that story to get rid of me. Everyone could be lying. How did I know Tate was telling me the truth? I ponder that. The only answer I have is admittedly weak. Tate is hot. More than that, he is hot but doesn't seem to be overly aware of his overwhelming hotness.

Monalisa will not be impressed with this logic. Even I am not particularly impressed.

I realize the world is full of good liars. Good or even middling liars have a major advantage when people want to believe their lies. The fact is I wanted to believe it was time to go. Surveillance, especially on a bike, is tedious.

Have I pulled another fail?

A knock on my door interrupts this pleasant reverie.

"Sweetheart?"

It is Moorea, and she never says sweetheart unless she has something unpleasant to tell me.

If I pretend to be asleep, I wonder if she will go away. I close my eyes. A few seconds later, she says, "We need to talk."

Although I am in bed, the earth lurches below me. My empty stomach hurls acid into my throat. I hate this particular phrase. Even Moorea saying it triggers the same feelings I had when I heard these words from my cosmetic surgeon's sleazy lawyer.

I straighten out the comforter. Dipping down over the side of the bed, I grab my plush hedgehog, Hedgie, off the floor and smooth his fur. I prop Hedgie next to me and sit back against some pillows, assuming a more professional upright position. I open my laptop, and study my desktop screen.

"Come in," I respond.

She opens the door and stands in the doorway.

I glance down at my laptop. "I'm working."

She smiles. I feel a twinge in my gut. Something is amiss.

She asks, "How is your new job going?"

"Great," I say. "I'm helping Monalisa find a missing person."

I wait for the frown and tumble of questions.

Moorea rubs her chin and says, "That sounds perfect for you. Do you feel like this job is working out?"

This is not the mother-daughter interrogation I expected.

"So far so good," I say, still bracing myself. Will she mention church?

"I want to let you know that Roy and I can help you. We were thinking you might want to get some additional training for a profession."

"I'm fine," I say. "Work is going exceptionally well."

"Okay." She backs from the doorway. "I'll leave you to it."

The door shuts. My thumb hovers near my lip. I yearn to gnaw on the nail. Could Moorea and I be entering a new positive phase in our relationship? For a moment, I wonder what I would do with all the energy that currently goes into being irritated.

I hide my hand under my thigh for safekeeping as a terrible thought smashes a window and breaks into my mind: What if I never find Kevin?

More windows break. What if I fail at this job and never move out from Moorea's house? I visualize myself with grey hair, cowering in my power cocoon, dreading Moorea's knock on my bedroom door. This vision turns my stomach. My mouth goes dry.

After two days of investigation, I am no closer to locating Kevin than I was at the start. I have no promising leads. Fear takes over, and I go back to my power cocoon, agitating, poaching in my glorious fluffy white comforter.

After about an hour of this, I decide on a course of action. It should not be difficult, I tell myself. There can't be many Lady Gaga impersonators trolling around Phoenix.

5

I sit upright on my bed and grab my laptop. It's time to find the Lady Gaga lookalikes. Zoltan from the American Egg assumed they were part of a bachelor party celebration. This would make them hired help. Having watched the YouTube video several times, I also suspect they were professional lookalikes. For starters, their confidence was striking. It's one thing to wear a mini dress that barely covers your hot stuff while rocking it in a dark boozy club. It's another to take that outfit into a civilian setting.

Another factor that cries professional is their clothing. Most people can't go into their closet and dig out five-inch stiletto booties and corset dresses concocted from pillow tassels, parachute fabric and tent poles.

Fingers hovering over my keyboard, I wonder whether you can get these outfits on-line. If so, the ladies might just be talented amateurs who know their way around Google. I Google Lady Gaga costumes. The answer is clear. Yes, you can buy certain items online. On one of the Halloween sites, I pause to contemplate the horror that is a tiny American flag bikini with a matching glitter eyepiece.

I continue scrolling through the sites with Gaga costumes for sale. After a minute or so, I realize the selection on-line is limited. The same outfits and accessories are on display across other sites. These include a balloon-sleeved gown, several asymmetrical mini-dresses, a few bathing suit outfits, and a butch tuxedo. Accessories include a pair of blue gloves, a hair bow on steroids, wrap-around sunglasses, and wigs in all the lovely pastel shades of Easter, including yellow, pink, and aqua.

Most importantly, these outfits look nothing like the get-ups sported by the ladies at the American Egg.

Next, I Google companies that rent out celebrity lookalikes. The first few sites that appear in the listings are slick L.A.-based operations. Initially, I wonder if you can make money being a fake celebrity. From the long line-up of faux stars on the websites, the answer appears to be yes. The available rentals range from Beethoven to Boy George, spanning centuries and even planetary systems. You could throw a cautionary tale party with Jimi Hendrix, Janis Joplin, and Jim Morrison.

As I scroll, I learn more about celebrity rentals. For singers, you have the option of renting either a lookalike or, for extra cash, an impersonator who can perform songs. The websites indicate that celebrities are rented for meetings, conferences, parties and team building. Team building? Clearly, I have been working at the wrong places.

One of the L.A. companies has a Lady Gaga lookalike on offer. In the on-line photo, she wears a red glitter eyepiece. It is impossible to tell if she is one of the American Egg Gagas. She may as well be wearing a burka. Anyhow, I doubt she is one of the lookalikes working in Phoenix. She probably gets plenty of work in L.A.

I continue searching the internet, shifting to the celebrity rental companies in the Phoenix area. The range of rentals shrinks considerably. One local company, which seems to do a lot of casino business, offers up Wayne Newton, Rodney Dangerfield, Dolly Parton, and Bono. Another local business has twelve Elvis impersonators. As I click along, I find plenty of Barbra Streisand and Cher on offer.

No Lady Gaga.

I take my search into the web backwater of oddball business directories. Several minutes later, I am stunned to find my persistence is rewarded. In Phoenix, I discover a directory listing that reads: "NB Entertainment: M. Jackson, J. Timberlake, L. Gag."

I Google "NB Entertainment." I scroll and scroll and scroll, wearing out my finger pads, but cannot find a website for this company. Odd. I return to the directory listing. It has a phone number. My laptop says it is a few minutes past six p.m. I don't expect to reach anyone, but I'm curious whether they're actually in business or not.

A man picks up almost immediately. "Yeah."

Even I can do a better impersonation of a receptionist. "Do you have Lady Gaga lookalikes?"

"How much?"

I mentally correct him: *how many?* Then I wince, realizing that I am turning into Moorea.

"I'd like two," I say.

There is a pause and he says, "Two what?"

"Two Lady Gaga lookalikes."

He doesn't respond.

I add, "I'd like them for a bachelor party."

As soon as these words leave my mouth, I realize my tactical error. Women aren't generally in the business of helping organize bachelor's parties.

"A bachelor's party," the man repeats.

"Yes," I say, realizing this sounds lame. Perhaps it would help if I explain that I am a super-controlling fiancée.

"How did you get this number?"

"The Phoenix business directory. It says you have Lady Gaga lookalikes."

Technically, it says they have L. Gag on offer, but I'm trying to help this guy out, support a local business.

He snorts. "Try a party planning place."

"What do you do?" I am honestly curious at this point.

"We don't have what you want," he says. "Don't call here again."

He clicks off, as if that's an acceptable way to end a call with a potential customer.

In moments like these, I yearn for the civil exchanges that characterized the day spa experience. *How was your thermal mud wrap, Mrs. Wexler?* A beatific sigh would issue from Mrs. Wexler. *I feel like a new woman, Angela.* Every exchange was so upbeat: *Mrs. Gleason, did you enjoy your harmony facial? Heavenly, Angela. I'm walking on air.*

In my white faux medical jacket, I became accustomed to a certain level of respect. This all changed, of course, when the fake Botox hit the spa. But for a while, it was truly magical. Life in a medical day spa is refreshingly unreal. The truth is, I want back into the magic kingdom. My impeccable nails are scratching at the sustainable bamboo door.

In a quest for a new life path, I wander out of my bedroom and into the kitchen. On the kitchen island I find a grilled tuna steak and green salad on a plate covered in plastic wrap. The tuna steak has the dimensions of a playing card, which Moorea has informed me is the proper serving size for protein. A yellow sticky on top says "HELP YOURSELF."

Thank you, dear goddess, for Roy and Moorea, who keep me in low-fat protein. Please bless this food to my body, and my body to thy service. Amen.

The lovebirds usually take a loving, heart-healthy walk after dinner. Tonight, though, they are watching TV, serious, heart-healthy TV. From the living room, I hear a deep voice on TV say, "NASA takes the threat of asteroids very seriously."

Personally, I don't think much about asteroids. I clean the

plate, wash it down with a diet Dr. Pepper, and stow the dirty dish and fork in the dishwasher.

With the business of eating and tidying concluded, I return to my office (bed) and open my laptop. I tap the screen, which returns me to the Phoenix business directory listing for NB Entertainment.

It's clear to me this company doesn't do weddings or parties. They don't do websites either, as far as I can tell. The question is, do they do abductions?

Mr. NB Entertainment has laid down the challenge by telling me not to call them again. I can hear Monalisa's words. *He told you not to call again so you didn't?* That's right, I didn't call them again, I will say. I will smile and tell her what I did instead.

After a thirty-minute bike ride, I am within screaming distance of NB Entertainment. The retail environment is not attractive. I am surrounded by exterminators, off-brand tax offices, spay and neuter outfits, bail bond places and tobacco shops. I would like to wave a fairy wand and make it all go away. Then again, in the midst of this grubbiness, the siren smell of grilled chicken permeates the air. Perhaps I won't use that magic fairy wand quite yet.

The undeniable smell leads to a small, ramshackle supermarket-restaurant, Mercado Temixco, where two men in hoodies tend a grill in a shadowy front courtyard. The Mercado sells chicken and who knows what else from a drive-through side window. Their neighbor to the left is NB Entertainment, a jaundiced stucco bungalow landscaped with pea gravel and an empty Big Gulp cup.

I ride by NB Entertainment slowly. The lights are off. The windows are shuttered. It looks like the company went to bed in the 1970s and has only been reluctantly conscious since that point.

On the bright side, grilled chicken is on offer next door. I wheel my bike into the Mercado's parking lot, passing the drive-through window. The driveway extends behind NB Entertainment before leading back onto the main street. I stop my bike, leaving a good ten feet between me and the dumpster at the back of the lot.

The smell of chicken is stupefying. Garlic. Pepper. Annatto. Oh my. Never mind the tuna steak and green salad I ate for dinner. Those are but a distant blip in my food memory, a forgettable low-protein pit stop on my way to chicken nirvana.

As I start to pedal out of the driveway, fleeing the temptation of grilled chicken, a Buick pulls up to the carry out window. A hand-written sign advertises chickens with two sides for twelve dollars. On Saturdays and Sundays, the price is ten dollars. The driver orders a chicken, and the window man takes payment then disappears. Seconds later, he emerges at the market's front door, where he yells something to the grill men.

Oh dear goddess, the price of deliciousness is not high. The voice of reason counters that twelve dollars should go to my long-term happiness, namely the Honda Coupe fund. Before I can get a single purr out, my mouth cries out for chicken. My tush screams for padded shorts. My stomach howls *chicken!*

I am frustrated and thwarted at every turn. This must be a sign of maturity, that state of being wise elders speak of so highly. One of the hoodie guys from the grill chops the grilled chicken with what looks like a machete. Several moments later, a white paper bag full of heavenly grilled chicken is exchanging hands through the carry out window. Twelve dollars. For only twelve dollars I—

"Are you okay?" a man's voice asks.

The driver at the carry out window is craning his head toward me, frowning. In this moment, I realize I have been staring. Not a casual gaze either, but the focused, intense stare of a hungry dog. I have been stalking his dinner.

"How's the chicken here?" I ask, taking possession of myself.

The driver waits a beat and says, "Fantastic."

I nod, knowing I didn't need to hear that, and wheel my bike back to a shady corner of the parking lot, where I can torture myself in peace. In the shadow of two concrete block walls, I decide that I will not purchase chicken. I will defer this particular pleasure until after I've earned at least two paychecks. I congratulate myself on my adult-like behavior and take a few deep chicken-infused breaths to prepare for the ride home.

An Elantra pulls into the lot, passing the drive-up window. Dearest dad in heaven, Justin Timberlake is behind the wheel. I stifle the urge to fall to the ground. I hold onto my bike for dear life. He's a perfect lookalike.

Not a chicken customer, Justin goes straight to the back of NB Entertainment and parks the car, leaving the engine going. This is somewhat odd behavior. In the dead heat of summer, people sometimes leave the AC going while they run into a store to make a quick purchase. This way, when they return, they won't need potholders to steer their broiler-hot cars. But it is not the dead heat of summer. It is a reasonably comfortable spring evening.

Justin, toting a small black nylon gym bag, enters the company's back door. He doesn't knock or use a key. Several minutes later, he comes out, still toting his gym bag, and gets back into the car and drives off.

My skin tingles. I shake my palms, trying to release some of the voltage. With Justin there and gone, Lady Gaga can't be too far off.

Forty-five long minutes later, Kenny Rogers arrives in a Honda Fit. With all due respect to Mr. Rogers, this is not who I want to see right now. Kenny also pulls to the back of NB Entertainment and parks his car. As opposed to Justin, he cuts the engine before going inside the building. A few minutes later, he emerges with his gym bag and takes off.

After Kenny leaves, I wait thirty minutes before Cher arrives. She is decked out in white feathers. I start to giggle, thinking of chickens. She runs the same drill as the other fake celebs, a quick in and out of NB Entertainment.

I watch for another ninety minutes. No one else shows up. It is after ten o'clock at night. I decide the Gagas will probably not appear this evening.

As I wheel the bike out, my phone pings. I glance at the e-mail. Tate, Kevin's fetching brother, has accepted my Friend request. My smile could light up a city block.

I immediately pay a friendly visit to Tate's timeline, where I quickly see he hasn't mentioned a word about Kevin.

On his timeline, I write, "Howdy," but I don't post it right away. I am going for short and sweet, but this is missing something. I ponder a different salutation, professional with a hint of spice, when I spot the chicken drive-through guy leaving.

"Howdy" will have to suffice, and I post the message on Tate's timeline.

I pedal toward the drive-up window employee, who is already on the sidewalk heading toward the intersection with Thomas.

"Hello," I say.

He turns and crouches, ready to fight.

I brake. "Sorry," I say. "Didn't mean to startle you."

Lines radiate from the corners of his eyes. "I don't have any money."

I sigh, tired of being viewed with suspicion. Then again, I am the woman who's been huffing chicken fumes all night in the corner of the parking lot. Perhaps he noticed.

"I'm not a robber," I say. "I'm actually looking for someone."

His shoulders relax slightly. "Oh?"

"Have you seen a woman who looks like Lady Gaga around here?"

His mouth twists. "Gaga."

"You know," I say. "The singer."

"Yes, I seen her."

"Here?"

"MTV awards. A while ago."

"Not the real Lady Gaga but someone who pretends to be her."

"Pretends to be her?"

My words don't seem to be translating well. Also, even I have to admit the question is a little odd.

"Someone who looks like her, but isn't actually her," I say. "Have you seen anyone like that around here?"

His hands make a dramatic sweep of the parking lot, the same gesture one might make at the South Rim of the Grand Canyon. "Gaga here?"

I nod.

"No," he says, squinting at me with puzzlement. "Lady Gaga likes chicken?"

"I don't know," I say. "I'm pretty sure she likes feathers."

His gaze wanders. "I'll watch for her."

"Thanks," I say but I'm speaking to his back. He's running across the street.

On that promising note, I point my bike east and order my weary legs to pedal homeward.

6

Armed with some exciting non-developments, I check-in with Monalisa first thing Wednesday mid-morning. She is hunched over her desk, examining a wooden sword. Boo is in the far right corner of the room, slobbering over what looks like a femur. An average day at the office.

I point to the sword. "That for forensic accounting?"

Her head tilts in puzzlement. "What?"

"The sword."

She looks at the wooden sword and back at me. "It's a bokken, a training sword I use in Aikido." She peers at it more closely. "I think I need a higher grade of wood." She runs a finger over a stretch of the bokken. "To better sustain impact."

Oh. A training sword. I tell Monalisa about how I heard Kevin was attending a medical conference in Europe, but determined this to be untrue through a quick but brilliant bit of investigative work. She is not particularly impressed. She believes the medical conference was an obvious lie.

"He would have told Charise he was at a medical conference," she says. "There's no reason to keep that a secret. You don't run off to a medical conference like you would, say, to a secret love nest in Cozumel."

No, I agree, one wouldn't do that. Never. I wonder what Monalisa knows of secret love nests. As usual, she is the picture of sensible fashion, wearing a crisp white cotton button down shirt, quiet silver jewelry, cargo pants and black flip flops. This is an outfit that could go from work to swordplay in a snap. On the surface, she doesn't appear to be a woman with personal experience in love nests. Maybe love nests belong to some obscure branch of forensic accounting.

I tell her I've also looked into celebrity lookalike rentals. Monalisa lifts her right brow, as if daring me to impress her. I decline the challenge, mentioning only that Lady Gaga does not seem to be a popular rental option in the area.

I do not tell her about last night's sightings at NB Entertainment. It is not, as a lawyer might say, a premeditated omission. Yet I feel better for having withheld the information. Inside, I've created a happy little room where the secret lives, a sunny, flower-filled space with wicker furniture and the occasional light breeze. When conditions become bleak, I can escape into this room and tend to the flowers.

"What's next, Angela?" Monalisa asks.

Good question. I gaze at Boo, who is no help at all as he is still deeply engaged with the femur. Monalisa, waiting, takes a slow draw of what looks like Krakus. This is so unfair. I did plenty of thinking yesterday! Now I need to think again today? I mentally empty out my pockets, thumbing through the lint and gum wrappers for some ideas.

"Kevin is not going to show up at his mom's place since she's claiming he's in Europe. His brother Tate is in town from California. He seems to be staying with mom."

Monalisa sets the mug down and folds her hands on the desk, giving this her full attention.

"Tate and I are Facebook friends," I say, unable to stop this senseless sequence of words from coming out. "He also doesn't say anything on his timeline about Kevin disappearing."

My face heats up. I realize I am looking for any excuse to say Tate's name out loud. Monalisa's alien sensory system is registering the uptick in blood flow in my skin, which is characterized by increases in saturated hemoglobin and capillary engorgement, manifesting in redness.

Monalisa takes pity on me and merely says, "His brother is the one who gave you the bogus medical conference story."

"Being friends on Facebook doesn't mean much."

"It's a start," she replies.

A thunderbolt hits me. "Kevin's uncle is local. I'll see if there's any sign of Kevin at his uncle's house."

Monalisa gives me a wry look. "Is his uncle a Facebook friend as well?"

I smile. "A very dear Facebook friend, in fact."

BEFORE I STAKE out the house of Kevin's uncle, I do some intensive Facebook research. Alas, Facebook is not the path to enlightenment about Uncle Dave Newman. It indicates that he likes *Golf* magazine, has no comment on the link to ninety-nine best golf jokes someone posted on his timeline, and went to Koh Samui, Thailand, on vacation last December. The dots do not quite connect, at least on Facebook. How does a man go from ninety-nine golf jokes to Thailand, a trip he appeared to take by himself?

With respect to surveillance, I may need to watch out for errant golf balls.

He's been uncharacteristically communicative in posting around thirty-five photos from Koh Samui. Thankfully, the focus is not on golf courses but the crystalline turquoise waters of the Gulf of Thailand. Like parched desert dwellers everywhere, he may be obsessed with gorgeous bodies of water. I linger on the photos. As a connoisseur of web images of paradise, I have to say these photos rank highly on the heavenly scale.

I am, of course, quite knowledgeable about Thailand, which is famous for its destination spas. Kamalaya Koh Samui is one of the leading resorts in the world. I detour to its website, which notes that its name means "Lotus Realm."

I close my eyes and follow the scent of lemongrass and coconut oil and kaffir lime all the way to Thailand. After a bracing royal Thai massage, I pad down a wooden walkway to my hotel room, where I dip into an infinity pool Jacuzzi. After, reclining on a chaise lounge, I sip warm bael tea with ginger and honey and gaze out at the palm-fringed beach.

Le sigh.

Eventually, I tear myself away from the Lotus Realm. One thing that surprises me about Uncle Dave is that he lives near downtown Phoenix, in an historic district full of bungalows and cottages from the 1920s and 1930s. They are inevitably described as "charming." This is another word for bathrooms with no space for skincare and beauty products, and bedrooms with tiny closets fit for a nun's wardrobe. I would have placed Uncle Dave in a swanky golf-course house.

About forty panting minutes later, I pedal down to Uncle Dave's block, coming to a stop across from his house. I pause for a drink of water. His house is yellow with white trim and black shutters. It is taller than a ranch, with large windows. A leafy, non-native tree holds court in the middle of his emerald green lawn. A stone walkway leads to his door. This house looks like it belongs in Connecticut or perhaps England.

No car is in the driveway. The drapes are shut. The lights are off. On the surface of things, it does not appear that anyone is home.

I return my water bottle to its holder and, determined to go beyond the surface of things, pedal to a house near the end of the block. From here, I watch the block for several minutes. Not so much as a single soul is out taking a walk. Undoubtedly, most residents are hard at work at their offices, earning money so that they can enjoy evenings and weekends in their charming but costly historic homes.

My ankle itches. Several minutes later, I watch what appears to be dryer lint tumble through the air. I sneeze. Maybe I am developing an allergy to surveillance.

My mind flashes back to the YouTube video and Kevin's cool, unimpressed expression when the Gagas visit his table—the way he got up and went with them without making a big deal of it. I have a hard time imagining this same cool character deserting his fiancée without a word. I have a hard time believing he's hiding in his Uncle's house, curtains drawn and lights off, tail between his anesthesiologist's legs. He doesn't seem the type.

I feel the creepy touch of a spider's web cross my arm and swat it away. Soon my entire body is involved in escaping from the spider. This would be a good time to leave, before I go completely loony.

I take inventory. Based on a single two-minute video, I have decided Kevin isn't the type to run off and hide from his fiancée. Oh, goddess, please give me more brain cells. Monalisa might offer me a final cup of Krakus before she kicks me to the curb.

Speaking of curbs, I decide to see if I can spot Kevin's silver Camry in the vicinity. I take to the open road, looping around the pleasant, leafy streets, soaking in all the charm I can handle without gagging. I spot a black Camry. The black Camry is the black sheep of the Camry family, way too slick and sexy to fit in with its practical siblings.

Other cars I spot include a Benzi sedan and a sprinkling of late model German and Japanese vehicles, all tucked neatly into driveways.

Soon I am back under another non-native tree on Uncle Dave's block. A light breeze ruffles the leaves above me. I am conducting surveillance on a ghost town.

Several minutes later, I decide to actively look for ghosts. I
bump along Uncle Dave's charming cobblestone driveway to his
house. Charm is overrated in a driveway. I pedal through the
empty carport to the back gate, which is locked. No wonder, as
beyond the gate and its swirls of wrought iron is paradise. A
yellow casita, painted to match the main house, opens out to a
long rectangular pool with heavenly blue water. Lounge chairs
with black and white striped pillows are positioned around
the pool.

No sign of life disturbs this magazine-perfect image of tranquility. Not a ripple in the still blue surface of the pool. Not a
single white Egyptian cotton towel draped over the back of a
chaise lounge. Not an issue of *Golf* magazine on a side table. Not a
light on in the casita.

If I were Kevin, I would be here. He could have the pool plus
the entire casita to himself, all day. I linger, willing the gate to
unlock and a special pool pass to materialize in my hand. Public
pools are full of toddlers with water wings. Ah, the glory that is
the private backyard pool. I can see myself reclining on a lounge
chair—alas, no magic pool pass manifests. My powers of mind
over matter seem insufficiently strong.

In the evening, I will return to see if Kevin turns up.

I pivot my bike around, steeling myself for the clattering ride
down the driveway. Where the driveway intersects the sidewalk
stands a man wearing a white polo shirt, worn jeans, and black
athletic flip-flops. He is one of those people who can wear aviator
sunglasses successfully.

I feel a tick of annoyance. Where did he come from? He
wasn't anywhere to be seen a few minutes ago, when I decided to
trespass. Nevertheless, I pretend he doesn't irritate me, and do
the ride of shame down the driveway, gathering up aggravation
with each banging rotation of the wheel. Sir, how dare you catch
me on the slippery slope toward breaking and entering? Good

thing I have the cause of righteousness on my side, the sacred cause of the wronged fiancée.

Another positive is that he is tall. Some people would feel threatened by his size and apparent strength. In my experience, most tall men are of limited capacity, not due to some innate lack of intelligence, but because being a tall male is all you need to be in life. People automatically think you're smart and capable. You get paid more than other people just because you're tall. And when you give orders, people tend to jump to it. With nothing to prove, tall men don't have to strive for more. Of course, there are notable exceptions such as Abraham Lincoln.

The tall man gives me a lazy grin. Nothing is more annoying than a tall man smiling his entitled, self-satisfied smile. This is especially the case as I am not girded with my usual armor of impeccably ironed hair, a spritz of perfume, and a darling dress that goes from day to evening with ease. As I try to display grace under cobblestones, I consider a quick diversion to the right, looping around him and speeding away, detective tail between spandexed legs.

He raises a palm, as if I don't see him already. The palm, which starts out friendly in a native-American sort of way, soon angles downward, as if I'm a jumpy terrier. Despite the offensive down-girl motion, I scrap my plans for a speedy getaway. Sadly, I doubt I could escape him in my current state of chafing and fitness, even with him on foot and me on bike. He looks like he could run fast. Those long legs probably lope. I lower my feet onto the driveway and come to a stop a few feet from him.

He says, "May I help you."

He is not Kevin. He is not Uncle Dave. Thus, he cannot help me.

"No."

He points to Uncle Dave's house. "Do you know who lives at this house?"

Of course. We're dear Facebook friends. "Dave Newman."

"Then you know he's at work right now." The lazy grin turns into a more menacing smile.

I resort to a lie. "He was going to leave something for me, an envelope."

"An envelope at the gate to his backyard?"

Mr. Neighborhood Watch crosses his arms, assaulting me with a smirk. Of course, after making a minor observation, he thinks he's master of this situation, yet another tall genius. Having been on the receiving end of many an interrogation, much more expertly delivered, I am prepared for this would-be inquisitor, this neighborhood nanny.

My face registers bland boredom, and I lift a foot onto a pedal. *Ho-hum. Tall man, you bore me. Let others worship at your large feet.* "I didn't see anything at the door so I looked around," I say.

"Why wouldn't he put an envelope in the mail?"

He speaks English with an accent, which I can't place. I also can't readily answer his question.

I smile, and he grins. As an interrogator, he is not in Moorea's class. That said, he has the advantage of looking like the unholy love child of river rocks, a classic Mustang, and a baseball bat. "It's no problem for me to pick up the envelope at his house," I say. "Are you his Neighborhood Watch associate or something?"

"I keep an eye out for the criminal element."

"I suppose everyone needs a hobby. You live nearby?"

"Trust me," he says, "there's no envelope for you at my house." The lazy grin returns. "But we could always work something out. If an envelope is what you need. Shall I leave an envelope for you at my house?"

In an instant, this exchange has gone off-road. He seems to think I'm a thief and he seems to think it's cute. My circuits scramble, and I nearly fall off the bike when a tabby cat brushes by my leg.

Mr. Neighborhood Watch laughs.

I pivot the bike around him. "Nice chatting with you."

"I think I've seen an envelope around the neighborhood. It's lost. Are you offering a reward?"

I shake my head.

"I'll make sure you get your envelope," he says as the cat twines his ankles, purring happily.

I skedaddle, detective tail between spandexed legs.

THE HEARD MUSEUM has an impressive collection of American Indian art. It also has striking Spanish colonial architecture. At the moment, its particular draw for me is that it's near Uncle Dave's house and has a reasonable restroom.

After the exchange with Mr. Neighborhood Watch, I can almost taste the stress hormone, cortisol, coursing through my system. At the spa, we learned that stress hormones cause premature aging. Luckily, I've learned how to metabolize these hormones to prevent long-term damage. My low-cost anti-anxiety regimen involves fussing with my hair and reapplying lip gloss in a hygienic setting. Inevitably, it also involves relieving my bladder. At home, the power cocoon is my treatment of choice.

After I use the facilities, I exit the museum and stroll through the arcade into the courtyard. I am admiring a water sculpture when, lo and behold, I realize that the museum store is right in front of me. Coincidence? I think not. The store windows feature Hopi Katsina dolls and Navajo rugs. I want to press my nose against the glass and cry.

I've learned that impulses, like cravings, usually pass in five to seven minutes. I drag myself away from the store window, deciding to abide by the personal restraining order I've got with all retail establishments. My first paycheck has Moorea's name all over it. The second one will also be Moorea's, but there may be a little left over for the car fund.

On the other hand, I could pick up a post card at the store. For old time's sake?

Iona and I used to visit the museum together. We spent many happy hours taking in the Hopi pottery, Navajo jewelry, Katsina dolls, and beaded boots. We would giggle for no apparent reason at the large display of bolo ties. We would visit the museum store, where Iona would linger over the postcard rack, selecting new cards for her collection. We would then take a table at the patio cafe, where Iona would order tea, and I'd drink diet soda even though it's terrible for the skin.

The pea-sized part of my brain in charge of budgeting agrees to allow me one post card. Further, I am permitted to take twenty-five breaths in the store. After that I have to leave.

I dash into the store and select a card featuring a red and black Navajo rug. After my purchase, I race out of the store and sit on a bench under the dappled shade of a Palo Verde tree. A roadrunner scoots past, disappearing around the side of the museum.

I grab a pen from my bag and put the card on my thigh. "Dear Iona," I write. *I wish you were here.* "I have conducted two stake-outs for my job with Monalisa. Still no fiancé. I know you're thinking that he got the "milk" so he doesn't have to buy the cow. But I don't believe that's why he's missing. Life is different now than when you were young. Hope you're enjoying heaven. Love, Me."

My phone dings.

Tate has sent me an e-mail that says, "We need to talk."

I reread the message. My mouth goes dry even though Tate can't break up with me or tell me there's been a misunder-standing about some fake Botox. He could, however, report me to the police for stalking his family. I wonder if he somehow heard about my visit to Uncle Dave's house.

The cortisol is making a comeback. I shut my eyes, trying to conjure happier thoughts. That doesn't work so I try to reason with my amygdala, the almond-sized director of stress hormones. The last thing I need is premature aging. I visualize Iona's purple ceramic unicorns. That's better. Who on earth would manufacture purple unicorn salt-and-pepper shakers? I smile. The world is a better place because of them.

I e-mail Tate my cell number and wait five long minutes. He doesn't call. For a moment, I stare at my postcard, thinking I'd better get a stamp. Then I remember. I put the card into my backpack.

Somewhere on the museum grounds, I hear drum beating. I follow the sound. In a plaza on the other side of the store, a group of Hopi men sit around an enormous drum, each hitting it at the same time. I am transfixed even as my DNA suggests a preference for string bands with guitars, panpipes, and ukuleles.

My phone rings. It's Tate.

The concert goes into high gear, the men chanting and wailing and whacking the drum. This is music to wake the dead or destroy your enemies or call for rain from the withholding god of the desert. Tate is saying something. I can't hear him.

I dash out toward the parking lot, where it is quieter. He has hung up. I call him back.

"What was that?" he asks.

"Pow-wow music," I say. "I'm at the Heard Museum."

He laughs. "Glad you're taking some time from your stalking for some culture."

Glad I am such an amusing stalker.

"You wanted to talk?" I ask, my voice frosting over.

"I'll meet you at the museum, in front of the store. I'm at a climbing wall nearby."

With that, he's gone. I make a quick dash back to the restroom. Looking in the mirror, I know what I would say about this woman if I didn't know her. Unkempt is one of the kinder words I'd use. Life would be so much more pleasant if I maintained unrealistically high standards only for others, not myself.

Sadly, bike riding does nothing to enhance my best features. I look swollen, greasy, blotchy.

There is one bright spot, my nails. They are immaculate. The gleaming purple-black color transports me to a happy place. It's hard for me to imagine what life was like before nail wraps and gel lacquer.

Working quickly, I do my best with water, paper towels, and finger combing. Then I return to the pow-wow, unable to resist loud, insistent music. Several minutes later, Tate is standing beside me. He gives me a gap-toothed smile, and brain fluid leaks out of my ears.

We wait out a song and head to somewhere quieter, where we can talk. Personally, I'd rather pretend we are on a date, listening to pow-wow music, but if Tate wants to talk, I am the consummate professional. Talk is what we will do. Still, I'd feel more comfortable skipping over the small talk and heading straight into the living happily ever after phase.

We sit at a bench on a quiet side of the museum. Nearby, the sun lasers the cheeks and forehead of a bronze sculpture of a native-American woman. Her body, the shape of a bell jar, is draped in voluminous robes.

"I found out where Kevin is," he says, turning so we are almost face-to-face.

"Yes?"

"If I tell you, will you promise to leave my family alone?"

"It depends."

A slight ripple forms between his eyebrows. "On what?"

This strikes me as obvious. "On whether Kevin is where you say he is."

"He's at the Bellagio Center in Italy. There's a conference on anesthesiology."

Bellagio. Bell-agio. I slide down the middle of the word and land in a vat of dark chocolate gelato. Kevin needs to be rescued from Bellagio, where he is in the clutches of some depraved anesthesiologists. Of course, all anesthesiologists are depraved. Otherwise, how could you conk people out all day?

"Did you hear this directly from Kevin?" I ask.

"My mom did," he says. "And I believe her."

Not being a blood relative, I feel no such obligation to believe Mrs. Sherman. This also doesn't explain the Gaga lookalikes. I couldn't imagine they'd accompany Kevin to a conference in Italy. Bellagio in Vegas, maybe.

"Why is Kevin being so secretive?"

Tate shrugs. "Maybe he needs some time alone."

And a unicorn is my best friend. No, I remind myself, a dead woman is my best friend. Iona wouldn't have any patience for this foolishness.

"None of this makes sense," I say. "It's less than a month before the wedding, and he takes off without a word to his fiancée. He was last seen leaving an all-night diner with two Lady Gaga lookalikes. Now you're saying he's in Italy."

Tate flips his palms upward. "People do crazy things all the time before weddings. Some of them don't even show up at the altar."

Pre-marital insanity. I wonder if this is an official syndrome, recorded in the *Diagnostic and Statistical Manual of Mental Disorders*. I might have stayed in the nursing program if it had been on the curriculum. It's way more interesting than pre-menstrual syndrome although it's probably in a related family of illnesses.

Tate continues. "I like Charise. I'm sorry my brother is behaving this way. This is totally uncharacteristic. The only explanation is temporary insanity."

"That's going to make Charise feel better."

"Charise," he says, groaning. "She's out of control. No offense, but hiring a detective?" He gives me a wide-eyed stare. "They need to resolve this between themselves, not involve other people."

"She can't find him to resolve anything. Otherwise, I'm sure she would have preferred to keep this private."

"He's been found," Tate says.

"We'll see."

He juts his chin out. "You don't believe me?"

Of course I want to believe this fetching gap-toothed creature, this handsome son of Poseidon. I feel a twinge from the vicinity of my heart, only, since Dr. Fantastic, my heart no longer lives there. It was replaced by ashes and thick brown crud, the caked-on sludge at the bottom of a coffee pot that's been sitting on a burner too long. Sometimes I still perceive sensation there, a little like people with amputations who suffer from phantom limb syndrome. I have phantom heart syndrome.

Time to move on and find my inner badass. Fortunately, righteous anger is healthy.

"Charise isn't paying me to believe you. She's paying me to find Kevin."

Tate leans back, putting some distance between us. He says, "You'll make someone a wonderful pit bull someday."

Better a pit bull than a deserted fiancée. I think of Boo and smile and say, "One of my best friends is a pit bull."

BACK AT HOME, I go to my office (bedroom) and learn that the International Anesthesia Society is indeed meeting in Bellagio, Italy. Thank you, Google. The meeting is "a multidisciplinary review of current evidence and challenges." The topic is important enough to warrant a five-day meeting, which ends tonight. I suspect all topics take on great importance when they're discussed in Italy. What could be discussed in Columbus, Ohio, in an hour or two takes five days in Italy.

The meeting is being held in a seventeenth century Palazzo with a commanding view of Lake Como. Palazzo Como. This is

almost inspiration enough to make me want to become an anesthesiologist. Then again, perhaps "multidisciplinary" includes
the perspective of a nursing program dropout. Unlikely. Anyway, I
have no desire to associate with a gaggle of anesthesiologists,
especially those who go to Bellagio to engage in multidisciplinary
reviews of evidence and challenges. What a waste of Italy.

Using Google voice, I call the Palazzo. A woman answers,
saying something very beautiful in Italian. I take a wild guess and
assume she is saying Palazzo Como, good evening, how may I
help you? I trot out the only Italian I know, having heard people
are friendlier when you first attempt to butcher their language.

"Buongiorno," I say, failing to keep a little laugh out of my
voice. "Do you speak English?"

"Yes." There is no laughter in her voice. Perhaps Americans
call her all the time wishing her good morning after nine p.m. in
the evening.

I tell her I am looking for Dr. Kevin Sherman, one of the
participants at the meeting of anesthesiologists.

"The doctors," she says. "They are still at dinner."

Ah, Europe and its late dinners. I imagine the anesthesiologists lingering over tiramisu, monitoring each other for airway
obstructions as they drift off into a collective grappa haze.

"Could you connect me to his room so I can leave a message?"

"There are no phones in the room. Have you tried his cellular
phone or e-mail?"

"He's not responding."

"I will take a message for you."

"It's very urgent," I say. "He needs to call Charise." I spell
Charise's name and repeat that he needs to contact her immediately.

"These doctors have been in meetings all day. But they will be
finished with dinner soon. I will give him the message."

This seems too easy. I can't quite believe Tate told me
the truth.

I say, "So Dr. Sherman is there, at this meeting?"

She makes a clicking sound. "Why else would you be calling if he's not here?"

"I'm not sure he's there."

"Ah," she says. "You are trying to locate Dr. Sherman."

"Yes."

"And who are you?" I don't say anything for a moment. She adds, "What relation to him are you?"

"Charise is his fiancée."

"I understand," she says. "Hold a moment."

A few minutes later, she returns to the line. "There is no Dr. Sherman registered here," she says. "Where is he from?"

"Phoenix, Arizona."

"We have some Americans at the meeting, but there is no one from Phoenix."

Of course not. I thank her and lose no time in sending a text to Tate.

"Kevin not at Bellagio conference. I called. What gives?"

Optimist that I am, I expect a response pretty quickly. *Tick, tick, tick.* Nothing. More ticks and a long tock. Still nothing.

This goes to show that you can't judge a man by the dreamy gap between his front teeth. Of course this is no surprise. Still, my phantom heart smarts a little.

At Monalisa's house, Boo smothers me in dog love. In a few minutes, I get my recommended annual dose of dog slobber. This is the one chink in my germ-free bubble. I can't resist dog affection. This is probably why I am still demonstrating such good work habits as checking into the office regularly. Employers everywhere should have an office dog.

"Boo down," Monalisa says, standing up from her desk for emphasis.

Boo gets in one last wet lick up my arm before racing to Monalisa then tearing from the room, nails clacking on the floor.

"What's the latest with Kevin?" Monalisa asks.

Kevin, Kevin, Kevin. I am starting to tire of this tedious man. "He's not at his mom's house. He's not in Bellagio."

A right eyebrow shoots up. "Bellagio?"

I tell her that Kevin's mom said he was in Bellagio but that I discovered otherwise. By the time I finish speaking, Monalisa is gazing out her window. Tracking her gaze, I spot a hummingbird feeding at the Chuparosa bush in the front yard. It darts in and out of the brilliant red tubular flowers.

After a moment, her gaze returns from wild kingdom. "Do you think he's trying to get Charise to break up with him?" she asks. "Convince me this isn't just some craven act of male cowardice."

I'm not feeling up to defending Kevin at the moment. "Charise wants us to find him."

"That doesn't answer my question."

"He doesn't seem like the type to run off," I say, knowing I'm in for a lawyerly skewering. I gaze toward the wall cabinet, where the two majestic purple ceramic unicorns smile at me. Gathering positive energy around me, I beam them a request.

Oh, unicorns, kind mystical creatures, please help me. Send me some magical insights.

A moment later, they transmit a message back to me.

Dear Angela, sweet princess, we are only novelty salt-and-pepper shakers. Do not look to unicorns when you have so many powers within you.

"You don't even know the man," Monalisa says.

"He drives an old Camry." In case this isn't telling enough, for emphasis I add, "A silver one."

Monalisa tucks her chin into her neck, giving me a doomsday stare, and I know I'd better offer up something else and pronto. I dig deeper. "Kevin has made it through medical school and a residency. This demonstrates he's conscientious and careful. He's not a deserter."

"I'm willing to grant he's conscientious and careful." She nods, this lawyer and accountant, acknowledging the character-building aspect of advanced degrees. "Maybe he's a saint in almost all aspects of his life except for his relationship with Charise. He's trying to force a break-up."

The forced break-up is a well-known maneuver in the yellow-belly toolkit. The gentleman behaves so badly that the lady has no choice but to break up with him. This saves him trouble, and gives her the satisfaction of dumping the bastard. The yellow-belly undoubtedly sees this as a win-win. He never thinks of the collateral damage, the corrosive effect of rage on digestion, cortisol levels and fine lines. What a cruel way to go: riding alone into the sunset, spitting tacks.

Monalisa continues, "If Kevin was truly missing, his family would be concerned. They wouldn't be telling you stories about medical conferences."

"Something isn't right."

"Something stinks, I agree," she says. "Unfortunately, we have nothing concrete on Kevin's whereabouts. And nothing interesting has turned up about his family, right?"

"Interesting?"

"Any suggestion of criminal behavior among his family members."

I give this a spin. His mother is criminally adorable. His brother Tate is criminally cute. His uncle has a criminally lovely house. Alas, all these are figurative, not literal, forms of criminality.

"No one in the family seems to be a criminal."

Indeed, I am running out of rocks to look beneath. Still, I want to moan and groan about how I only started this job two days ago. The grown-up inside me, the one I trot out on special occasions, agrees the clock is ticking. My phantom heart gets into the act, making me feel pity and shame for wasting a scorned woman's hard-earned money.

"I'll swing by his uncle's house tonight."

Monalisa shrugs. "I'm going to talk to Charise about her options. If we're not turning up anything concrete, she may not want to continue."

No, no, no. "I agree."

"My guess is he'll turn up eventually, after she's cooled off," Monalisa says.

"Probably."

I almost say something about my plan to track down the Gaga lookalikes. My mouth opens and shuts. I'm afraid Monalisa is going to squash the idea. If she does, I will have nothing.

"You look upset," she says.

"I want to find him."

I want to keep this job. I need the money. I also need to be good at something. Anything. There comes a time in life when the line blurs between happy-go-lucky and total loser. It's time for me to get real, as horrible as that sounds.

"Sometimes people won't be found," she says. "Sometimes cases won't be solved. That's the way it goes."

There's a stone in my throat. I swallow it. "I know."

I AM IN BED, in the power cocoon. My laptop has been banished to the night table, along with my iPhone, a trial separation. Hedgie has fallen to floor, a common occurrence as I gather up the comforter and enter the power cocoon. Although technically no one can harm me right now, I am anxious. I am having an anticipatory failure attack. This triggers fond memories of my most recent spectacular failure.

I hit an all-time low when my Dr. Fantastic tried to implicate me in his Botox fraud. His lawyer thought he could get my ex a reduced sentence if he claimed I was the mastermind of the scheme, and despite his claims of love to me, he went along with his lawyer.

Dr. Fantastic said I was the business manager of his practice. This was laughably untrue, but he found an aesthetician and a masseuse to agree to this lie. I would have loved to have been the business manager or, better yet, services director. My business card said I was a "spa associate." The truth was that I was a low-level employee who took some initiative to improve the services and environment of the spa. The market for spa services is brutally competitive in the Phoenix metropolitan area, and I worked hard to help us keep up.

On a day-to-day basis, most of my work was humdrum. I scheduled the occasional appointments that came by phone rather than the automated Web system. I took payments and gave patients brochures and price sheets. Occasionally, I'd peddle the potions that do battle with all the familiar enemies of youthful skin: time, sun, facial expressions, alcohol, fun. Other times, I'd peddle potions that sounded like they should have their own aisle in Home Depot, gunk that claimed to repair integrity or firm underlying structures or build tensile strength.

After hours, I dated the boss.

I had to fight the legal charges on what amounted to a recep-tionist's salary. Fear gnawed away my insides. Cortisol and adren-aline ran rampage in my body, undermining years of disciplined skincare practices. When I pondered the possibility of prison, one thing popped into my mind.

Dad.

I wanted my father. He was the ultimate unavailable male, having died in a car accident when I was four years old. Although I never really knew him, I did pray to him when I was a wee girl. At church I thought they were teaching me to talk to my dad when I was praying. My father, who art in heaven, I would say, hands folded, eyes shuttered, sure I was dialing up my dad.

Moorea rarely spoke about him. By the time I was three years old, he'd left her, returning to a former girlfriend in San Diego. He didn't forget me, though. He sent me stuffed animals and Christmas and birthday gifts, and child support.

Although Moorea was generally tight-lipped about him, she did tell me about how he tried to teach me phone etiquette when I was a toddler.

What do you say when you're finished speaking to someone on the phone, Angela?

I love you.

That's right, honey. I love you too. After you say I love you, you say goodbye.

I love you and goodbye.

Perfect sweetheart. You got it.

I can't help it. I want my dad. I would never tell Moorea, especially since I owe her big time. For starters, I am on this planet because of her. She raised me. She's put up with me and my clothes and my Italian-made footwear all these years. She's tolerated my skincare and beauty products, which, in times of plenty, would overflow into the linen closet. She's even been good-natured when I've offered her tips about eliminating sunspots.

Most recently, she found me a lawyer. He gave me a good price because he is the brother of one of the doctors at Moorea's hospital. Moorea also took me into her house when I had nowhere else to go. She has fed me and made sure I have a roof over my head and an iPhone and health insurance and gleaming nails. For this and more, I am grateful.

Still, I want my dad. I want him to tell me I'm going to find Kevin, that it's all going to be fine, and that if I don't find Kevin, he still loves me. If this job with Monalisa ends, he'll tell me that I'll find another, even better job. And when I do, he'll help me find an apartment, scouting the neighborhood and testing the doors and windows to make sure everything passes muster. He'll help me move in, putting up white shades on the windows and installing shelving on the back of the bathroom door for my skincare essentials.

I have daddy's girl written all over me. I always have. I even have a beguiling expression that would be good for at least forty dollars and the car keys from dad. While this expression has occasionally served me well in the workplace, it is completely lost on Moorea.

Get out of bed, I tell myself. I say it again, out loud. "Get out. Now!"

ON WEDNESDAY EVENING, I am back in Uncle Dave's neighborhood. About a block from his house, I lock my bike to a stop sign and continue on foot until I have an angled view of Uncle Dave's house. On one side of me is a brick Tudor and on the other is a Cape Cod. Conveniently, the houses have a dense, gnarled Ironwood tree between them. The tree says have a seat, kick back, watch the show. I take a load off my bike-weary limbs, and fold my windbreaker onto the ground before sitting on it.

Uncle Dave's house is dark. No car is in the driveway. The street feels deserted. Despite myself, I try to enjoy the quiet. Only a few stray toddler-yodels in the distance disturb the peace.

After a half-hour of crazy-making quiet, a woman appears across the street, walking a black ball of a dog with manic stick legs. The dog stops to pee at every tree or bush along the walk. This is when it occurs to me my hiding place under the Ironwood tree may have its vulnerabilities.

I get up slowly, trying not to pull or strain anything, and hobble over to the sidewalk. Aching all over, I do some stretches, trying to coax the knots along my legs into loosening. As I torment myself, a woman walking a Lab-like mutt comes by on my side of the street. The dog rushes over to greet me.

"Clancy, get back here," the woman says.

"Hi, pup," I say, eager to make a new friend.

Clancy laps up my hands. I'm pretty much one big salt lick after cycling across the city. The owner pulls Clancy back, using both hands on the leash.

"Nice night for a run," she says.

"Yes," I lie.

In my opinion, running is a perfectly fine way to spoil an evening, which could be better spent drinking a Milano gimlet or getting a reflexology treatment. The dog owner continues down the block, Clancy protesting every so often, craning back toward me. I wave, and Clancy barks.

I check my phone. Sadly, no exciting work-related text or e-mail traffic has come my way. On Facebook, someone has posted a video of a six-year-old doing an impersonation of Aretha Franklin. I'm about to power this up when I spot a man on the sidewalk in front of Uncle Dave's house. The lit end of his cigarette pokes orange holes in the darkness. A multi-tasker, he is also speaking on his cell-phone.

His voice is familiar. I creep down the block for a better view, careful to stay in the shadows. The man is annoyingly tall. Yes, it is Mr. Neighborhood Watch, the guy with a thing for burglars. On cue, my face heats up, residual embarrassment from my last encounter with this gentleman. He stands in the driveway as if he owns it.

I turn into a statue, content to watch him from a safe distance across the street. We don't need to meet again, especially since I'm fresh out of excuses for being in the neighborhood. I'd be hard-pressed to duplicate the brilliance of the story about Uncle Dave leaving an envelope for me at his house. And Mr. Neighborhood Watch probably wouldn't buy me as a jogger.

A few minutes later, he ends his call. The cigarette snuffs out. Soon, he walks away, disappearing around the corner at the end of the block.

Back at my watching post, the Ironwood tree, I check my

messages again, realizing I am still waiting for Tate to get back to me and explain why Kevin is not at the medical conference in Bellagio. Tate has not written or called. Good thing I am not holding my breath. At this point, I'm not sure why I even bother to be disappointed.

A friend has sent me a picture of some new jeans she bought. They are two hundred dollar jeans that tug at my phantom heart. As I'm texting her back my sincere congratulations on the jeans, a Ford Focus pulls onto the street. It slows before turning into Uncle Dave's driveway, where it goes almost as far as the carport.

Speaking of the devil, Tate gets out of the car, strides over to the front door, and knocks. He knocks loudly. After, he waits in front of the door. The door doesn't open. The lights remain off. A minute later, he raps on the door.

He seems angry. The knocking seems loud and emphatic. Or is it that I'm bored and creating my own bit of reality TV?

Tate waits at the door for about thirty seconds. Then he walks around to the side of the house and peers through the gate. He kicks the gate, which rattles in response.

Several seconds later, he is back in his car, pulling out of Uncle Dave's driveway. He speeds off into the night.

Finally, Tate and I have something in common: irritation with Uncle Dave. This is probably insufficient common ground for a relationship, especially since we've gotten off to such a poor start. But, from a professional perspective, it is interesting.

More time passes. I stick to my post near the Ironwood tree, exploring a state beyond boredom. For several minutes, I clear my mind sufficiently to reach a semi-meditative state. But a soft chirrup from my iPhone sounds, and I soon find myself enmeshed in a passionate debate among my acquaintances about the merits of strawberry caipirinhas versus mint caipirinhas.

At around eleven p.m. Uncle Dave finally appears, pulling into the driveway at the wheel of a retro Thunderbird convertible, which is an arresting turquoise blue color. I forget my grievances against Uncle Dave, who has come home so late. Something stirs from deep inside my pelvic cradle. It takes hold of me, and all I can do is stare slack-jawed at that car.

Eventually, my brain function returns and, with it, a sense of injustice. Cars like these are lost on the middle-aged male. I would put that gorgeous machinery to much better use, seeing how I have more hair for the wind to blow through and more spare time for driving.

Uncle Dave rushes into his house, the front door opening and shutting in the blink of an eye. I've occasionally moved that quickly when I've had an urgent need for the bathroom. I assume that is why Uncle Dave has sprinted into his house. A half-hour later, however, the house remains dark. There is no sign of Kevin. Uncle Dave may be hiding something but he does not appear to be sheltering Kevin.

My arms prickle with cold; my legs ache. I have come up with nothing. It is time to head home, detective tail between legs. Tomorrow, Monalisa will talk to Charise about options. Charise may decide to pull the plug on the investigation. We have nothing concrete to offer her about Kevin's whereabouts. We are spending money that could go toward a better cause, such as an understanding therapist or a single's supplement for a tour of Italy.

I unlock my bike and pedal onto the street. I intend to head home, but find myself heading to Uncle Dave's house. I head up Uncle Dave's charming cobblestone driveway. This is my last chance. I'm going face-to-face with this man.

If I can't glean information by stealth, maybe I will get further by being a pest. At this point, I don't have much to lose.

I leave my bike at the back gate and approach Uncle Dave's front door. There is no doorbell. My first few knocks are polite. I give him ample time to get to the door.

The house remains still and dark. I rap at the door, loudly.

"I know you're home," I yell.

With the side of my fist, I hammer the door.

Nothing.

I grab a scrap of paper from my backpack and scribble a note to him, "Urgent: Contact me about Kevin. Angela Cray." I add my phone number and tuck it into the narrow crevice between the door and its frame.

I return to the Ironwood tree, where I watch the house. I wonder if he'll be able to resist a quick peek out a window or door. Ten minutes later, he has not appeared, proving stronger and more obstinate than I would have been under the circumstances.

I am getting the distinct impression that Uncle Dave wants to be left alone.

A soft purr draws my attention. It is a tabby cat, perhaps the same one that I met earlier on Uncle Dave's driveway. I kneel down and let it sniff my fingers.

"Hi kitty," I say.

The cat noses my leg, and I pet its head. The cat hums. Finally, something I can do well. A minute later, my new friend takes off, and I'm alone again, left to my unpleasant thoughts.

Before I hit the street, I hydrate, forcing down some lukewarm water. It tastes stagnant and metallic. Next time, I will slice some lemons into the water bottle. Next time? I realize there probably won't be a next time.

I stretch my neck backward, releasing this negativity. The sky is a grey-black glaze with a dusting of blinking stars. The air is cool and smells surprisingly fresh, like newly cut wood. I glance at my phone, and see that it is closing in on midnight.

I have tried my best to find Kevin, and that is all I can do.

At a good steady pace, I ride back home. The streets are empty. Without traffic noise, I am free to tune into the voice within. Unfortunately, that would be Monalisa's voice.

Sometimes people won't be found. Sometimes cases won't be solved.

Eventually, I pass a vacant building that used to be Maggie's Pizza. Before that, it used to be a sub shop. Before that, it was vacant for a long time. It is one of those locations where businesses go to die.

I wonder why certain locations seem cursed with a pattern of retail failure. More to the point, I wonder if I am doomed to fail in all my professional endeavors. Soon, without coming up with any answers, I turn onto my block. Home sweet home.

As I ride toward the house, I hear a car behind me. Traffic this late on a Wednesday night, or technically, extremely early on Thursday morning, is rare. I edge to the side of the road, concerned this may be a drunk person.

The car, a black BMW, is moving slowly. It appears to be driving in a straight line. Still, I am wary and turn up a driveway and ride onto the sidewalk. As the car passes, the driver glances over at me. He gives me his lazy grin and a quick wave.

It is Mr. Neighborhood Watch.

My heart thumps. I stop the bike, planting my feet on the sidewalk. We are miles from Uncle Dave's neighborhood. The BMW stops at the end of the block, where there is a stop sign. After a long pause, he takes a left.

This is so odd that I wonder if I've made a mistake about the driver. Maybe it wasn't Mr. Neighborhood Watch. Maybe I'm turning my life into reality TV. Too much surveillance is messing with my head.

I ride to the end of the block and take a left. Blocks ahead of me, I see the BMW's glimmering taillights. A minute later, they're gone, the BMW having turned to the right. I pedal for a few blocks, scanning the streets, making sure the BMW is gone.

I decide that I really did see Mr. Neighborhood Watch. His grin is unmistakable.

Pedaling hard, I race back home and stow the bike in the garage. Keeping the lights off, I run into the house directly from the garage. I am seriously tachycardic. In the kitchen, I realize I need to metabolize the cortisol and adrenaline.

It's impossible to panic when you're breathing deeply, or so

I've told clients at the day spa. I take a deep breath. One, two, three, four. Chest puffed with air, I wait another four seconds. When I feel strong pressure at the back of my neck, I do a slow, noisy release. I repeat several times. It actually seems to work.

With my heart rate back in the sane zone, I put a mug of cold water in the microwave and extract a chamomile tea bag from a cabinet. As the water heats, I wonder how Mr. Neighborhood Watch found my address. He did not follow me from Uncle Dave's house. I would have noticed him. The streets were almost devoid of traffic.

I stare at the microwave. Mr. Neighborhood Watch knows where I live. The water starts to bubble. I pull out the mug and drop the tea bag into it. How could he know where I live? I remind myself to breathe. I jiggle the tea bag around in the water.

Maybe he took my note from Uncle Dave's house. Starting with my name, he could track me to Moorea's house. This would take a little internet digging but it's not impossible. During the Botox incident, Moorea spoke to the press on my behalf. He could do a search on Moorea and find her address. But how would he presume that I could be found at my mother's house?

I take a drink of the tea. Down the hall, I can hear the light snuffle of someone snoring. Moorea and Roy are asleep. Padding quietly into the living room, I peer through the blinds.

No BMW.

Still, I sleep with one eye wide open.

7

*A*t the ungodly hour of nine a.m., my phone wakes me up with an offensively cheerful chirruping. It is a text from Monalisa.

"News?" she asks.

Good question. It is the one-week anniversary of Kevin's disappearance. I crawl out of bed and sleepwalk into the kitchen, where I study my celebratory breakfast options of plain yogurt, rice cakes, oatmeal.

These are not the food items to lift my spirits. But Moorea did not raise me to be defeated by minor setbacks. I shift my attention to the coffee maker, dumping the brown-infused water brewed earlier in the morning. Feeling better by the second, I fire up some rocket starter coffee. For food, I settle on rice cakes and almond butter.

I take my breakfast out onto the back patio, where I ponder exactly what Monalisa means by "news." A hummingbird zips into the yard and feeds at a tall, purple thistle flower. In the bright, sanitizing morning sun, I can't help but wonder again if I was mistaken about seeing Mr. Neighborhood Watch on my block.

Why would he be following me? I drink some coffee, hoping the caffeine will get the brain cells moving. My mind flashes back to the grin and the wave. Mr. Neighborhood Watch seemed to be toying with me. Playing. Regardless, none of this has any obvious link to Kevin's disappearance.

In short, I have no news to share with Monalisa.

My fingers refuse to text Monalisa three simple words, "Sorry, no news." Texts leave precious little room for nuance or, in my case, excuses. This leaves me no choice but to see Monalisa in person.

I finish my breakfast and return to my bedroom, where I consider my wardrobe options. After several minutes, I pull on an adorable pair of navy capris and a crisp white shirt, my first non-biking outfit in days. After ironing my hair to sleek, seal-like perfection, I start putting on the makeup. I am glossing a second coat of mascara on my right eye when I realize this is futile.

In the past, a sharp outfit and impeccable makeup typically translated into mercy and forgiveness at work, especially if my boss was of the masculine persuasion. My sharp appearance is not going to impress Monalisa. I seriously doubt she's a sucker for an elegant white shirt.

Nevertheless, being a consummate professional, I finish putting on my face. When I reach Monalisa's house, I linger at the side fence, where I take in the sad state of Iona's garden. The snap peas writhe in a tangle. The withered tomato vines resemble razor wire.

I can almost hear Iona saying, "What mischief have we here, my pretties?" The garden is beyond mischief; it is dying. Soon enough, Monalisa will probably hire landscapers, who will uproot the garden entirely.

Keep moving, I tell myself. *Go.*

But I don't move. I keep staring at the yard.

The hard part with this case ending is that I have tried my hardest and still failed. This is disconcerting. I am quite comfortable with the notion of failing because the job was stupid or my boss was useless or I didn't care enough to put forth the effort. But coming up blank after I have truly applied myself? After I have rubbed my thighs raw with cycling? This is something new and awful.

A sorrowful ache is coming from my phantom heart. My inner coach kicks into gear. Somewhere I read that if you fail and learn something from it, you have not failed. What have I learned? *Sometimes people won't be found. Sometimes cases won't be solved.* Hardly reassuring.

My mind reaches back for other, more reassuring lessons from premature job loss.

At a gift basket company, I worked in customer service. I was fine with the service part of the job. But it is amazing how many ill-tempered morons turn out to be customers. I learned that public-facing jobs are a challenge if one is not a big fan of the gift basket purchasing public.

Working at a small bookstore in the lobby of a hospital, I learned it was possible to die of loneliness. One day, in desperation, I purchased a plush ground hog from the gift shop to keep me company. We became close, and I named him Hedgie. In talking business with Hedgie, I landed on the idea of selling books to patients door-to-door. I listed several titles on an order form, including those I thought particularly helpful for patients, soothers like *Chicken Soup for the Soul* and life-affirming romances like *Born in Fire* and, one of Iona's favorites, *A Knight in Shining Armor.*

After a brisk morning of sales, a hospital administrator accosted me in the hallway, obviously threatened by my success. Apparently it's perfectly fine to peddle grossly overpriced opiate derivatives to a captive audience. But books, which feed the mind and elevate the spirit, have to stay in the bookstore and rely on walk-in customers.

In waitressing, I learned that I have a keen memory for hairstyles and unfortunate fashion choices. I could care less about who ordered what and even less about people with endless questions about food preparation or an irrational hatred of perfectly inoffensive foods like cucumbers. Waitressing was hell on my nails as well.

I'm sensitive to smells. This I learned at a car rental office, where it stank of burnt rubber. It made me nauseous. The last straw was when my chin broke out.

When I walked into the day spa for my first interview, I could almost hear the angels sing. This was my place in the world. It smelled right, like tropical flowers after a fresh rain with a touch of lemongrass. It looked right, with warm, complexion-flattering lighting. And it performed a vital function, leaving customers happier and more youthful and rested looking.

While there, I helped create something truly special, an immersive experience that rejuvenated clients. I replaced the soft jazz soundtrack with the soothing sounds of ocean waves lapping the shore, whales breaching, and the distant ring of Asian wind chimes. To the decor, I added textural organic elements such as decorative branches and Japanese viewing stones. I upgraded the towels to a sumptuous level of plush.

I took the job seriously, and although the environment suggested complete relaxation, behind-the-scenes the place ran with the precision of the Swiss train system. Everything was running beautifully, that is, until it all turned into a spectacular supernova of crap.

Every time I care about something, it turns to crap. This is my big insight. Part of me shrugs. No one said the world is fair.

At the front door, Monalisa ushers me inside without the usual fifty-point inspection. Boo is delighted, absolutely delirious with joy, to see me. He does a spectacular half-twist X Games maneuver in the foyer. I embrace him, hoping it's not our last meeting.

Monalisa walks into her office, where she sits behind her

desk. I take a chair directly across from her. Boo circles me. I wonder if I can have visitation rights to Boo after I no longer work for Monalisa.

"Boo," Monalisa says. Boo trots over to her and sits down. Monalisa nods at me.

I tell her about not spotting Kevin at his uncle's house the night before but seeing his brother Tate bang on the door.

"Tate," she says, drawing out his name like it's made of taffy.

I wait for her to offer up some other kind of response. She doesn't. Okay, onto the next piece of news. I tell her about Uncle Dave coming home late and leaving the lights off, and how he didn't answer the door even after I knocked loudly on it.

She slowly rotates her palms upward into sign language for "so what?"

"Haven't you had days like that? You get home late, you're tired, and you want to be left alone," Monalisa says.

Another strike. Saving the best for last, I tell her about Mr. Neighborhood Watch, how we met at Uncle Dave's place and how I spotted him on my block last night.

Her brows squeeze together. Her index finger taps at her lips. She's looking at me like I'm a piece of furniture she just bought and doesn't know where to put yet.

"You're sure about this man tracking you down?" she asks.

"Pretty sure," I say.

"You were watching David Newman's house by yourself for a few hours. That can play tricks with your imagination. Humans are pattern-seeking animals. We're always trying to extract meaning from what happens to us, even when there might not be any."

"He slowed to a crawl and waved at me," I say.

"Did you get his license plate number?"

I shake my head and exhale brain cells. *Of course not. No. Sorry for taking your time. I'll just be on my way to find another job now.*

"I was so surprised, I didn't think to get the license plate number."

"Most people would have reacted that way."

Most people. I want to say that I am not like most people. Unfortunately, I don't have a leg to stand on at this moment.

"He might be watching Uncle Dave's house," I say.

"How would that connect with Kevin?"

"I don't know yet."

Boo gets up and stretches, and Monalisa smiles at him. "We'll go out in a minute." She shifts her gaze back to me. "It is what it is, Angela. Some cases end this way."

No! I may be a quitter but I don't take losing well. I hate to lose. This is what I am learning from this experience of failure. My teeth sink into my lower lip, which provokes an idea. The Gaga impersonators. This is the lead I have stowed away in a safe haven deep inside me, the room with flowers and pretty throw pillows and afternoon light.

"It's a long-shot," I say. The flowers in my little mental room wilt at the doubt in my voice. "But the impersonators were the last ones to see him. I could resume my watch for them."

Monalisa sighs and sits back in her chair. "I don't mean to suggest we've completely run out of investigative steam. We could have you pursue the impersonators or, for that matter, park you outside his mother's house for the next month. Unfortunately, we have no indications that these are promising investigative directions. Is that a fair statement?"

I exhale long and hard. "Yes."

She taps her fingers on her desk, all business. "Hold off on charging any other time to the case. I'll review what we've learned with Charise and see what she says."

So it goes. I shutter the windows on my secret little room. Maybe next season I'll get to open the room up again, air out the place, invite hope back inside.

ON THE WAY HOME, I think about finding another job. A new day spa has opened up on Camelback. I start to walk faster, intent on submitting a job application as soon as possible. The competition will be fierce as everyone who has ever been to a day spa thinks they can work at one.

As I near the house, my immediate goals shift. I decide I'll feel much better if I take some time in the power cocoon. It's a truly restorative wellness treatment.

I change out of my outfit and into my casual loungewear and crawl into bed, pulling the comforter around my body and over my head. Soon, there is a silence. The world outside has disappeared.

Several minutes later, a knock on my door interrupts my treatment.

"Sweetheart?" asks Moorea, who has an uncanny sense of exactly when I'm feeling most lost.

I pull the comforter off and say, "Is this important?"

"Yes, I need to speak with you."

I grab my laptop and sit up straight, trying to appear semi-presentable. After many years, I have finally trained Moorea to wait for me to tell her it's okay to enter my bedroom. At the hospital, health workers have this terrible habit of barging into rooms at all hours without knocking. This may pass muster in the hospital but it is unacceptable behavior in a home environment.

"Come in," I say.

Moorea enters the room, closing the door behind her. She sits on the edge of the bed.

"What's up?" I ask.

Her eyes are shiny. "I have some news."

In my head, I hear a terrible cracking noise, like an ancient tree falling.

"You're not sick are you?" I ask. "Tell me you're okay."

"No, baby," she says, her eyes welling up. "I'm happy."

I hear myself exhale. "You scared me."

She laughs, wiping her eyes. "Roy and I are very much in love."

"That's great, Mom."

"He's tired of driving in from Chandler," she says. "He's ready to take the next step. I am too. It's time."

It is not like Moorea to be indirect. "He's going to move in with us?"

He's already here most of the time so this is not a big deal. Once or twice a week they stay at his house. I wish he made stronger coffee, but otherwise he's not a bother.

She locks eyes with me. "We're getting married."

I push the laptop aside and lean over to give her a big hug. "Congratulations! That's wonderful."

"It's still a bit away. We're thinking a fall wedding, when the weather won't be so hot."

"Do you want me to help plan it? I'll go dress shopping with you. We can get our hair and nails done. Oh, and flowers—"

"No, we're going to do something small and simple. We don't want a formal wedding. We're putting our money into buying a place together. A place that will be both of ours."

Now I understand why she called me sweetheart. I realize I will be moving as well. They will not be building a love nest for three. I will be on my own.

I take a deep breath and say, "You should have your own place. Just the two of you. When are you thinking you'll move?"

"Soon," she says. "We found a house a few days ago. I didn't want to say anything to you until we decided to put in an offer. We weren't actively searching, but we both fell in love with this house."

"You put an offer on a house?"

"Yes, and they accepted it. They want to settle quickly."

"How quickly?"

"Next month."

I'm already sitting in my bed, otherwise I might have collapsed onto the floor. "That's quick."

"Now that you have this job with Monalisa, I feel it's a good time for all of us to start fresh. You can get a cute place of your own."

I stare at her, trying to keep the smile on my face. What happened to her hating my job with Monalisa? I hear myself say, "Well, congratulations again."

Moorea gives me a soulful look. My toes curl.

"You're going to be fine, baby," she says.

No, no I'm not! "I know."

"Everyone goes through rough patches. You're out of the woods now."

I can't trust my quivering mouth to release words. *Please, goddess, please don't let me blubber.* I think of fires and earthquakes, and of my distant Samoan ancestors who barbecued their enemies for dinner.

"You can take care of yourself again. That's how I raised you. And I did a darn good job."

Tears stream from my eyes. The smile has slipped off my face, sliding down a stream of salt water before bungee jumping off my chin.

"I want you to be happy," I say, the words coming out wet and slurry.

Moorea holds me against her. "I know you do. But you don't look too happy at the moment."

"I'll miss you."

"I'll miss you too, baby."

Her face glows with happiness. She resembles a blissed-out saint from a religious painting. She's been struck by a heavenly thunderbolt of happiness.

After giving me one last vise squeeze of happiness, Moorea floats out of my room.

I SPEND the afternoon with my laptop at the lovely library in downtown Scottsdale, which isn't far from Moorea's house, and search the job boards. The new spa on Camelback no longer has a job available. But there's another new place called Cactus Flower, which is looking for an assistant-level whatever. When I call they ask me about my grooming experience. I find this odd until I learn they are a dog spa.

I try to talk my way into an interview. I tell them about my talent with all types of hair and my long friendship with Boo. My deep interest in grooming. My ability to sooth angry and irrational clients.

No dice.

I message all my friends, telling them I'm looking for work. By the end of the afternoon, I've got no leads. Three of my friends ask if I want to go out for drinks. Now those are some great friends. Alcohol pairs so well with unemployment.

Late afternoon, Monalisa texts me, "Charise says okay to continue."

I read the text twice, not quite believing it. Then I write back: "Will do."

Will do. Can do. Must do. A reprieve. I got a reprieve!

In a celebratory mood, I bike home and find Moorea and Roy in the kitchen, which smells earthy, like plant roots. They've been chopping carrots and broccoli. A large square of quivering tofu sits on the kitchen island. The wok sizzles on the stove.

Moorea gives me a radiant smile. "Hi, honey."

She looks so happy, my heart wobbles. The mask of worry is gone; the only evidence it ever existed is in the faint webbing around her mouth and eyes. The dents and hollows of worry and stress have diminished.

I've seen similar results with Botox and filler. In Moorea's case, love and a truckload of vegetables seem to have done the trick. Roy is looking well, too. He's lost at least thirty pounds since the cardiac event put him in Moorea's hospital.

"Do you want to join us for dinner or will you be working tonight?" Moorea asks.

I gaze at Moorea then Roy. They both look so content.

Roy smiles and says, "You've got to take some time out for dinner."

I find myself saying, "No, sorry, I've got to work tonight."

Around six p.m., I set off to the office of NB Entertainment for an evening of celebrity watching. When I arrive, Mercado Temixco is doing a brisk business in grilled chicken. Three cars are lined up at the drive-through window.

I pull into the far corner of the lot and straddle my bike. The smell of grilled chicken makes me realize I should have had some vegetable and tofu stir-fry before I left the house. When you are watching every penny, it is important to never leave the house hungry.

A skinny black dog trots into the parking lot and, head down, sniffs the pavement. When the dog is a few feet from me, its head jerks upright. We stare at each other. A moment later, the dog takes a wide detour around me on his trip to the dumpster, perhaps recognizing me as a formidable competitor for chicken scraps.

Sixty minutes come and go with nary a celebrity sighting. Even the dog has left, giving up on chicken scraps. I pull out my phone and page through Facebook.

"When is Lady Gaga coming?" says a heavily accented man's voice.

It's the man in the drive-through window, peering out at me.

I smile. "If I see her, I'll ask."

"No chicken for you tonight?"

I glance down at my hands. "I'm on a budget."

He shakes his head slowly, faking great sadness. "You're going to stand in our parking lot and not buy anything?"

"Yes," I say. "It's my job."

He smiles. "I've got a special price for you, a special for crazy women."

I wheel my bike closer to the window. "What's that?"

"Ten dollars for chicken plus two sides. That's our weekend price, but I'll give it to you tonight."

Ten dollars. I glance down at my chipped nail. Is ten dollars going to make a difference between me getting an apartment or not? No. I'm an entire job away from being able to move.

"Deal," I say, cycling over to the front of the market, where I lock my bike to the side of a worn wooden bench.

Inside the store, we introduce ourselves. His name is Ramón. He pronounces my name as Anhella.

I sit at a single white plastic table jammed up against a refrigerated cabinet of sodas. The chicken is delicious. Occasionally I pause to breathe and slurp some Diet Coke. I am $11.50 poorer, but I am happy.

Ramón folds his arms across his chest. "You pretty normal-looking for a crazy person," he says, with a faint hint of a smile.

I suppose that's a compliment. "Thank you."

"Usually the crazy ones smell bad. They come in here, scratching their arms and yelling. They're angry." He eyes turn into slits. "So angry. They're punching and kicking at the air, beating up invisible people."

"I'm not crazy," I say, draining my Diet Coke.

"Why are you looking for Lady Gaga in our parking lot?"

His expression betrays no hint of amusement or skepticism. He appears to be genuinely interested.

"I'm looking for someone else, someone who was last seen with a woman dressed like Lady Gaga." On my phone, I page through photos, looking for the one Charise sent me of Kevin. "He disappeared a month before his wedding."

Ramón laughs. "It's simple. He don't want to get married."

When I've found the photo of Kevin, who is wearing a white

polo shirt, I get up and show Ramón, who studies the screen of my phone.

"I've seen him."

"Are you kidding?"

His nose is inches from my screen. He appears to know Kevin on a pixel-level.

"Last week, he came in around closing time." He hands me back the phone. "He was wearing something else."

"Do you remember what?"

"The kind of clothes they wear in the hospital. You know, the blue shirt with the short sleeves and the pants that tie with a string."

"Scrubs," I say.

"That's it," he says. "And he was *borracho*." Ramón fans the air around his face for emphasis. "Very drunk. I was watching him, thinking he was going to vomit."

"That drunk?"

"He was mumbling and swaying. His head kept nodding, like he was going to sleep. He wanted to know if we had any coffee."

"Was he alone?"

Ramón rubs the side of his face. "I think so. We get a lot of people come into the store."

"Was there someone waiting for him in the parking lot?"

Ramón shrugs. "I don't know. I sold him two bottles of water. We don't have coffee."

"After that?"

"He left."

Outside, with my stomach full of chicken and Diet Coke, I intend to unlock my bike and head home. Instead, I sit on a bench near the front door of the market, taking a moment to celebrate this new information. Kevin was here. There's no doubt in my mind. Ramón even remembers the scrubs.

I mentally retrace Kevin's steps. Kevin exits American Egg with the Gagas and drinks with wild abandon. For some reason, the lookalikes take Kevin back to NB Entertainment and he stumbles into Mercado Temixco for coffee.

Stumbling drunk. This would help explain Kevin's whereabouts Thursday night and perhaps a good portion of Friday morning. It would not explain why he'd still be missing a week later. It wouldn't explain why his car was missing or why he hadn't withdrawn any money from his accounts.

Still, Ramón's observations don't suggest Kevin was abducted. He appeared to be alone trying to buy coffee at Mercado Temixco. And, if Kevin was abducted, at least two people were involved, including the two Gaga lookalikes and maybe someone from NB Entertainment. This suggests planning, organization and teamwork. In general, people don't engage in these unnatural activities unless they're getting paid or going on vacation. It doesn't appear that Kevin's family has been hit up for money by kidnappers.

I dash off a text to Charise, telling her about the sighting of Kevin in his scrubs and drunk. I can already guess that she will express surprise and no small amount of doubt. My best guess is that Kevin is not much of a drinker. You'd probably never find him in a bar, red-faced, wearing a Hawaiian shirt, bellowing for a final round of shots at last call.

Maybe the lookalikes poisoned him and stole his car. Humiliated, he's fled Phoenix, unable to face Charise or his life.

Somehow, I doubt it.

A Kanye lookalike drives by and disappears into the parking lot. I walk along the side of the lot, threading around cars, until I'm in the back, where I watch him from the shadows of a desiccated palm tree. Kanye hops out of the car, leaving the engine going, and disappears through the back door of NB Entertainment. He carries a small black duffel bag. A minute later, he emerges with the same duffel bag over his shoulder and gets back into his car and drives off.

This is the same drill all the fake celebrities seem to follow. It is so odd. Why would the lookalikes have to check-in at the office? They're in and out so quickly most don't even bother to turn off their car engines. I try to think of reasons they would need to visit the office. There doesn't appear to be any adorable dog greeting them there. They could file their invoices and expenses electronically. They wouldn't need to pick-up their paycheck.

Paycheck. Maybe they don't get paychecks. If paid in cash, they would be motivated to stop by the office. Tax-free income is a powerful draw.

Dolly Parton pulls into the parking lot in a green Kia Soul. Be still my heart. I love this car. Dare I say it may be a love I can afford, a love within grasp, a love that actually might be attainable? Attainable, that is, after I get and keep a decent job.

I will always have a special feeling for the Honda Coupe. Even so, there comes a time in every girl's life when she needs to be realistic. As I am in the dark side of my twenties, this appears to be that time.

Dolly pulls around to the back door of NB Entertainment. A song by Taylor Swift warbles from the car. Swift is singing about a mean person.

Leaving the engine running, Dolly gets out of the car. Immediately, I see she is too tall and thin to pass for Parton. She has overcompensated in the chest area, with mountainous bosoms straining against a ridiculous Daisy Mae gingham top. These twin mounds are an architectural wonder of the world. Bags of sunflower seeds? Tempur-pedic pillows?

As she struts toward the back door, I am transfixed. She wears black stiletto booties with killer heels. Those suckers must be five inches high. Somehow, I recognize these booties. Somehow, my legs are taking me toward the Kia Soul.

Dolly disappears inside NB Entertainment. She is wearing the booties the Gagas wore the night they encountered Kevin. Those shoes are unforgettable.

Taylor Swift is still singing about this abusive guy who doesn't think she can sing. The driver-side door of the Kia Soul is unlocked. I open it and hit the universal unlock.

Taylor calls the mean guy a liar. And a cheat. *That's you, Kevin!* Humming along with the music, which shuts up the voices protesting in my head, I scrunch into the back seat of the car and shut the door quietly. Taylor sings away, about leaving the mean person and moving to the big old city.

The back seat of the Kia Soul is a little tight, a good thing when you're trying to hide. It's even tighter because of the trash. Dolly Gaga is a bit of a slob. I maneuver three empty containers of coconut water and a takeout bag from Kepi's Vegan Cafe out from under me. A Spark Fitness water bottle rests on the back seat along with several used gym towels.

There is a terrible smell. I quickly identify the culprits, a hideous pair of black gym shoes. They are stiffer than most gym shoes, with three velcro straps along the top instead of shoelaces. Could this be some terrible new athletic fashion? I grab them, ready to toss them out the window, when I hear the clack of stiletto heels.

Dolly Gaga opens the front door, gets inside, and pushes a black nylon zippered bag into the back. It lands with a plop onto the seat. I release the gym shoes.

As the car pulls out of the lot, I can see a slice of the world through the back window. A few minutes too late, I wonder what on earth I'm doing. Dear dad in heaven, this is insanity.

Focus. I'm in a Kia Soul with Dolly Gaga. *Focus.* A voice inside me protests: *How will I get information about Kevin from this woman?* My major superpower is calming down frequent frowners! *It's going to be okay*, I reassure myself. *The doubters are wrong. She's going to tell you where Kevin is hiding. Stop breathing so loudly.*

Luckily, she's still got Taylor Swift playing, loudly.

I divert myself with happy thoughts about where we're going and how I'm going to get home without a car. I am having some stow-away regrets. This is seriously off-road, beyond the comprehension of Monalisa and well outside the agreement with Charise.

I hate to lose. This is kind of funny given how many jobs I've lost. But when I care about something, I really hate to lose.

Several few minutes later, the Kia slows down. *Hallelujah!* We are taking a left. We pull into the parking lot of a 7-11. Never in my life have I been so happy to see the unflattering fluorescent lights of a convenience store.

Dolly Gaga parks the Soul, locks the doors, and walks into the 7-11. I start to clamber out of the car, pushing aside Dolly Gaga's black zippered gym bag. But the bag gives me an idea. A second later, I am outside the car, with her black nylon bag looped around my shoulder. I am not a thief; I just appear to be one at the moment. I figure Dolly Gaga will be more helpful if I offer her an incentive for disclosing to me Kevin's whereabouts.

Usually, I would not stoop to extortion, but desperate times call for desperate measures. That back seat is vile, and I can't tolerate any more stowing away. My lack of progress on tracking down Kevin is becoming an embarrassment.

Inside the 7-11, I watch as Dolly purchases some blaze orange bottled beverage at the counter. When she comes out of the store, I am in the obvious act of admiring her Kia Soul, circling it, gazing lovingly through its front windshield. Her clacking booties return to her car.

"What are you doing?" She gazes at me, lips pursed, only slightly hostile, perhaps concerned I am casing her vehicle. I've not set off any major alerts with her yet. She doesn't seem to have noticed that I have her gym bag. Luckily, it is black nylon and nondescript.

I decide to warm her up with some small talk before hitting her up for information on Kevin.

"I'm thinking of getting one of these cars. How do you like it?"

"It has four wheels. It takes me places."

She's so sour, exactly the kind of person who receives a gift basket and calls customer service to complain. I doubt she'll become friendlier when she realizes I've swiped her gym bag.

"Wow, that's pretty great for a car. It takes you places," I say. "Is it fun to drive?"

She gives me a look. Safe to say, she is not a car lover. Usually people brighten when I ask about their cars. They are flattered. It's almost like complimenting their child or dog.

I press on. "Are you in a bad mood because you've wearing five-inch heels?"

She swings the car door open, ignoring me. But she doesn't get inside the vehicle right away. Instead, she looks down at the oil-stained pavement. I wonder if she's going to realize the car door should have been locked. I wonder if she's going to realize I've got her black gym bag looped over my shoulder. She already must have noticed that I am unusually burdened, wearing both a backpack and a gym bag.

"I've got another question for you," I say.

She doesn't say anything. She's still looking down at the pavement. Her brain is probably sending her signals that something is awry but she hasn't processed them yet.

"I'm looking for a man named Kevin Sherman," I continue. "He was wearing surgical scrubs when you encountered him."

"No idea." She leans inside her car and puts her energy drink in a cup holder.

I raise my voice. "I saw you with him last week. You were dressed like Lady Gaga. You're wearing the same shoes. It's on YouTube."

She slowly backs out of the car and straightens. She stares at me with new interest. "Have you been following me?"

"Good question." I smile.

Her gaze sweeps over me and rests on the black bag looped around my shoulder.

A storm system hits her. She points at the bag. "Give that back to me."

"Where's Kevin?"

She glances at the 7-11. Two people are waiting at the counter, their backs to us. The clerk is busy with the register.

Her left hand juts out while she pulls a small gun from her purse and points it at me. "Put the bag in the car."

I see the gun. My mind takes a moment to process the gun. It appears real, unlike the fun gun she waved around in American Egg. Still, I don't think she's going to shoot me in front of the 7-11. Any moment now, people inside the store will notice the gun. Her slender left hand, attempting to block the view of spectators, isn't quite up to the job.

"I'll give you the bag when you tell me where Kevin is."

"You idiot, give me the bag."

The name-calling doesn't help. A bell dings as a customer exits the 7-11. She gives the man an exasperated look and lowers the gun, muttering sweet nothings under her breath.

I unzip Dolly Gaga's gym bag. My hand plunges inside, and I feel a lot of plastic bags.

"Where's Kevin?" I ask. "Speak up. I can't hear you."

I peer inside the nylon sack. It is full of glassine bags that contain white powder. The bags are stamped with blue ink that says "Obamacare."

Dear dad in heaven. I've seen these types of bags before, on the TV news. Stories about drug busts. Drug dealers brand heroin this way. Heroin.

"We dropped him off at the office," Dolly Gaga says, her voice even and calm. Her gun is upright again, aimed at me. I look at Dolly Gaga. I feel no fear. I feel nothing at all. Out of the corner of my eye, I spot a man inside the 7-11 pointing at us.

"I don't know where he is," she continues. "You can't keep that bag. You're going to get killed."

An alarm sounds. I gaze behind me. The counter guy at 7-11, mouth gawping, is hunched over, hands above his head. I spot a customer crawling away from the door. Safe to assume they saw the gun.

I sprint out of the parking lot. Behind me, the Kia's engine roars. I pound ahead, onto the street. The Kia's wheels shriek as it backs up and around.

I'm on a familiar street, but more than a mile from Mercado Temixco and my bike. The Kia zooms past me, heading east. I run the same direction until I reach the next intersection, where I veer to the right, into a residential area. The siren is still going.

I race up a block with small tract houses. *Faster*, I tell myself. But I am no runner and the block is long. It dead-ends into a fenced industrial area. I take a left and jog along another long block. On my right, the fenced industrial area continues. If the police spot me, my hiding places are limited. At the next intersection, I go left, heading up another street of houses.

My gait has become sloppy. It's unclear whether I'm stumbling forward or running. My muscles are spent. My lungs burn. The backpack and gym bag feel heavier by the second. I have already ridden a number of miles on my bike today.

I will not escape through physical speed. This means I need to be smart. In a minute, maybe less, the police will find me. They'll find me with a gym bag full of heroin.

About ten feet ahead, I reach an unlit stucco ranch and hustle through its side gate, entering the yard. Somewhere down the block a dog is barking. At the back of the yard is a garage and another gate, which leads to an alley. The barking becomes louder.

Much as I would like to stay in the dark back yard, I decide I must leave. I enter the alley, which smells like rotting garbage. My stomach churns. But I realize the smell probably keeps people from spending much time here. I pass by a dumpster with a warped top.

After I put some distance between me and the dumpster, I pause to catch my breath. I drop the gym bag on the ground so I can gulp down more oxygen. Soon I find myself leaning against a dusty garage door for support.

I should have given Dolly Gaga the gym bag back. At the clang of the alarm, I should have swung her car door open and tossed the bag inside. If I weren't so exhausted, I would kick myself.

With shaking fingers, I call Monalisa. It goes directly to voice-mail. I leave a message, telling her I've run into some trouble. I don't, however, mention drugs.

Heroin. I need to go to the police. But I can't go to the police alone. I don't want to get blamed for dealing heroin. I've already faced accusations of trafficking bootleg Botox. Even being innocent of these charges, it was costly to mount a defense. I can't afford a lawyer. I can't even afford to move into an apartment.

I need to get back to Monalisa's house and explain everything to her. She will know what to do. She will help me.

I continue down the alley, which leads directly to the street I have been trying to avoid. Great move. What a brilliant escape. The 7-11 is only a few blocks away.

To the left of the alley is an assisted living community called Sunview Square. It is a sprawling colonial structure with a wide drive leading to the front and parking at the front and around the sides. It offers up some greenery, trees and shrubs, along with a meandering walkway.

I'm about to turn back down the alley when I spot a man sitting at a bus stop. A bus strikes me as the perfect getaway vehicle. No one would think to look for me on a bus. The only issue is that I can't sit next to this man at the bus stop. I'd be spotted in a few minutes.

I take a closer look at the grounds around the assisted living place. The walkway has a bench about every five feet, which is perfect for elderly people who can't manage more than a few feet without needing a rest. At the moment, this would be me.

At the corner of the property, I sit under a pergola with a

lovely view of the parking lot and a view of the bus stop. I scan the area, looking for people in the vicinity who might be curious about my presence there. A breeze rustles some shrubbery, which gives me a scare. To my left, I can see into a large dining room. At this hour, it's deserted, except for four people and their walkers seated at a round table. They appear to be playing cards.

I pull out my cell-phone. Monalisa has sent me a text: "Kevin's car found near Apache Junction. It's full of chips and empties. Police think it was stolen. Call me."

I tap on Monalisa's number. Again, it goes into voicemail. I hear myself exhale loudly.

I sit back, waiting for the bus. For fifteen minutes I wait patiently. At this time of night, I realize the bus could be a long time in coming. Using my phone, I search for bus schedules. Even if it's a long wait, it's better to know how much time is involved.

As I click on the bus schedule, an arm loops around my neck. I scream. The arm fastens harder. I jerk back and forth, trying to free myself. My arms swing up and back, fighting. In the process, my phone flies from my hand and lands somewhere behind me, rustling in the shrubbery.

I howl, digging my nails into the leather jacket of my captor. He presses down on me, the weight pinning me into the bench. My yell comes out a gargling sound. I kick my feet against the ground.

Mr. Neighborhood Watch appears in front of me. "Hello, Angela. I'm going to have to ask you to use your indoor voice. You know why?"

"Help!" The words barely make it out of my mouth.

I turn my head, toward the crook of my captor's elbow, trying for more air. But I can barely maneuver around the thick leather of his coat. The world turns fuzzy for a moment.

"Good thing our closest neighbors are mostly hard of hearing," Mr. Neighborhood Watch says. "I'm going to have to insist you settle down."

This is a cue for me to writhe again. I gargle out a yell.

"We have a colleague posted outside your mother's house. Do you want him to introduce himself to your mom?"

I try to shake my head. My chin barely moves.

He continues, "Moorea is such an interesting name."

I rock back. The arm around my neck loosens slightly.

"Take the bag, I don't want it," I say. "It was a big mistake."

Mr. Neighborhood Watch smiles. "Too late. You've already seen what's inside. Fortunately, you didn't probe deeply enough to find the tracer." He turns and nods. Another man appears and collects my backpack and the gym bag. He is wearing a black t-shirt, pants, and gloves. Gloves. Dear dad in heaven.

Mr. Neighborhood Watch says, "We always add a tracker to a delivery this size."

"I only want to find Kevin."

He offers up a smiling grimace. "About Kevin..."

"What?" I ask.

"Oh, nothing," he says, flipping his hand through the air. "I don't want to spoil your evening."

The man holding me lifts me upward. I am now standing, my back arched, as if against a powerful wind. My feet are pushing away from the pavement.

A black Mercedes rolls up in front of us. With the driver, that makes four men abducting me. I nearly faint. The doors unlock. Mr. Neighborhood Watch opens the trunk.

One of the men tosses my backpack and the gym bag into the back seat.

"No," I say, realizing the trunk is for me. "No!"

Still in a heavy neck lock, the man wearing the dark gloves pats me down.

"Where's her phone?" Mr. Neighborhood Watch asks.

"I dropped it when you grabbed me," I say.

"Excuse me," a female voice says in the distance.

"Help!" I cry.

Mr. Neighborhood Watch nods, and the man holding me pitches me into the trunk. I bang my head against the top of the lid and land on my wrist. A bolt of pain shoots through my arm. I scream. A second later, a fist hits the side of my shoulder.

"Shut up," a man says.

I push myself deeper into the trunk.

A fist hits the side of my body. Hard. For a second, I don't breathe.

"Gentlemen," Mr. Neighborhood Watch says. "Try to be gentle with our guest. Show her some hospitality."

"I can't move my arm. Oh my God!"

"There should be some rope in the car," Mr. Neighborhood Watch says. "And don't forget to tape her mouth."

I can still move my arm. But I don't want to be tied up. I start sobbing.

"Anything broken?" one of the men asks.

I let my breathing go jagged. "My wrist. I can't move it."

"Good," he says.

I hear someone in the car, opening and shutting compartments, looking for a rope.

"Angela," Mr. Neighborhood Watch says. "Please forgive my friends. They're not cultured. They don't know how to treat a lady."

The men laugh. I don't.

"Hello?" a woman's voice calls. She sounds fairly far away. Maybe she is standing at the front door of the assisted living residence.

A hand reaches in and tightens against my mouth.

Footsteps shuffle over the pavement, like someone jogging. Several seconds later, Mr. Neighborhood Watch says something to the woman. They exchange some words, but I can't make out what they're saying.

I pretend to pass out, letting my head droop, letting the fight go out of my aching body, letting my mouth go slack under the weight of the hand pressing against it. This is not easy. If they think I'm out, maybe they won't tie me up.

A minute later, Mr. Neighborhood Watch is back at the car and says, "Let's go."

The hand releases from my mouth. "She's not secured."

"There's no time. The night manager of the old folk's home is going to call the police."

"I think she's passed out," a man says. "She says her wrist is broken."

That gets a skeptical grunt from Mr. Neighborhood Watch. "I sincerely doubt it."

The trunk shuts. My world turns into a grey-black smear.

8

I am curled up in the trunk of a car. I think I've been here in here for about a half-hour but it could be more or less. I've lost track of time. The trunk smells like wet dog, although that could be me. My mouth is dry, so dry I might choke on my tongue.

I have been asking myself why I didn't give Dolly Gaga the gym bag back after I saw the heroin inside. More than anything, I guess I had to win. Why did I have to win, I wonder. Because I am tired of losing?

I run a test of different body parts. I open my hand and close it. I wiggle my toes. My fingers tingle. My ribs ache. My arm hurts. My face is wet. My nose is running. My teeth are rattling.

The Mercedes seems to be moving through quiet streets. I don't hear many other cars. We are probably going somewhere dark and deserted. They will not kill me while I'm in the trunk. That would make a mess. And the trunk feels clean. The cropped carpet is smooth, with no sticky spots or crumbs. Perhaps I'm its first inhabitant.

Oh, dad, who art in heaven. Help me, please. When I was a child, and Moorea overheard me praying to my dad, she explained that people in heaven can't communicate directly with us. But this would be a good time for a change in policy.

The car speeds up. I hear the hum of expensive machinery gliding down the desert autobahn. We are on a highway.

The tears break through the dam. Moorea is so happy right now. Why do I have to ruin things for her? After several minutes of slobbering I consider the bright side: I don't have to worry about getting a new apartment. About keeping a job. About finding the love of my life. About getting a life.

A small laugh escapes me. This triggers a stabbing pain from my ribcage. Something broken? I exhale hard. The pain makes me dizzy. I have an ice pick caught in my ribs.

This doesn't bode well for my escape. I close my eyes, knowing I need serious assistance. I call upon the gods and goddesses of my distant ancestors. *Tagaloa, let all things conspire toward the good and pure. Tuli, creator goddess. I beg you for a spark of inspiration. Mahuika, goddess of fire and earthquakes, please give me strength. Mother of the sun, moon, and sea, let this humble creature live.*

The car zips along. When the car stops, they will pop the trunk and ask me to get out. Then they will shoot me and hide my body.

Laughter leaks out of me. My ribs shriek. I groan. I'm losing it.

Oh dad who art in heaven. I clasp my hands. I can move my hands! They did not tie me up. Now I remember. There wasn't time. I hear a woman's voice, the woman from the assisted living place, calling to Mr. Neighborhood Watch.

Mentally, I tied myself up.

I frisk the trunk, hoping for a tire iron. The trunk is empty. I pull up the cover for the spare tire and scratch at it with my fingernails. The tire is heavy, and I quickly realize it is not going anywhere, especially not with me above it.

I maneuver around, turning toward the back. A green button

catches my attention. I move closer to it. It is a trunk release button, on the inside of the trunk lid.

Thank you, German engineers, for your consideration. For good measure, I also thank my dad who art in heaven and Iona. I thank the pantheon of gods and goddesses belonging to my distant ancestors.

I stare at the button until I'm seeing four of them. There's a minor hitch. We are going highway miles at a supersonic Mercedes speed. At some point, I can pop the trunk and hurl myself out. Then what? I will have to run. And hope that I can outrun four men who don't happen to have an ice pick lodged in their ribcage.

ROUGHLY A THOUSAND YEARS LATER, the car slows down. It has been at least an hour, probably more. We take a few turns and the engine noise intensifies. My guess is that we're going into the mountains. The turns feel like switchbacks. I plant my hands into the carpet, trying to keep myself still.

This road is rougher than the highway. With each jounce, I emit ghost-like moans, smothering them as they leave my mouth. My captors need to think I'm conked out.

My only hope is the trunk release button. But I will have to time it perfectly. If I press the green button too early, I'm finished. The Mercedes probably has multiple efficient ways of alerting the driver when the trunk is open. A flashing yellow light. An exacting voice with a German accent that says, "Your trunk is open. Your victim is trying to escape."

The Mercedes slows. The wheels kick up some grit as we pull off a road. The car crawls. The car is gliding, coming to a stop.

I hit the button and push at the trunk. It bounces open. As the Mercedes comes to a complete stop, I clamber out of the trunk. We're in the mountains, at a scenic turn-off.

I can hear the men inside the car. They are arguing about something.

I stagger onto the ground, onto my knees, then onto my hands and knees. Flecks of gray dance around my vision. The ice pick in my ribcage twists, digging deeper. I heave up liquid, which spells down the front of my jacket.

There is nowhere to go!

I take my jacket off and whip it into the brush at the edge of the pavement. Then I slither under the Mercedes, scooching into the thick dark center of its undercarriage. My chest feels like it's full of broken glass. I shove a fist in my mouth to keep from making noise.

The car doors open.

Mr. Neighborhood Watch's voice is saying, "She won't find out. If she does, tough. She can do it herself."

Another man's voice says, "She's going to be furious."

Mr. Neighborhood Watch laughs. "What else is new?"

Perhaps the green trunk release button doesn't alert the driver. This would make sense. Who else would be in the trunk of a moving car but some sort of captive?

The men stand around the car. I take stock of their positions. One is standing by the driver's side. Another is near the trunk. I don't know where the others are standing.

"You're not going to believe this," one of the men says. His voice has an oddly flat quality to it.

"What?" Mr. Neighborhood Watch asks.

"She's gone. The trunk is open."

"You said she passed out."

"She can't be far. She's got a broken wrist or arm or something."

"She's in excellent condition. She bikes everywhere," Mr. Neighborhood Watch says.

A flashlight clicks on, and I watch thin lines of light loop around the pavement. The feet standing around the car tromp off in different directions.

Several seconds later, from a distance, a man's voice says, "Damn."

"What?"

"Thorns."

"Be careful out there," Mr. Neighborhood Watch says, laughter in his voice.

A minute later, one of the henchmen says, "Here's a jacket. I bet it's hers."

"Where?"

"Over here, on the Manzanita bush."

Mr. Neighborhood Watch says, "No way."

"Musta' got caught when she went over the side. It's a steep drop. But you can't see that without a flashlight."

"You're sure she's down there?" Mr. Neighborhood Watch asks.

"I think so." The man laughs. "The undergrowth is thick. We won't be able to see anything for sure until morning."

"You'd better go and check," Mr. Neighborhood Watch says. "I want proof."

Someone makes a muffled snorting sound, as if he's trying to stifle laughter. I'm so glad my demise is of amusement to someone.

A henchman says, "Even if she's still alive, she's injured, with no water or phone. If she's not dead, she will be soon."

Another replies, "Saves us a bullet."

A minute later, the men are back in the car and the engine comes to life. A terrible thought hits me: They're going to pull away then get out of the car and shoot me. They've known I've been hiding under the car all along. This is a game. I can hear it in their voices. They've been acting.

A car door opens. I knew it. I shut my eyes, preparing for the inevitable.

I hear a whoosh and a thump as something hits the ground. Mr. Neighborhood Watch says, "This way they'll think it was an accident."

The car door shuts. I open my eyes. The car pulls away, crunching over gravel. I watch it turn onto the road. It keeps going.

Unbelievable. I slowly turn over and gaze at the spackle of stars overhead. Life. I think I'll take it.

I try to stand upright. The ice pick in my rib cage objects, and I emit a sound that scares even me, and gently settle back onto the pavement. I lower my ambitions. Slowly, I roll onto my side then onto all fours. As long as I don't breathe much, I feel okay.

I listen for the sound of the Mercedes, returning to get me. The high woods are alive with yips and yaps and rustling sounds. I don't hear the sound of any vehicles.

I crawl toward the edge of the turn-off. Soon I spot a lump of dark on the ground. My jacket! My eyes have adjusted so that I can make out gradations of black. I grab for the lump. It is nylon, thick nylon, not my jacket.

It is my backpack. I unzip the top, making sure my wallet is still inside. Yes! Blinking back tears, I clutch the backpack.

This way they'll think it was an accident. The guys thought I was dead or close to it. They could presume that when the authorities found my body, they would look for a backpack or some personal effects. If they didn't find anything, they might presume foul play.

A moment later I spot another lump hanging off a shrub. Soon, I am reunited with my vomit-stained jacket. It smells sour. I hug it to me anyway.

I shift onto two knees, whoa horsey, and put one arm through first one sleeve then the other. Leaning forward, I push upward, rocking onto my feet. I immediately celebrate by heaving up bile, which scours my throat raw. The ice pick turns and I scream something incoherent.

Now that I'm vertical, I decide I should enjoy the scenic view and, not coincidentally, avoid the Mercedes, should it make a return trip. A trail from the turn-off cuts through forest. The trail leads to a small, denuded lookout area with a bench. Sadly, I don't spot a vending machine with Vitamin Water Zero or Snicker's bars or extra-strength pain reliever. The scenic view is unsettling, at least at night. It's like looking through a hole in the sky.

I make myself comfortable on the bench. It must be well after midnight. A small voice within suggests it may not be the best idea to loiter alone at a mountainous scenic lookout area in the middle of the night. I stretch out on the bench. My eyes shutter. *Just a few minutes of rest*, I tell myself.

I WAKE WITH A START. The holler and jangle of the White Stripes vibrates through the night air. I heave off the bench, stress hormones gushing, arms out, ready to fight. A few seconds later, I curl over. *Ouch.*

A vehicle has pulled into the scenic view turn-off. It's not a Mercedes. But it sounds powerful, like a spaceship.

Probably teenagers. It's dark, late, and remote, perfect for pot smoking and messing around. They have no idea they're about to become heroes and return me to the nearest center of civilization. They have no idea I'm about to save them from a world of trouble. All those risks associated with drug use and sex.

Using both arms for balance, as if I'm on a surfboard, I hobble toward the turn-off area. The ice pick in my ribs gives me a needling. Ignoring it, I press on toward the vehicle.

It's a Ram pick-up truck. The engine is chugging away. The headlights ignite an insect riot.

I move closer, for a better view. A lone man sits inside, age indeterminate, but not a teenager. His arm is flopped out the window, a lit cigarette between two fingers.

Hello, goddess? Not to sound ungrateful, but I'd strongly prefer being rescued by a nice couple or, better yet, a frequent frowner. A single man in a pick-up truck, especially a smoker, is worst-case scenario.

The music goes from a shout to a whisper. I freeze. My gut rumbles unhappily.

The man in the pick-up truck says, "Yeah." His neck curls around a cell-phone.

"I told you I had to work ...we're still cleaning up," he says.

He's a bit of a liar, but who hasn't told the odd little lie? The important thing is that it sounds like someone at home is waiting for him.

Using the truck's side panels for balance, I make my way around the back of the truck, avoiding the front beams. I don't want to surprise him and get run over.

The driver says, "Probably a half-hour ... big night ... the band was great."

I pause a few feet from the driver's side door. The orange tip of his cigarette catches my attention. It bobs up and down. Watching it, I almost fall over.

"Okay, okay ... as fast as I can get there ... I promise."

I press onto the side of the truck, trying to maintain my balance. Specks of gray dance around the edges of my vision.

"Love you too," he says.

A few feet more. I lurch forward, wanting to make it to his door. I don't want to startle him from behind.

He cranks the White Stripes and tilts his head back, immersing himself in a deafening power cocoon of sound. I'm guessing his eyes are closed.

I knock at his door. "Excuse me."

He doesn't move.

"Hello?" I tap my knuckles on the window. "Sorry to bother you."

Still nothing. I hit the door with the side of my fist.

He snaps upright, arms flailing. The cigarette missiles through the air.

"Hey!" His eyes are saucers. "What?"

"Please," I say, holding up my palms.

This is all I manage before the frayed cord holding me up snaps, and I crumple onto the ground.

AFTER THE INITIAL SURPRISE, the pick-up driver, a bartender commuting from Jerome back home to Prescott, decided he'd better make sure I was okay. He assumed I was drunk. Experienced dealing with horizontal people, he figured he'd help me over to the edge of the turn-off, where I could safely sleep off my overindulgence without getting run over. When he got out to investigate, he was surprised not to smell any alcohol. This is when he became confused.

He helped me into the vehicle. Although I told him I'd been abducted, I don't think he quite believed me. I'm not sure I believed me. It all seemed so insane.

I asked him to drop me off at the police station in Prescott, which he did. He offered to stay with me but I waved him off. After using the restroom, I told the reception person that I lost my cell-phone in an altercation and really needed a cup of coffee. Did I want to make a report? Okay, I said. But first the coffee?

As the caffeine started to pump through my cells, I realized I did not want the police to pursue Mr. Neighborhood Watch and his henchmen. If the police gave chase, the heroin traffickers would realize I survived the evening. I was perfectly happy with them thinking I'd fallen down a ravine and perished. This was probably best for the health of my mom and Roy as well.

I told two officers that some men in a dark sedan tried to grab me, which is when I lost my phone. I might have lied and led them to believe that perhaps I'd imbibed a few too many drinks.

They must file lunatic reports every so often from drunks in the wrong place at the wrong time.

The police asked me some questions, which I couldn't answer. No, I didn't get a license plate number. Not their names, either. And what did they look like? Let's see, Mr. Neighborhood Watch was white, taller than I am, with a shaved head. Oh, wait officer, I've got it, the telling detail: he was mean. I couldn't conjure any details about the henchmen, except that one of them had a hairy arm, which was roughly the circumference of a tree trunk.

One of the officers let me use his cell-phone to call Moorea. Not surprisingly, she was full of curiosity: how did you end up there, what happened, did you get robbed, raped, hurt? The rush of words made me dizzy. With my head bowed, I delicately suggested we discuss these troublesome details later, that I was on a borrowed cell and needed her help. She promised to come and get me.

After we hung up, I wondered how I was going to lie my way out of this one.

ON A BENCH just outside the police station, I wait for Moorea in the grizzled pre-dawn light. Once she sees me in person and realizes I'm basically fine, she's going to be furious. And, by forcing her to make an emergency trip to Prescott to rescue me, my already considerable debt to her has deepened. In short, I will owe her an explanation.

Unfortunately, a truthful explanation will make her head explode. After she recovers her brain matter, she'll march me into the police station, where she'll force me to make a full confession. This will be shameful and humiliating as I lied in the official police report, which is also probably illegal and may mean I'll need a lawyer. After that, I will lose my job.

Limping along on caffeine fumes, I decide I will tell her I hit my head last night and remember very little.

With that settled, I ponder the potential link between Kevin's uncle and Mr. Neighborhood Watch. Why would this man pay so much attention to Uncle Dave's house? I have no answer.

It dawns on me that I might be way over my head in this investigation.

Moorea is walking toward me. Her face is half-melted with exhaustion, but her eyes are wide-awake, twin beams that sweep over me. I immediately realize I can't tell her I hit my head the night before and don't remember anything. "Mom," I say, slowly easing onto my feet. "I'm so sorry."

Her arms open, and I fall into her.

"Oh, baby," she says, smoothing my hair.

I come apart at the seams, the bolts holding me together pop, and fear and worry liquefy from me in a gush of tears.

"It's okay, honey," she says. "I'm here."

I say something unintelligible. All this breathing and emoting is torture. I exhale slowly, as if through a straw, trying to placate the ice pick in my ribcage.

"What's wrong?" she asks.

I explain about my ribs. She conducts a quick inspection, gently patting and probing my ribcage for dents or bones sticking out. Two women walk by, ignoring the medical exam unfolding in public. They probably think I'm being frisked.

Moorea soon determines everything seems to be in its right place. We discover that I can take a deep breath, but it's not something I want to do very often just yet. Moorea decides I can see a doctor after we get home.

I follow her to the car, where she hands me a glass jar containing a cloudy liquid. She tells me it is an oral rehydration solution. She is concerned that I am dehydrated. With all the evening's excitement, hydration didn't even occur to me. The solution is concocted from sugar and salt and water. It has saved the lives of millions of babies in Africa who become dangerously dehydrated from diarrhea.

Although it is clearly a noble liquid, it tastes rotten. At the first large drugstore we see, Moorea pulls over to get some ice for my ribcage. I ask for ibuprofen but she says that I can't take any pain medication until tomorrow morning as it can cause bleeding. The mention of bleeding piques my curiosity. But I decide that I may be better off not knowing more about that. I also repress my urge to ask her to see if the store has any strawberry lemonade Pedialyte.

On the road, with an icepack on duty, I feel better, even well enough to enjoy the ride. Stands of Ponderosa and Pinyon pine trees surround us. The air smells of pine and wood smoke. Someday I will have a cabin in the mountains. First, of course, I have to keep a job and get an apartment and buy a bold red Kia Soul.

I take a nip of the rehydration solution. All I can tolerate is the tiniest homeopathic size dose. Moorea eyes flick over at me. She shakes her head.

"Don't sip it," she says.

I take my time, not wanting to gag and also knowing she is still concerned about my health. The moment her concern wears off I'm in for an epic grilling.

"It hurts to swallow too much."

This is, incredibly, the truth. Of course I am lucky and grateful to be alive. At the same time, I can tell this rib injury is going to quickly grow tiresome.

I dutifully drink my baby diarrhea cure, thinking of all the lives it has saved. When Moorea sees me making an effort, she gives me a small smile. I take this opportunity to ask if I could borrow her cell phone for a moment. She rolls her eyes and hands me the phone, which I use to send Monalisa a text.

I write, "Lost phone outside Sunview Square, asst living place. Long story. Back in touch later."

As soon as I've sent the text, Moorea reaches her hand toward me. "My phone," she says. I place the phone in her palm. "Just don't want you to get too attached."

Eventually, we reach the valley. I say a mental goodbye to the mountain air and the pine trees. I also say goodbye to peace and quiet.

It begins when Moorea gives me a sidelong glance. Her eyes peek through cushions of swollen flesh. The dull glaze over her retinas suggests the thrill of seeing me is gone.

"What happened, Angela?" she asks. "How did you end up out here?"

I recount the evening in broad strokes, leaving out some of the gnarlier details. Me getting into the car of a perfect stranger, for example. Me finding a zippered bag full of heroin.

I tell her about my surveillance of one of the women who was last seen with Kevin, the missing person I'm trying to track down. I tell her the woman dropped a gym bag in the parking lot of NB Entertainment then sped off in a Kia Soul. Curious, I peeked inside the gym bag, at which point some men confronted me. I airbrush the contents of the gym bag, saying I think I may have spotted some marijuana in it.

When I finish, Moorea shakes her head. "I don't get it. Why did they grab you? You gave them back the gym bag."

These are difficult questions but not completely unmanageable.

"They believed I was trying to steal the bag."

"I'll bet it was some sort of secret exchange of illegal drugs."

"I was in the wrong place at the wrong time."

"The police will find these people and punish them."

Tired of lying, I study the view out the window, mostly stunted scrubby bush.

Moorea pats my leg. "Hang in there."

"I'm sorry you had to come all this way to pick me up." The tears start rolling. "I'm sorry to worry you."

Moorea stares straight out the windshield. Her jaw tightens. "Last night, when you didn't come home, I called Monalisa."

I sense a storm system on the way, a wild one. "Oh?"

"Do you know what that woman said to me?"

I shake my head. I can only imagine. Monalisa isn't exactly a mistress of social graces.

"I told her you'd gone missing. It was two in the morning and you weren't home. Did she know where you were? She said she didn't know. She said she bore no legal responsibility for you."

I say that technically that is true.

"Technically?" Moorea chops the air with her right hand. "So I asked that woman, what about moral responsibility? How could she let you do dangerous work late at night by yourself?"

I don't respond.

"You know what she said? She said you've been trying to find a man who has gone missing before his wedding. She said he's probably run off because he doesn't want to get married. She said this search shouldn't have involved any danger or late nights."

"Oh."

"Oh is right. What a bunch of boloney." Moorea thumps the steering wheel. "That woman. Hard to believe she and Iona share the same bloodline."

"Yes."

Moorea jabs at the air with a finger. "She knows all I've got in the world is you. Well, now I've also got Roy." Her eyes are welling. I grab a tissue from the glove compartment and hand it to her. "But you're my baby. My only one. And the best that woman can say is that she's not liable for you." Moorea shakes her head. "That's a lawyer for you."

AT HOME, I sleep until late morning. When I get up, I notice a spectacular bruise blooming on the middle of my forehead. It has all the vivid colors of a desert sunset. The odd thing is I don't even remember bumping my forehead. I've got a few angry scratches on my arms. My wrist has a purple-green bruise, and two of my nails are chipped. This does not bode well for my job prospects with day spas.

On the bright side, I'm still alive.

I reach for my iPhone, thinking I'd check my messages. As my hand clutches at air, my phantom heart sends up a sorrowful wail. *It's gone forever!* I grab Hedgie and remind myself that I am alive.

Phoneless but alive. I try a positive spin: phone-free. Nice try but no dice. It's amazing how quickly I have adjusted to survival and am once again focusing on relatively trivial matters. Survival is the important thing. I am alive.

Where there is life, there needs to be caffeine. I hobble into the kitchen, going straight to the coffee maker. As my rocket-fire brew drips into the carafe, I take a moment to reflect on my nails. Although two soldiers are down with chips, I have to admit the polish has held its own, surviving an armed encounter, a foot chase, a hostile abduction, and a cordial chat with the police.

I pour a cup of coffee and add sugar. This is the secret to intelligent life

"Angela?" Moorea calls.

I didn't realize she was home. She must have switched shifts, which makes sense since we both had a long night.

I take a long draw on the coffee, then say, "Yes?"

Moorea doesn't answer. I set off from the kitchen, following the sounds I hear coming from the family room. Moorea is taping the bottom of a cardboard box. The coffee table holds stacks of books, along with an opened pack of moving tape.

I'd forgotten that we're moving. I take another dose of my sugar coffee.

"How are you feeling?" Moorea asks.

"Okay," I say. "Thanks again for rescuing me."

I feel great for someone who should be dead. By another measure, as an actual live person, I feel like I've been through a rock tumbler. But I've learned that unless I'm literally dying, Moorea considers me fine. You have to be in rough shape to warrant the attention of an emergency room nurse.

"Sleep is the best medicine," Moorea says.

Alcohol, of course, is a close second in the medicine department, along with coffee. I smile at Moorea and make a noise that could be interpreted as agreement.

On the coffee table, among the books waiting to be packed, are several novels. The rest are Spanish instruction manuals. Moorea is always talking about how she needs to know more Spanish, especially working in Arizona. She also dreams of going to Mexican beach resorts and speaking like a local. This is quite noble of her, especially as thousands of Americans go to Mexico each year and seem to do quite well with their two words of Spanish.

The various manuals speak volumes about her progress with the delightful Spanish language. Her initial ambitions are reflected in two weighty tomes, *Designs for Spanish Grammar* and *Teach Yourself: Spanish Grammar*. Probably partway through this serious regimen, she picked up *Practical Spanish for Beginners*. After this turned out to be less practical than she'd anticipated, she picked up the guide equivalent of a breakfast pastry, *Spanish in 10 Minutes a Day*. Last but not least, she's got a matchbook size production that could fit in your pocket, *Spanish Phrases for Tourists*.

"What's funny?" Moorea asks.

"*Cómo estás?*"

She laughs. "Take a hike."

"I will," I say. "I'll hike right into the kitchen and eat something."

She clears her throat. "Monalisa wants you to call her. She's left several messages on my phone."

Monalisa, the woman who is not legally liable for me.

"Do you want to use my phone?" Moorea asks, working hard to keep a neutral tone to her voice. Too bad she can't control the angry steam coming from her ears.

"No."

I'll use e-mail until I get a replacement phone. This will keep the peace on the home front.

"Okay." Moorea's shoulders relax.

I tell Moorea about leaving the bike locked in front of Mercado Temixco. She says she'll have Roy bring it back home with his sporty new Outback Subaru. What did we do before Roy?

After I eat some low-fat treats, I return to my bed and flip open my laptop. Monalisa has written me an e-mail. She asks me to check-in with her immediately.

No legal responsibility. Not my fault. This is why people despise lawyers. I can't blame Monalisa for the trouble I got into the night before. It wasn't her fault. Still, her response to my mother wasn't quite human.

I send Charise an e-mail, asking for more details about Kevin's stolen car. Next, I activate the Find My iPhone app. A map shows that my phone is no longer at the assisted living facility. A green dot blinks on the map. The dot shows the phone is nearby.

How could this be? I zoom in on the dot, thinking I must have made a mistake. Still puzzled, I track its path. The map shows a straight line from the assisted living facility to Monalisa's house.

9

*A*s I enter Monalisa's house, Boo love-taps my hip. The force nearly breaks me in half. He doesn't realize I'm made of glass at the moment, with an ice pick lodged in my ribcage.

"Boo. Light of my life."

Boo jumps and twists, making a gymnasium of the front hallway.

Monalisa puts her hands on her hips. "Boo, settle down."

Boo rushes over to her, nose-butting her leg. With Boo darting around us, we make our way into the office, where I pull a chair up to Monalisa's desk and sit down much more slowly than usual. The wooden sword is propped against the side of her desk. I wonder if it is a gift for me. Lovely, thanks. I'll be sure to carry it with me next time I conduct surveillance.

Apparently, this is not what Monalisa has in mind. She opens a desk drawer and pulls out my phone. I blink several times. Could it be? She nudges the phone across the desk to me. Yes, it is. I grab it and hold it against my heart. My beloved phone.

I fight the impulse to kiss its screen. The goddess is laughing. Monalisa is smiling. Not my legal responsibility. At the moment, I don't care what she said to my mom. Monalisa found my phone. In the scheme of things, that counts for something.

Pressure builds behind my eyes. I can't believe it's such an emotional reunion. I can hear Moorea's disapproving voice in my head. *Angela, it's an inanimate object. It's not going to love you back.*

I don't care. I count the ways the iPhone has proven better than Dr. Fantastic: It doesn't make promises it can't keep, it's never too tired to hang out, it's happy for me to stay the entire night, it's there whenever I need it, it takes my questions seriously, it doesn't try to implicate me in a felony.

"How?" is all I can manage to mutter.

Monalisa gives a small shrug. She's a cool one. Still, I can see the self-satisfied smile twitching on her lips, the pleasure peeping through her emotionless mask.

"After I got your text, I went over and got it," she says.

Just like that. "How long did it take to find it?"

"Not long," she says. "One of the maintenance men had already turned it in at the front desk."

"I thought it was gone forever."

Monalisa sits back and clasps her hands. "Tell me about Prescott."

Inwardly, I groan. My chest hurts. My wrist hurts. My head hurts. Monalisa stares at me, her face betraying no sympathy whatsoever.

I sigh. "There was a bit of a misunderstanding with one of the Gaga lookalikes. But it's resolved now."

Although I have been planning to tell her the truth and nothing but the truth, I can't summon the strength for an interrogation. Monalisa would not be impressed to learn I stowed away in Dolly Gaga's car. She would not be pleased to hear I stole a gym bag full of heroin and ran off with it. She would be upset that I almost got killed at a scenic overlook. All this would translate into an immediate stop work order.

Of course, the pea-sized part of my brain governing common

sense suggests I should cease and desist with the investigation anyway. If heroin is related to Kevin's disappearance, this would be a case for Supergirl or the police. Either way, I should bow out.

"Abduction is a serious offense," Monalisa says.

I can only imagine what she'd say about Obamacare heroin.

"I agree," I say. "But it was a big mistake. I was following one of the Gaga lookalikes, thinking she would lead to Kevin."

"And she led you to her security goons instead?"

Thank you, Monalisa. In an instant, she has made my story more credible. And, if you squinted hard, you could almost spot a little truth in there.

"Yes, they were her security guys." Next, I find myself saying, "They were only trying to give me a good scare."

In an instant, I realize this could be true.

How did they miss me under the car? The obvious answer: they didn't. They gave me a pass. The obvious place to search would have been around and under the car. Mr. Neighborhood Watch is no fool. If he'd wanted me found, I would have been found. And then there was the courtesy of returning my backpack.

While I'm having my aha-moment, Monalisa is thinking about the Gaga lookalikes. She says, "A responsible company would have someone accompanying those women to parties. It can't be safe for them to walk around alone dressed like that."

At this moment, I am sorry that I haven't told her the truth. I am deeply curious to know what she would think about deploying celebrity lookalikes to distribute heroin around the Phoenix metropolitan area.

Monalisa is shaking her head. "Still, security personnel should have given you a verbal warning. They crossed a serious line. We could press charges."

I hold a hand up. "It's okay. Really."

We stare at each other for a moment, something passing

between us, perhaps something akin to understanding. *Don't ask, don't tell.*

Boo trots over to me, and I pat his head. He nuzzles my hand. *Yes, Boo, I want to spend the rest of my days with you. We'll go chase squirrels together into the sunset.*

"Kevin's car was found," I say, changing topics.

She nods. "One of my police friends says it looks like some kids took it for a joy ride."

I can't help but smile. What imbeciles would take an old Camry for a joy ride? Phoenix has so many fun, sexy middle age man mobiles around, cars that truly put the joy in ride.

"The police haven't caught the joy riders," I say.

"Correct."

I tell her about the sighting of Kevin at Mercado Temixco.

"Where did he go from there?" she asks.

"I don't know yet." Since Monalisa doesn't look impressed I feel compelled to remind her about the significance of this discovery. "It's the first information I've gotten about his whereabouts after leaving the American Egg."

"Charise wants you to continue the search. Given what happened last night, I've decided to get you a rental car for the next few days."

This hits me like a thunderbolt. "A car?"

"Your mom told me you've been doing all the investigation by bike. If you're going to continue, you need a car."

First she finds my iPhone. Now, she is getting me a rental car. These acts of kindness are probably her way of apologizing for the missteps with my mom. Of course, she had me with the iPhone. The rental car merely seals my everlasting devotion to her.

"I don't know what to say. Thank you."

Monalisa stands up. Boo runs a few laps of excitement around the room.

"I'll take you to the rental place," she says.

The three of us pile into Monalisa's Volvo. Boo gets into the back seat and rustles up a chaw bone from the floor. Monalisa loads up some classical music. Minutes later, to the somber strains of Chopin, we pull up to the rental car office. I am in awe of an entire lot filled with automobiles, any one of which I might be driving within the next fifteen minutes.

Monalisa pulls a piece of paper from her small tote bag. "This has the reservation and other details on it. I've prepaid."

I take the paper and mumble something about my everlasting gratitude and naming my first-born child after her. She says something in response, but my attention is diverted. A white Kia Soul sits among the rental cars. It calls to me.

"Angela?"

I force my neck to turn back to Monalisa. "Yes?"

"I need you to stay close. I want regular texts, calls and visits. Don't worry about over-communicating. I want to be fully informed about what you're doing."

"That's fine. I'll keep in touch."

As I step out of the car, I find Monalisa isn't finished quite yet.

"This isn't about a lack of trust," Monalisa adds.

What? I rewind. Oh yes, she wants more communication from me.

I nod.

Okay, I get it. You trust me. That's why you want me to tell you my every move.

Monalisa continues, "It's about you having back-up in case there's trouble. I know you like to operate independently."

I smile. I haven't considered that I actually have a work style. "I guess so."

"We've seen things can get tricky. I need to be in a position to help if there's any more trouble."

"I appreciate that," I say.

After I give Boo a quick air kiss, I waltz into the car rental office.

How often in life does something turn out to be as good as you imagined? The Kia Soul does not disappoint. The goddess smiles as I carefully settle into the driver's seat. The driving experience is buoyant and joyful. The car is nimble. It is so wonderful I forget about my battered ribcage for a while. I even forget about the heroin.

I return to an empty house. The iPhone gets plugged into its charger. With that pressing priority out of the way, I prepare an icepack for my ribs. With one hand icing the ribs, I use the other to fork stir-fry leftovers into my mouth.

I have two texts from Charise. In one of them, she takes issue with Kevin being drunk at Mercado Temixco. Kevin is not a drinker. She's never seen him drunk. And she's known him for many years.

I text Charise, "Okay, thanks."

I could waste my breath by arguing with her. After all, Kevin has engaged in a number of uncharacteristic behaviors of late. Participating in a friendly abduction with two Lady Gaga looka-likes. Not answering calls, texts or e-mails.

Charise can think what she wants. My bets are with Ramón from Mercado Temixco. He saw Kevin last Thursday night. He even remembered the scrubs.

The other text from Charise warms my heart. "Tate wants to talk to you. Concerned since Kev's car was found."

The thought of Tate makes me take a deep breath, which gives me a lovely stabbing sensation in my chest. *Ouch.* On the bright side, to the extent that I learn to associate Tate with pain, the better off I'll be.

I will have to tuck myself in, batten down the hatches, and remind myself that I am the consummate professional. No joke. I'm a different person than I was last year. I will not mix business with pleasure. Plus, I've got an apartment and security deposit to think about now. Responsibilities!

Unfortunately, I don't have a good record in keeping my impulses in check. Tate's Facebook picture pops into my mind. The smile. The chunk of sun-bleached hair falling over his forehead just so. The masterful way he stands on the wooden sailboat.

I pour a self-administered bucket of cold water over my feverish mind. Tate, I tell myself, has given me false information about Kevin's whereabouts, threatened to call the police on me, and insulted my client, Charise. It occurs to me that this meeting request may not be about him helping me find Kevin. It may be about him trying to find out what I know.

I text Tate and ask him to let me know when he wants to discuss Kevin.

A few minutes later, he texts back, "U around now? Meet me at the botanical garden gift shop?"

Botanical garden. My mind doesn't waste a second, conjuring up images of Columbine, Bougainvillea, Bells of Fire. Oh my. A hummingbird garden. Succulents. Why the botanical garden? It has such romance potential. People get married there.

Enough, I tell myself. His brother is missing. Finding Kevin is the priority.

I text Tate back. "C U soon."

I go into the bathroom and set the stopwatch on my iPhone to five minutes. This is all the time I'm allowed to spend on makeup. I must triage. This means no eyeliner. No second coat of mascara. No hair ironing. Covering up the bruise on my forehead is the priority. After a few layers of makeup, I realize I need a cap to shadow the bruise. I find a crisp white baseball cap.

Exactly twelve minutes later, I set off for the botanical garden.

IN THE GARDEN STORE, Tate is shelving books. When I reach him, he is holding a children's classic in his hand, *Who Pooped in the Sonoran Desert?*

"This is the best guide for scat out there," he says.

I smile. "I've been searching for a good guide. All the others are so—"

"Inferior? Lacking in graphic detail?"

"Exactly," I say. "Do you work here?"

I am confused. His Facebook timeline—*and FB doesn't lie, hah*—puts him in San Diego.

"I work in San Diego, but I've taken some leave to stay with my mom," he says. "Since she hasn't been feeling well, she's not been doing her usual volunteer hours. I offered to help."

"You're a natural book salesman."

He points to a small stack of books. "I need to finish shelving. Do you want to look around while I wrap up here?"

"Sure."

I purchase a postcard of a stunning yellow flower blooming from a prickly pear cactus, then stroll to the far end of the store, where I examine a garden torch shaped like a barrel cactus. Wedding gift? It isn't exactly cute and cuddly. I decide the best wedding gift I could give Moorea and Roy would be to find a job and leave them in peace.

When Tate is finished shelving books, we leave the store and stroll down a wide walkway. Two oldsters in electric scooters drag race by us. I smile at the wise elders. We pass a Chihuly glass sculpture, which glows eerily in the sun, looking like an explosion of blue glass eels. "Gorgeous," I say.

Tate glances over at the sculpture but doesn't say anything. He steers us toward a small round table just off the walkway.

"You know about Kevin's car?" he asks.

"Yes," I say. "Do you and your mom still think he's in Italy?"

He gives me a sad smile, flashing that tooth gap at me. "Now mom says Kevin is hiking in the Matterhorn. She says he called her two days ago."

I pause, wondering how to tactfully ask Tate if his mom is delusional.

"Do you believe he's in the Matterhorn?"

He shakes his head. "But I do believe he's been calling my mother. I think he's telling her lies, and I want to know why."

I tell him about the Kevin sighting at Mercado Temixco and how Kevin appeared to be drunk.

Tate's mouth twists skeptically. "I've never seen Kevin drink more than two beers at a time his whole life."

"Odd."

I wonder if Kevin was drugged. This would help explain things. I'm about to voice this suspicion when I see Tate rubbing his temples, looking drawn. He doesn't speak for a moment. I hold my forked tongue, not wanting to agitate him further.

"My entire family has gone haywire. My mom isn't well. Now Kevin is gone."

"I'm so sorry."

He takes a deep breath. "Something must have happened to Kevin. Something serious."

"Not just the wedding."

"No."

On impulse, I decide to dip my toe into some potentially dangerous waters. I tell him about watching his uncle's house for Kevin and encountering a strange man there.

Tate angles his head at me. "A strange man at my uncle's house?"

"He seemed oddly protective of your uncle's house, almost as though he were guarding it. Maybe he's a neighbor."

"A neighbor?" Tate's eyebrows knit. "What's he look like?"

"Shaved head, white, probably around six-foot-two, wiry, smokes."

Tate says, "I think I've met him."

"You do?"

"Just a few days ago, I went over to borrow my uncle's road bike. My uncle was having a drink on the patio with a guy who fits your description."

"Did you get a name?"

"If I did, I don't remember it."

No name, but Uncle Dave and Mr. Neighborhood Watch know each other.

"You don't know anything more about this man?" I ask.

Tate makes an exasperated sound. "Why does this matter? He's some acquaintance of my uncle. My uncle has *nothing* to do with Kevin's disappearance."

"I saw you at your uncle's house, banging on his front door. You seemed upset."

"You're kidding." His arms cross against his chest. "You seriously think my uncle is involved?"

"I'm investigating a number of leads."

"That's the best you can do?" A bitter laugh escapes from him. "That's all you've come up with in your so-called investigation?"

I don't respond. I'm finding his anger interesting.

"That's pathetic," he says.

As I prepare an icepack in Moorea's kitchen, angry thoughts spark from the hard flinty edges of my mind. Kevin, the lying cheat. Tate, the jerk. Dr. Fantastic, the slimeball. In the end, these thoughts fail to ignite. I sink into the sofa with my icepack. I stare out the window until the street becomes a blur.

The nap lasts about a half-hour. When I wake up, my entire shirt is soaking wet. Proof that I am still alive. A sharp pain from the ribcage is another sign of life.

In the kitchen, I brew some half-caff, hoping this will help. The fumes inspire more thoughts about heroin and Uncle Dave and the Lady Gaga lookalikes and Mr. Neighborhood Watch. Somehow, they're connected. This is exciting news. My texting finger is itchy. But I have no one to contact. I sit at the kitchen island, staring at a trio of browning bananas. At this moment, I feel truly alone.

Monalisa asked me to over-communicate. I imagine going to her house and doing just that. Her alien eyes would laser holes into me. She'd either fire me or make me go to the police or both. A police investigation would tell Mr. Neighborhood Watch that I hadn't taken his warning at the scenic overlook seriously. In his eyes, I'd gain a new, more exciting identity: living, breathing witness.

Internet research, I tell myself, is safe.

To get reacquainted, I visit Uncle Dave's Facebook timeline. He hasn't added any news since my last visit. I take another peek at his Thailand vacation shots. I am looking for some sign that Uncle Dave knows drug traffickers. The photos offer up no such clues. They seem to document the literal order of his days: breakfast buffet, Buddha temple tour, curry lunch, beach slumber, massage, fish dinner, evening stroll on the beach.

My gaze lingers on a beach photo. The blue-green water is the color of heaven. My fingers tingle. This water is in my DNA. I am an island person. I am not designed for the desert. I add Koh Samui, Thailand to my bucket list. It registers somewhere down the list from American Samoa and even a bit after the Kia Soul.

Next stop: Google. There are many David S. Newmans in the world. A few of them are doctors and hog the first page of Google results. Among all these David Newmans, I think I find my David Newman on page two of the search results. Only one David S. Newman directs the city's transportation department and is on the pointy end of an angry rant by the New Sons of Liberty. This group is urging their members to contact Mr. Newman and protest the latest assault against American values. They've staged protests at the Department of Transportation.

I wonder what particular assault against American values is at issue. Are they fighting for data privacy or the abolishment of the income tax or even the right to bear shoulder-fired rocket grenades? According to Wikipedia, the original Sons of Liberty were the colonists likely behind the Boston tea party. The modern-day New Sons of Liberty fight the good fight against red light and speed photo-enforcement cameras. On a seriously amateur website, they lay out their case against these travesties of life, liberty, and the pursuit of happiness.

"These cameras are the tools of a POLICE STATE. They VIOLATE the 6th and 14th amendments of the Constitution. They are a LICENSE TO STEAL!"

If I could afford a car, I could probably bring more passion to this issue. I keep going through the website. It crackles with insane conviction. It's studded so heavily with all caps that I'm tempted to use earplugs.

"Traffic cameras are CRACK COCAINE for addicted governments who want to steal more money from hard-working citizens. They're a tool of a federal empire that robs Americans of hard-won liberties. HIGHWAY ROBBERY!"

Near the bottom of the homepage, I see a heading says: "Big Brother Coming Soon." The dateline is from last Wednesday, the day before Kevin disappeared. I click on the link.

The city is in the final stage of selecting a new company to add five hundred new traffic cameras throughout the city. This represents the most serious assault on citizens we've seen in years. Do you want this company taking photos of you and your loved ones? Accessing your private data from the DMV? The parasites in city government project these new cameras will generate one third of a BILLION dollars in revenue. In other words, they're a license to steal.

Folks, the city parasites are supposed to come to a final decision soon. They've not held a single public hearing. How's dat for democracy? Do you want your voice to be heard? HELL YEAH! This means WAR. By any MEANS necessary, we have to defend our rights:

1. Sign our petition to the Transportation Department Official David S. Newman. Let's march on Dave!

2. You can also contact this SOB through snail mail, e-mail, and phone.

By any means necessary? War? I wonder how far they'd go to stop these cameras from being planted all over the city.

The website has no "contact" button. I check out their Facebook page but this doesn't have any contact information either. I return to the website and click on "subscribe." I enter my e-mail address and, in a field that asks how you heard of the group, I mention that I know of David S. Newman and would like to learn more about his role in the traffic light decision.

After I submit my subscription request, I click on an "Events" button on the top menu. The website is so cluttered I didn't spot the button earlier.

One event is posted. The headline says: "Friday happy hour protest at the Department of Transportation. Tell 'em what you think of traffic cameras!"

The date is for today, starting at four-thirty p.m.

THE BICYCLE HAS ITS CHARMS, but nothing can compare to the Kia Soul. How I adore thee! Let me count the ways:

1. I get downtown in a snap;

2. I don't need to put on black lycra to get anywhere;

3. The Kia Soul responds with pep and verve to my every whim, without requiring the active participation of my tush and thighs; and

4. The Kia Soul slides without complaint into a tight spot only a half-block from the Department of Transportation.

I walk around the office building of the Department of Transportation but fail to spot any protesters. The sidewalks bustle with employees fleeing their offices on a Friday afternoon. I enter the lobby. The lighting is horribly unflattering, giving everyone a case of the ugly office flu. Would it kill the architects to put in some flattering light?

At the day spa, we believed that if you looked better, you felt better, and if you felt better, you'd be more effective. Today, I have taken this to heart. Before setting out, I changed into a crisp white shirt and a dark blue pencil skirt. My hair is freshly ironed and my chipped nails are repaired. I plastered makeup over my forehead bruise. I'm wearing a light spritz of Daisy perfume.

There are no protesters in the lobby. What gives? A man sits behind a security desk near the elevators. He smiles at me. I smile back, looking confident and full of purposeful direction as I head straight to the elevators. The protesters must be at the office of the Department of Transportation.

The directory says reception for the Department of Transportation is on the fourth floor. On the fourth floor, a receptionist glares at me from behind a tall counter. I would bet money this woman has never been to a day spa in her life. Or a gym. Or a hairdresser.

I scan the area, looking for fellow protesters. No one else is here. Not a single person carrying a sign or shouting a slogan about freedom and liberty. The website suggested these people were serious. If so, where are they? This is no way to conduct WAR against David S. Newman.

I keep my expression all business as I search out the protesters. As I ponder my retreat, the receptionist's face breaks into a wide smile. She asks how she can help me. She sounds so genuine and so sweet and so sincerely caring that I am tempted to ask for a job, an apartment, a life, an icepack for my ribcage.

Instead, I say I have an appointment to see Dave Newman. This is an odd thing for me to say, but since I'm in the neighborhood, maybe I can ask about Kevin's disappearance.

"And you are?" She flashes me that smile again. I want to curl up at her feet. I am such a sucker for maternal.

Still, I am cautious. I tell her I am Iona Walker and concoct a business for myself, Walker and Associates.

She asks me to take a seat.

I sit in an armchair by the entrance door, staring at a scratched-wood coffee table. It offers no hospitality, not even a magazine. They wouldn't have to do much to make the place more inviting. The latest issues of *National Geographic* and *Car & Driver* might be a nice touch. The beat-up wooden table would have to go, replaced with an oval coffee table, a lovely glass one. Above it, one of those funky light fixtures that looks like a constellation of stars.

"Ms. Walker?"

I stand and approach the counter. "Yes?"

"Are you sure your appointment is for today?"

My eyes widen with fake concern. "Yes. Why?"

"Mr. Newman is in a meeting all day today and on Monday."

I press my lips together, expressing mild displeasure without actually frowning and racking up more mileage on my skin.

"I must be mistaken," I say, ready to retreat.

"Maybe your appointment is for next Friday?"

I pull out my phone and pretend to check my calendar. "No, I have it here for today."

She tilts her head. "What is the nature of your meeting with Mr. Newman?"

Great question. Hmmm. An envelope he was supposed to leave for me at his front door?

"His nephew is missing."

She cocks her head. "Kevin?"

I nod.

"Dave has not mentioned anything about that to me. He was going to meet with you here at the office on Friday afternoon to discuss *Kevin*?"

I may be imagining things but she seems to be staring at my forehead bruise, her eyes filling with suspicion.

I nod and say, "I'll be going now."

She gives me a warm, sweet smile. "That sounds like a good idea. You can see yourself out of the building, right?"

"Right."

MONALISA IS ENJOYING some iced Krakus on her back patio. I sit next to her. Between us sits Iona's ceramic Afghan hound, Aramis. Iona didn't have any live pets, but she kept a menagerie of faux creatures on her property. One of the things Iona and I had in common was our ability to smother inanimate objects with affection.

Boo has disappeared in the Jurassic tangle of greenery formerly known as Iona's garden. The back yard even smells wild, with a tinge of rotting green in the air. Iona would not be pleased at this state of affairs.

Monalisa offers me some iced Krakus from her pitcher. I surprise myself and agree to have some. I am desperately thirsty.

I am taking my first delightful sip when Boo emerges from the back, with bits of greenery sticking to him. After circling us, sniffing with wild abandon, he takes a seat beside Aramis. I'm glad to see the two of them get along so well.

"Any news?" Monalisa asks.

I tell her about my chat with Tate and how he believes Kevin is calling their mom.

"He's calling her but not telling her the truth about where he is," Monalisa says.

"That sums it up," I say. "He probably wants her to know he's okay."

"I don't know how long Charise is going to want us to continue. Have you told her what Tate said yet?"

"I'll let her know after we're done."

Monalisa glances over at me. "Charise may decide to end this case. We need to be prepared for that."

I nod and tell her about the New Sons of Liberty campaign against traffic cameras and Uncle Dave.

Monalisa stirs, sitting up straighter. "He's involved with the traffic camera deal?"

"He's the primary decision-maker."

"People hate those cameras. For a little while, it seemed like there was a protest every week. At the Department of Transportation, protestors even hung the CEO of a local traffic camera company in effigy. It's strange the issues people go ballistic over."

I tell her I've sent an e-mail to the New Sons of Liberty.

"Does this group think there's been fraud in the traffic camera contract?" she asks.

I think back to the website. Monalisa continues, "If you've got any evidence of malfeasance, you could report it to the Salvador Foundation. They offer a substantial reward for whistleblowers."

I like the reward part. I make a note to look this up later. The problem is the evidence of malfeasance part.

"I'm not sure about fraud," I say. "The New Sons of Liberty seem to be opposed to traffic cameras on principle. They see them as un-American, an assault on our rights. That's what leads me to wonder how far they'd go to influence Uncle Dave on this issue."

"You think they'd abduct his nephew," she says, skepticism in her voice.

"I know it sounds far-fetched. And it is. But it's possible. They've called for war on Kevin's uncle, war by any means necessary."

This also may explain why no protesters turned up at today's happy hour protest. If they've got Uncle Dave's nephew, why bother with demonstrations?

Monalisa smiles at Boo, who wags his tail.

"Where's the ball Boo?" His head tilts up. "Ball!"

He tears down the yard, plunging into some brush. Seconds later, he trots back with an object that at some point in recent history used to be a ball. It is a nub of its former self, and shiny with slobber. He offers this gift to Monalisa, who grabs it and tosses it back into the yard. He tears after it.

Monalisa turns to me. "Next steps?"

"I'm going to infiltrate the New Sons of Liberty."

"They let women join?"

"They do now."

On Saturday morning, I am eating low-calorie macaroons, drinking rocket-starter coffee, and reviewing my latest texts and e-mails. Charise has responded to my text about Kevin being in touch with his mother: "His mother, but not me. OK. Good to know."

I sense resignation in her tone, a sign that she's moving from white-hot anger to acceptance over his absence. While this is healthy, it doesn't bode well for her wanting us to continue with the case.

I take a stiff drink of my strong coffee. Resignation. Acceptance. Humbug.

I grab my backpack and dig out the postcard I bought at the Botanical Garden gift shop, with its close-up of a prickly pear cactus flower.

"Dear Iona," I write. "Gorgeous flower! It made me think of you. Work is okay. Still can't find the missing fiancé. Yes, I know there are other fish in the sea. I will tell Charise. Sometimes I miss helping people rejuvenate themselves. Love, Angela."

A few minutes later, I receive an e-mail from the New Sons of Liberty. Someone named Errol Todd has written, "Let's meet to discuss Newman." I write back, suggesting the front entrance of the downtown Scottsdale library at eleven this morning.

A few minutes later, he writes, "Roger, CU."

As this is a bustling library, I add, "I'll be wearing white shirt. I have long dark hair."

"I know what you look like."

Whoa. A crazy man who does his homework. This raises a red flag. A red flag that I quickly lower because, in my imagination, I am being interviewed by a reporter, who is congratulating me on leading police to the group that abducted Kevin Sherman.

A half-hour later, I pull into the municipal garage across from the library and the civic center park. Usually, I don't like crowds but this morning I am happy to see hordes of people going into and out of the garage, rambling down the sidewalks, chasing toddlers through grass. If the front man for New Sons of Liberty tries anything with me, plenty of people can come to my rescue. Or, more realistically, plenty of gawp-mouthed people would stand by and create phone videos of me being carted away by a ranting madman.

I head up the library stairs and stand near the entrance. Many people, some even walking without canes or other assistive devices, head into the library. I scan the area, looking for a man who appears to be looking for me. I don't see anyone.

Several minutes later, a grey-haired man with mutton chop whiskers approaches the stairs. I know this is Errol. He looks exactly like the type of person who would be leading the New Sons of Liberty. His safari vest and sturdy hiking shoes suggest he's prepared for anything: traffic cameras, snakes, dragons, radiation, peak oil. His pants are light beige, perfect for warding off tsetse flies, and a thigh zipper enables quick conversion to shorts in the afternoon heat. I half-expect to see a Land Rover drive up and whisk him away to Masai Mara for safari.

"Errol?" I call.

Mutton chops peers up at me warily, an expression that

suggests he has a bunker full of canned goods and water drums at home.

He points toward the park. "Let's walk."

Of course. The library steps could be monitored, infringing on our liberties. Despite myself, I take a quick gander for cameras. We walk around the side of the library and into the park. Errol walks with a slight limp. My guess is he is somewhere in his fifties.

Neither of us speaks. I point to a bench near the lagoon, with its sculpture of Don Quixote on his horse. We find a vacant bench near the sculpture and both of us slowly and carefully lower ourselves onto it. As soon as he's seated, Errol yawns aggressively, making a lot of noise. His breath smells like sour milk.

He says, "How do you know David Newman?"

"We're Facebook friends."

He snorts. "Spare me. What are you writing about?"

"Writing?"

"You're a reporter," he says. "You're some kind of dirt digger. Otherwise you wouldn't have to gussy yourself up like you do."

He all but spits out the word "gussy" as if grooming and hygiene are suspicious activities. I sit back and take in the splashing water of the lagoon fountain. This man has a distrust of good grooming. This is not something I ever imagined working at the day spa. He probably thinks his disgusting whiskers are a virtue.

"I'm interested in the traffic camera deal," I say.

"No." He shakes his head slowly. "No you're not."

"Why do you say that?"

"You're of the female persuasion, for starters."

I give myself a quick once over. "Very observant of you."

"Our movement has a real problem attracting women."

No wonder. The name of the group is New *Sons* of Liberty. This is not inclusive, twenty-first century language. Another problem, frankly, is that he is dirty and uncouth. I fight the impulse to suggest he wash his hands and shave. Still, I don't think that alone would do the trick. My sense is that the most serious barrier for women joining the group is that the cause is ridiculous. I can't see a woman foaming at the mouth about traffic cameras, which are intended to curtail speeding and red light running, thus saving lives.

My theory about the New Sons of Liberty is that dangerously high levels of testosterone are involved.

Errol examines his hands, perhaps noting the clots of dirt under his nails. His left hand goes airborne, heading to his mouth, and I want to cry out: *No! Do not put that filthy digit anywhere near your mouth.* He is going to give his finger a good chawing.

I say, "I tried to go to your happy hour protest yesterday, but no one showed up."

He lowers his hand. "It got cancelled," he says, wearing a small, embarrassed smile. "We should have got word out earlier."

"Do you think you're having any success with the traffic camera issue?"

"Absolutely not," he says. "We're at war with Newman for the principle of it."

"You're at war with him?"

"Excuse my rectal misfire." He grins at his witticism. Meanwhile, I try to block any mental imagery around the word rectum from materializing in my brain.

He continues, "The word 'war' doesn't quite cover it. We're making some noise about what's right. We had a pretty good turnout at the protest last week, about thirty-five people and a Lab named Barney. Basically we're blowing farts in the wind. The cameras are a done deal. Now it's only a matter of choosing which proctologist to administer the enema to the good people of Arizona."

I mentally rinse my brain out with spring water. "You've given up on winning?"

He shrugs and gazes at Don Quixote on his metal horse. I sense that Errol and his merry band of liberty's sons have not abducted Kevin. They can't even get it together to let people know a protest has been cancelled. Plus, I doubt he's even heard of Lady Gaga, let alone the concept of Lady Gaga lookalikes.

I take another tack. "Do you think there's been any fraud with the traffic camera process?"

His head knocks back. "Fraud?" He makes a growling noise. "The entire system is a fraud. Our government officials are frauds. They're dung beetles. Government for and by the people, what a load of dog diarrhea—"

I decide to stir the pot. "Don't these cameras save lives?"

He pumps his fist. "Propaganda! Lies!"

"It's all about profit, then."

He stretches his legs, warming up. "The city blundercrats are waxing their assholes over these cameras. These ball lickers stand to make a billion dollars over the next few years. Newman is as bad as the rest of them. He's the kind of guy who sucks the farts out of the couch cushions before his boss sits down."

I can't help but notice Errol wears no wedding band. Funny, that.

"Do you think Newman will profit personally from this deal?"

"Of course."

My fraud-hunting fingers are quivering. "How?"

"He'll suck at Mama Government's titties the rest of his life. Who else gets that kind of job security?"

"Do you know him personally?"

"No." He chuckles. "I know his type. What's your interest here? Give it to me straight, without the usual side of Grade A bullshit."

"I was hired to find Mr. Newman's nephew, who disappeared last week."

"Isn't that ducky." His whiskers twitch with amusement. "How old is this kid?"

"He's in his late twenties. His fiancée—"

"Fiancée?" He smiles and scowls at the same time. "He's getting married?"

"Next month."

"No wonder he's missing," he says. "Why would you invite two of the world's biggest, worst bureaucracies, the government and the church, into your personal business?"

Not having looked at marriage this way, I don't have an answer for Errol. Somehow I doubt Kevin has run off from fear of the church and government meddling in his personal affairs.

"His fiancée isn't the only one looking for him. His brother is also concerned."

"I don't know anything about this kid. I can't help you there. If you want to join the movement, we're always looking for a few good women."

I offer up a sickly smile.

"You don't have to tell me now," he says. "Constipate over it and let me know."

AFTER ERROL LIMPS OFF, I linger on the bench. I still have nothing concrete to give Charise about Kevin. If anything, the case seems to have become more complicated. I have some inflammatory ingredients but no recipe: Uncle Dave, the traffic camera deal, Lady Gaga lookalikes, heroin, Mr. Neighborhood Watch, Kevin.

Could it be that Kevin found out about the heroin and skedaddled? This is possible. But it wouldn't stop him from contacting his fiancée. He's calling his mother, after all.

I mentally diagram my pieces of information. I have a dotted line between Uncle Dave and Mr. Neighborhood Watch, knowing they're connected but not knowing how. There's another dotted line between the Lady Gaga lookalikes and Kevin. A solid line between Mr. Neighborhood Watch and a Lady Gaga lookalike. A solid line between Uncle Dave and the traffic camera deal. Solid lines between heroin and Mr. Neighborhood Watch and a Lady Gaga lookalike.

The dotted line that seems critical is the one between Uncle Dave and Mr. Neighborhood Watch. This must relate to Kevin's disappearance and uncharacteristic behavior. This is the key to understanding the other links better. Unfortunately, more contact with Mr. Neighborhood Watch might put me in an early grave.

I get up from the bench and meander toward Robert Indiana's love sculpture. I keep my gaze steadied on the blazing red letters, trying not to let my mind wander over to the nearby restaurant and bar, Frank, where I used to drink martinis with friends when I had money.

Oh, how I loved Frank's patio and chic white chairs. One of the bartenders used to send me a Christmas card. Yes, Frank loved me back, when I had money. I had friends to drink with when I had money. I stand near the sculpture. A child is on the "E" letter, red-faced and bawling. His father is trying to coax a photo out of him. The kid will not be cajoled into a happy face.

I whip my phone out and take a photo of the squalling child hanging despondently off the love sculpture. The father shoots me an irritated look. I grin back at him. I could join this kid, slipping between V and E and letting loose a scream that would break martini glasses.

No, I won't join this kid. Surprisingly, I don't feel like screaming and not just because of my rib injury. I look at the sculpture and I think about Dr. Fantastic. What we had was not love, no matter how hard I tried to convince myself otherwise.

I know love. This is what I have with Moorea and my dad who art in heaven. This is what Moorea and Roy have with each other. This is what I have with Iona, who art in heaven, probably growing string beans. If I listen hard, I can almost hear her thanking me for my postcards. She's probably still adding to her collection, delighting over images of heavenly cloud formations.

All this love makes me think about Charise. Poor Charise. I text her and tell her I hope she's okay.

I walk back toward the library, giving Don Quixote a last nod as I head to the parking garage. The Kia Soul, my trusty steed, awaits me.

I head to Monalisa's house, where I find her standing in the front yard, talking to a man in khakis and a button down shirt. He is holding a notepad and has the kind of tan that suggests he works outside. Behind them, on the front steps, Archie and Humboldt, the eyeless stone lions, stand guard. I strongly suspect these proud guardians of Iona's realm, trusty warriors who never minded being half the size of the decorative deer in the front yard, will soon be retired from service.

At the gate, I greet Monalisa, who peers at me with a studious frown, the one that suggests her alien sensory apparatus is taking my pulse and temperature.

Eventually, she says, "Angela."

"Present," I say.

She tells the man that I am an associate. The man tells me he is a landscape designer.

"You're not going to get rid of Iona's lions, are you?" I ask.

They stare at me. Guilty as charged.

I fight the good fight. "They're excellent for security."

Monalisa turns to the man, "I'll be right back."

She meets me at the gate and leads me onto the sidewalk. "Anything to report?"

I tell her the New Sons of Liberty are most likely not behind Kevin's abduction.

"Are they claiming any fraud in connection with the traffic camera contract?"

I hedge on this one. "On principle."

Monalisa's mouth juts to the side. "The Salvador Foundation might be interested if there is evidence of fraud. Do you have any evidence?"

I shake my head, sensing a knockout blow is coming.

She says, "Charise called this morning and left a message that she wants to talk about the case."

I run my finger horizontally along my neck.

"Yes, I think this is probably it," Monalisa says. "Stay tuned."

I PARK a half-block away from the house so Moorea doesn't see the Kia Soul. The less she knows about me continuing to work with Monalisa, the better. When I reach the house, I slowly crack the door open, trying to make a ninja entrance. My mission? Make it to my bedroom without encountering Moorea.

From the front door, I can hear the hiss and spit of a busy wok. The smell of cabbage saturates every pore in my skin. I wait until the sizzling sound intensifies—probably Roy dropping some low-fat protein into the mix—and click the door shut behind me.

"Angela?" Moorea calls.

Never underestimate the superhuman hearing of your mother.

"Yes?" I try to sound weak, like someone with a damaged ribcage.

"Where have you been?"

This is a long story. I decide to make it a short one. "Getting some fresh air."

"You must be feeling better."

Oddly, I am. "A little better." But definitely not well enough to join you for a family lunch. Not healthy enough for a lot of well-meaning questions.

"Why are we shouting? Why don't you come into the kitchen and be civilized?"

Because I prefer the life of a bedroom-dwelling savage. One

thing I can say about myself is that I have never lost touch with my inner brat.

I go into the kitchen and smile at Moorea, the woman who rescued me from Prescott bright and early yesterday morning. Roy is tending to the wok. Moorea hovers behind him, her face bright pink from the heat.

Three places are set at the kitchen table. I'm expected. Drat.

"Want a beer?" Roy asks.

Moorea gives him a sharp look. One of the mother-daughter myths we maintain is that I don't drink alcohol.

"No, thanks," I say.

Moorea's shoulders relax, and she exchanges a look with Roy, her eyes flickering with excitement. The voltage between them seems stronger than usual. They're up to no good. I can sense an ambush a mile away.

"Have you talked to Uncle Hiro lately?" I ask, desperate for a distraction. "I think the bedbugs may have come back."

"He's very popular lately." Moorea laughs. "He's also got a new girlfriend. And he got a promotion at work."

My mouth stretches to the right. I hoist the other side upward, almost grunting with effort. Smile! I am happy for Uncle Hiro, really I am. But I close my mouth lest a bitter noise comes out. With Hiro on the up and up, I have hit a new milestone. I am now the most wayward member of the family.

"I'm going to my bedroom to rest. My ribs are starting to talk to me again."

Moorea's face falls. "Angela, you've got to eat something. We're having a special lunch today. Roy has outdone himself."

Roy turns to me, scowling with mock-disappointment. "This is a special recipe, just for you."

How can I argue with that? "Thank you."

Moorea and Roy trade electric smiles. My stomach tightens. I pour myself a glass of water and down an ibuprofen, steeling myself for friendly fire.

When the stir-fry is done, Roy invites us to fill our plates. I take a modest mound of food, about the size of my balled up fist. In an emergency, I could shovel it down my gullet in seconds and flee to my bedroom.

"Is that all you're going to eat?" Moorea asks.

"My stomach is funny."

"No wonder, after all that excitement yesterday," Roy says.

At the table, Moorea and Roy hold hands. We bow our heads.

Moorea says: "For what we are about to receive, may the Lord make us truly thankful. Amen."

After the prayer, Moorea and Roy smile at me. Here it comes.

The gambler in me places a bet they are going to offer me a bedroom in their new love pad. This is better than being homeless, I tell myself. The dreamer in me is crying out for a loan for a security deposit and first month's rent. This would tide me over until my bright shiny future materializes.

Roy takes a draft from his beer. Moorea taps the table with her fingers.

"We'd like to help you get back on your feet, Angela," Roy says.

I raise my hand in protest. "You've already done too much. You don't have to help me anymore."

"We know we don't have to," Roy says.

"We want to," Moorea adds.

"I'll be fine," I say.

Moorea's jaw tightens. "Honey, it's time to think about a good job that provides a regular source of income and benefits."

"We want to do something that will give you a foundation for life," Roy says. "You know that saying, 'Give a man a fish and you feed him for a day—"

Moorea chimes in, " 'Teach a man to fish and you feed him for a lifetime.' "

This is not sounding like a security deposit or first month's rent.

"Wow," I say, staring down at my glistening medley of cabbage, chicken and snow peas. "This is so kind of you."

Moorea clears her throat. "We're going to help you go to beauty school."

Beauty school? "Beauty school?"

Moorea beams. "It's been so obvious all along. You were always such a bright child, reading everything, asking questions all the time. But I can see now that your true love is hair and makeup."

"I appreciate the importance of grooming."

"Exactly," she replies. "These are your gifts, and God wants for all of us to realize our special gifts."

I was never one of those girls who loved doing the hair of other girls. Instead, I was off to the side, judging everyone's hair. That sounds horrible, and it is horrible. I don't want to do hair. I only want to judge hair.

Roy raises his beer. "You're going to be the top haircutter in the city."

I prefer the term stylist but clink my water glass against his beer bottle and against Moorea's water glass.

"Thank you," I say. "I'm so touched that you want to help."

With the business portion of our meal concluded, they dig into their food. As I gum a mouthful of stir-fry, I wonder why they can't take more interest in their upcoming wedding. Their nuptials would make a much more pleasant mealtime conversation topic than my future. I would love to help pick out flowers, caterers, dresses, invitations and music. They don't realize how good I would be at staging a beautiful, unforgettable event, arranging every sight, scent, sound, and object to surprise and delight.

You'd think, being an emergency room nurse, Moorea might display the slightest interest in beauty, tranquility, or rejuvenation. She never even visited the spa once when I worked there, even though I could have gotten her a hefty discount on any service. She's completely uninterested in aromatherapy, body-work, cosmetic enhancement, or skin treatments. She's never even plucked her eyebrows. She's never put anything heavier on her lips than Chapstick.

Sometimes I marvel that we're related.

Without the wedding to distract everyone, I will need to focus on beauty school. Could that be the answer to my problems? Maybe I've never asked the right questions.

Sometimes I give perfect strangers makeovers. Mental makeovers. I'll correct a woman's brassy dye job with toner or swap out a man's wretched pleated khakis for more streamlined trousers. When I used to go to bars, I was always mentally erasing tattoos. I could never fathom why someone would destroy perfectly beautiful skin with a tasteless dragon rearing up from a pit of flames.

I've always considered mental makeover a common pastime, a way to while away minutes spent waiting in doctor's offices or for the Milano gimlets to arrive. Maybe this is only something I do for fun. Maybe no one else does this for fun. Maybe this is a sign of career potential. But my gut tells me that I'm an armchair stylist, not a real one.

"Let us know when you've selected a school," Roy says.

"Yes," I say. "Yes, I'll do that."

Roy and Moorea are both smiling. They are trying so hard. I also smile, but my lips are being held up with a complicated system of ropes and pulleys.

As my fork scrapes up the last of my stir-fry, I tell myself I will make a good-faith effort at beauty school. After all, cutting hair has advantages over getting tossed into the back of a power Benzi and being left for dead in the middle of nowhere. A stable income would do wonders in helping me secure an apartment and a bold red Kia Soul.

Could I be good at cutting hair? Truthfully, I don't know. Here is my inventory of superpowers: ironing hair, calming frequent frowners, dressing for success, and skipping past male security guards. I'm also a genius at flaming out at jobs.

A small thought crawls into my mind and takes root. Maybe I'd like to be a private investigator. Seriously, I ask myself. Have I actually been enjoying my job without realizing it? I'd thought my interest in finding Kevin was primarily fueled by desperation. But is desperation so powerful a force that it would have me biking all over trying to track down Kevin?

I think I've been enjoying my job. On the other hand, maybe this is about me wanting what I can't have. I can be a sucker for hard-to-get.

"Angela, would you like any dessert?" Roy asks. "We've got some mango sorbet."

I thank Moorea and Roy effusively but excuse myself from the table and go to my room. My intention is to engage in some negative visualization regarding flunking out of beauty school. But, instead, I decide on a Hail Mary move to locate Kevin and get some answers.

World, here I come.

11

*U*nfortunately, my new hobby, thinking, has led me to the conclusion that Dolly Gaga, the woman whose heroin I ran off with, is my last best hope for locating Kevin. I am not running with this idea yet, though. Surely, Dolly Gaga will be the slightest bit peeved at me for accidentally on purpose taking her heroin and getting her into trouble with her boss. In a perfect world, I would never have to see her again.

Desperate for other ideas for tracking down Kevin, I take an emergency treatment in the power cocoon, letting the narcotic sounds of grey whales breaching off the coast of Santa Barbara wash over me. After ten minutes in the cocoon, I disrupt my treatment and pad into the bathroom, where I doctor myself up with eight hundred milligrams of ibuprofen. After the ibuprofen kicks in, I hope that pursuing Dolly Gaga will seem like a better idea.

Five minutes later, it still doesn't seem like a better idea. She probably got fired after losing control of the heroin. Then again, do heroin distributors get fired? It's probably not the kind of position where you give two weeks notice and get a friendly send-off lunch with colleagues.

If she's still got a handgun, I decide I'd better meet her in a public space.

If I'm going to meet her at all, of course. First I need to locate her. She's probably no longer working as a celebrity lookalike for NB Entertainment. I wonder if any of the celebrity lookalikes are still on the job. It's possible. Mr. Neighborhood Watch and his henchmen may think I'm deceased or scared to death. Either way, they may assume they can safely continue their heroin distribution activities.

I sit on the edge of my bed, thinking. When my brain empties of thought, I rub at my face, transferring bacteria, viruses, and allergens from my hands to my skin. Not only is thinking a disturbing habit, it is undermining my good hygienic habits. I zip into the bathroom and wash my face, then moisturize. With hygienic order restored, I take a brief stroll around my bedroom, the headquarters of my soon-to-be global business.

I hate to lose. On the other hand, I don't want to tempt fate and trigger another run-in with Mr. Neighborhood Watch. On yet another hand, I want to find Kevin.

When your decisions require more than two hands, you are probably dithering.

Has all my searching, bike riding, and risk taking been for nothing? The back of my throat burns. I thump my fist into my palm. The sounds of the ocean trickling from my laptop are starting to annoy me. I turn off the meditation track.

I stare at my laptop screen, realizing I don't even know Dolly Gaga's real name. What do I know? She listens to Taylor Swift. She drives a Kia Soul. I hold my nose and take myself back to the cramped, dirty back seat of her car. For a moment I am overwhelmed by the injustice of someone like her owning that car. The neglect. The trash. If I were the owner, I would keep it in pristine condition. It's so unfair. The wrong people always seem to own the best cars.

I drag myself back to a more productive line of thought. The smell. Oh, those terrible gym shoes. They were hideous stiff black shoes with Velcro straps on top. You wouldn't run in these shoes. Personally, I wouldn't do anything with those shoes except toss them in the trash.

A glimmering idea flaps its fairy wings and alights on my shoulder. Maybe the shoes smelled because she used them. Maybe she'd even been at a gym that day. There was a water bottle in the back seat of the car. I shut my eyes. The water bottle. It was branded with the name of a gym. I can't remember the name. My eyes snap open.

I Google area gyms, hoping a name pops up that I recognize. Eventually, it does. Spark Fitness. The water bottle in the back seat was from Spark Fitness.

The website tells me Spark Fitness has three locations in the area. One is in Arcadia, another in Glendale, and a third way yonder in Fountain Hills. The gyms offer Zumba, free weights, yoga, abs, spinning. They are considerate enough to have a photo gallery. Zumba is taught with disco lights. In the free weights class, everyone appears to be on the heavy side. I find a photo of a spinning instructor teaching a class. Something strikes my interest here. I peer more closely at the photo.

The instructor is wearing white and silver shoes. They have three straps across, just like the black ones did in Dolly Gaga's car. I do a Google search on spinning, and learn that indeed, these are spinning shoes. They are one more offence against elegance in the sacred name of fitness. They are also a pretty excellent clue.

The closest gym location to me is Arcadia. This location also seems to have the largest spinning studio and number of classes. They offer a free three-day guest pass to people considering gym membership. My ribcage howls in protest. The pea-sized part of my brain that controls common sense cries out for me to stay in bed. Another, larger part of my brain, headquarters for the Kia Soul and apartment fundraising foundation, counters that Dolly Gaga will have no room for a gun in a tight spinning outfit.

AT SPARK FITNESS, a membership associate named Rebecca is giving me a tour of the premises. She wears the gym's team colors of red and black and seems oblivious to my hints that I don't want a tour. All I want is the free three-day trial pass for potential new members. Across a sea of clanging self-torture machines, I spot the spinning studio against the far left wall. In a few minutes, the one-thirty p.m. spinning class will begin, and I need to stalk that class.

She points at a rack of free weights. "Have you done much weight training?"

I gaze toward the spinning studio, all but whining like Boo. "I'm really interested in the spinning class."

She laughs. "We'll get there. Your membership includes a fifty-minute baseline assessment with a trainer. The trainer will go over free weights with you."

"Great," I say. The word virtually disintegrates as it hits the air. I stare at the weights, wondering how many grimy, slimy mitts have sweated on them. No cleansing wipes appear to be in the vicinity.

Rebecca looks at me like she's my physician. "To achieve optimal fitness you need to mix cardio with weight training. Some people believe weights are actually more important than cardio."

Behind us, the desperate cries of an orangutan distract me. Rebecca displays no concern for this ailing creature. When I take a quick glance over my shoulder, I am surprised to see it is not a great ape but an average-sized man on a weight bench, hefting a barbell toward the ceiling.

"In your thirties, you start to lose muscle mass," Rebecca says.

My attention snaps back to Rebecca. My thirties? Excuse me? That is a land far, far away. That troubled place, with its decay and fat and metabolic inefficiency, is three years off. Well, two and a half years off. I'd rather not think about that right now. In fact, I'd rather wait to the very last minute to cross that bridge.

Rebecca presses ahead, her sales pitch going down hill quickly. "In your thirties, you burn fewer calories every day than in your twenties. Most women see increases in body fat and weight. By building muscle mass now, you'll burn more fat."

"Mostly I ride my bike for exercise," I say.

"You won't believe the difference weight training makes. You won't bulk up. Women think they'll get big so they don't take advantage of weights. Arguably, women need weights more than men." She pauses, giving me a meaningful look. "They need bone strength."

Being the consummate professional, I will not run screaming from this gym. Bone strength? Must we discuss this? I am still a mere slip of a girl. Besides, ribcage notwithstanding, I've got bone strength up the ying yang in my DNA. Samoans are strong. Of course, it's the half-American part of my heritage that I might need to worry about. Someday. Not today.

"This is helpful to know," I say.

She glances at my forehead, where I probably didn't use enough concealer on the bruise. I catch a flare of amusement in her expression and a gleam of admiration. She is probably the type who coos over athletic injuries.

"You cycle outdoors?" she asks.

Ah, cycling is the proper athletic way of referring to bike riding. "Yes, but I injured my ribs."

If she's wondering why I am touring her gym nursing a rib injury she is too polite to ask. She smiles at my forehead. The bruise is definitely showing through.

"How did you hurt your ribs?"

"Accident," I say.

She points clear across the gym from the spinning studio. "Let's go see the pool. Low impact is what you need."

"I'm much better, actually. My main interest is in your spinning class."

No use. Seconds later we are marching through the steamy ladies locker room, which has a door that opens directly into the hothouse of a pool. It is not a fun pool with a cabana and drink service. This pool smells like chlorine and means business. People swim laps in marked lanes.

My excitement must be showing because Rebecca asks, "Shall we go back into the gym?"

We leave, my hair noticeably limper for the dunk in the steam bath, and I follow Rebecca into the machinery department. We stand in the center of the gym, surrounded by the rack, the prod, and the thumbscrew machines.

"As part of your fitness assessment, we orient new members to the equipment."

Out of the corner of my eye, I spot a grey-haired man in a silver spandex shirt entering the spinning studio.

"You'll learn how to strengthen and tone every major muscle group."

A blond woman in turquoise spandex fills her water bottle at a water fountain outside the spinning studio. Could that be—

"You're addicted, aren't you?"

Addicted. My mind flashes back to glassine bags of heroin.

Rebecca points to the spinning studio. "You keep looking over there."

Oh, right. My profound love for bike riding. I smile and say, "There's something special about biking. I mean, cycling. At first I hated it. My butt and thighs were screaming."

"I know! It feels like torture. But then it starts to feel great and you can't live without it."

Totally. I only wish I'd get past the torture phase.

We stroll toward the spinning studio. I try to not to skip along like a puppy. An African-American woman in purple spandex waves to Rebecca. The woman enters the spinning studio and closes the door behind her.

"That's Diane, one of our instructors."

Safe to say, she isn't Dolly Gaga. Conveniently, the studio is separated from the gym by a glass wall. We gaze inside. The instructor, mounted on a bike at the front, faces us. Luckily, the entire wall behind the instructor is a mirror. I study the reflections of eleven people mounted on bikes.

Among the students, I rule out the man. The rest of the spinners are women. I peer at them, wondering if I can even identify Dolly Gaga. Behind the wig and the makeup and the costume what do I really know about her features? As disguises go, the Lady Gaga get-up isn't half-bad. My best guess is that her real hair is blond based on her light blue eyes and blond eyebrows.

I rule out five brunettes, which leaves three blonds. One of the blonds looks like she's gone over to the Botox side, making her a little older than Dolly Gaga. That still leaves two blonds. Dolly Gaga is tall and thin. Both of these women are tall and thin.

"I'm surprised you've never been to a spinning class before," Rebecca says.

"Me too," I say.

Diane the instructor clips her shoes into the pedals of her bike. I ask, "Do you need spinning shoes?"

"They give you more powerful and efficient pedal strokes. The instructors use them but not all students do." Rebecca drops her chin to her shoulder, as if she's telling me a big secret, and says, "You can wait to get the shoes. See how you like it first."

I study the footwear of the two blonds that could be Dolly Gaga. Neither wears spinning shoes.

"When's the next spinning class?"

"Three." She laughs. "You don't waste any time, do you?"

"Never."

Oozing ninja glamour, I return to the gym fifteen minutes before the three o'clock class. Even if my rib injury prevents any actual exercise from taking place, I have dressed for success in a black t-shirt and exercise Capri pants. I display my three-day pass at the reception counter and am waved inside.

The class schedule is posted on the door of the spinning studio. I hope Dolly Gaga shows up for the three o'clock class. Otherwise, I will have to return Sunday for the nine a.m. class, which is a little earlier than is convenient for me. Worse, I may have to go to spinning classes at the other gym locations.

"You made it," Rebecca says, appearing by my side.

"I have, but I'm probably not—"

"I'll help you set up."

I am thinking: *No, I do not want to take this class. I cannot take this class.* My ribcage chimes in, trying to talk some sense into me. *It's bad enough that you're breathing! You cannot pedal a bike as well.*

Rebecca opens the door to the spinning studio. I walk inside, saying, "I don't think I'll last long in class. Maybe it's better if I stick to being an observer for today."

"Keep your own pace. You'll be fine."

The studio is the temperature of a meat locker. Rebecca selects a bike in the center of class.

"Maybe one in the back?" I ask. "In case I have to leave early."

"Don't worry." She pats my shoulder. "You're hard core, I can tell. A total badass."

She has me stand next to the bike, then lowers the seat height. "Fit is super important in spinning. Improper alignment will destroy your back."

She has me get on the seat. I maneuver myself aboard, moving oh so carefully.

"It won't bite," she says with a laugh.

She laughs alone. "Still tender from my accident," I say, giving her a warning smile, sort of like a cat's soft hiss or a dog's slight baring of teeth.

Rebecca, oblivious to my discomfort, kneels and asks me to pedal for her.

A moment later, she says, "Perfect. You're all set."

I thank her as she bounces out of the studio. This would be a good time for me to leave, but Rebecca is watching from the window. She waves at me. I manage a feeble wave in return. She pumps a fist in response. Great, I have a cheering section.

Meanwhile, two men enter the studio. One takes the bike in front of me. The other is to my left. They give me a quick nod, then tinker with the bikes, adjusting the seats. Their expressions are dead serious.

Three brunette women come in next, going straight to their bikes without so much as a nod. No one says hello. No one bumps fists. This is serious business. This is not fun. To make matters worse, Dolly Gaga is not among us.

I stay propped on my bike but don't dare move for fear of shattering. The class continues to fill. With less than a minute to start, I have sized up three blond women. None of them are tall enough. Plus, two of them are built like fireplugs, which also rules them out.

The clock strikes three. An intimidating hum emanates from the collective chorus of wheels turning. I take a test spin, holding my breath. Not so bad, as long as I don't breathe. The secrets of spinning success: Form, fit, oxygen deprivation.

Now that I've figured this out, I decide I can leave. I start to maneuver my right hip off the bike. As I shift into the next phase of disengagement, the long step onto the floor, the teacher rushes inside. I sit very still for a moment. She is a tall, thin blond woman. Could it be? I swallow. At the front of class, she swaps her flip-flops for black spinning shoes.

Ugly black shoes with Velcro straps.

She introduces herself as Nicole and welcomes us to class

without the slightest bit of welcome in her voice. I know this voice. It is a hard voice. A voice comfortable giving orders.

Check.

In my excitement, I inadvertently take a deep breath. The ice pick lodged in my ribcage twists. I grip the bike handles, trying not to cry out in agony.

Dolly Gaga does not notice me yet. She is setting up her iPod sound system.

A moment later, she gets on her bike and gazes out at her victims without much interest. She appears to be counting us.

I study her face, all but quivering with recognition. How could I have forgotten her transparent blue eyes? Her long, straight nose? She is in fierce, Ork-fighting shape, all muscle and no fat. This is especially clear without the fake Dolly Parton chest. She resembles a warrior avatar, an unearthly creature concocted in a video game lab; all she's missing is a gem-encrusted breastplate.

She asks, "Is anyone new?"

I raise my hand. She peers at me and blinks. Her watery eyes seem to freeze solid. For a few long seconds, she doesn't move. She does not appear pleased to see me.

She starts the music and says, "Everyone start cycling."

A second later, she is standing within inches of me. Close up, she looks even more ripped than from a distance. Her biceps jut sharply from her shoulders. She's got sinewy definition to her forearms. A less dedicated detective than I might have asked her about her weight-training regimen.

"It's a miracle," she says without a smile. "You're alive."

I do not have a ready response for her. "I'm already set up."

"Good for you."

She clomps back to the head of class, where she dons a mike and waxes on about climbs, sprints, and keeping your core engaged. She does not mention keeping your ribcage intact; I am on my own here. The various postures for spinning include bending forward, standing, or staying in the saddle. I listen hard for sitting perfectly still but she doesn't mention that option.

Within minutes, people are cycling as though they are trying to escape from a violent heroin trafficker. I keep my head down, pedaling every so often as I carefully control my breathing. The music blurs into one relentless electro pop riff.

Every so often, Nicole interrupts to demand that we climb or sprint or keep our pace. *Remember your core!* How could I forget it? As my shipwrecked body sinks, crashing on a bank of fractured ribs, I think, *Remember the core.*

Three hundred years later, when class is finally over, I ease myself off my bike, feeling like one of Iona's ancient teacups, veined with tiny cracks. The other bike bunnies hop away. Arms crossed against her steel abs, Nicole watches me as I hobble over to the front of class.

"What a surprise," I say. "You're a spinning instructor."

"It's an income."

I take this to mean an official, documentable source of income. "I can only imagine what the IRS would make of your other job."

She blinks. "I can't believe you're still alive."

"I appreciate your concern," I say. "Where's Kevin?"

She makes a disgusted noise but doesn't answer. She peels the Velcro straps loose on her shoes, making a violent ripping sound. She changes back into her athletic looking flip-flops and stuffs the spinning shoes into her gym bag—loose, without any protective shoe bag.

"I have a question." She stands up straight, towering over me. "But I want an honest answer. Will you give me that?"

"I can try."

"How did you find me?"

My gaze flits to the mirror, to the empty bikes behind us, awaiting the next class. Is there any reason I shouldn't tell her the truth? None comes immediately to mind.

"I pieced it together from the junk in the back seat of your car."

She throws back her head and grimaces at the pipe-laced ceiling. "You're kidding."

"No." That will teach her to clean up her slovenly ways.

"No one else has found me." She slowly shakes her head. "Yet here you are."

"I need to locate Kevin."

She picks up her gym bag, looping it over her shoulder. "Join the club." I follow her to the door of the spinning studio.

"You don't know where he is?"

She passes through the door. "He's with my sister, Joni."

"The other Lady Gaga lookalike?"

"Yes. The two of them have done a great job in disappearing. But I'll find them, and sooner than they'd dream possible."

Nicole veers to the right, toward the exit. The main gym area is teeming with sweaty people building muscle mass, and I struggle to navigate around them to keep up with Nicole.

"Why are they hiding?" I ask.

She taps her lip with her index finger. "Let's see," she says. "Maybe it's because my darling sister has taken some money that doesn't belong to her."

"Does it belong to—" I stop myself before I say Mr. Neighborhood Watch. "That tall guy with the shaved head?"

She gives me a look.

I continue, "You know his name. You work for him."

"I work for him?" She laughs. "You're not going to get his name from me. Not going to happen, pumpkin."

Her long legs seem to be picking up speed, and I feel like an injured Chihuahua trying to keep pace with a Greyhound. I could really use a brand shiny new ribcage at this point. A replacement model made of titanium.

As we pass the vending machines near the exit, I lob another question at her. "Who hired you to pick up Kevin?"

She slows, giving me an appraising look. "If I tell you, will you promise to go away forever and leave me alone?"

"What if I find Kevin and your sister first? Wouldn't you want me to let you know?"

She laughs. "You're not going to find them first. Believe me."

"Okay, if you tell me who hired you, I'll leave you alone."

Nicole puts her hands on her hips. "It was a favor to someone. I can't remember who, maybe a friend or relative. We don't usually entertain individuals. It was a one-off."

"You don't remember who hired you." I enunciate slowly, letting her know I think this is a lie.

"Now you have to go away." She makes a shooing motion.

"I could go away and let the authorities handle this matter. I'm sure they'd love to chat with you about your different *income* streams."

"Do you have a death wish?"

"How do you know Kevin went away with your sister?"

She wags her head in disbelief. "You're not joking."

"I need proof. For my client."

She extracts her cell-phone from her bag and taps the screen with her finger, producing a photo of Kevin with his arm around the shoulder of a Lady Gaga lookalike.

"I took this before they left town."

I all but press my nose against the screen. Kevin and the Gaga lookalike are sitting in a booth, looking cozy and bleary-eyed. Three cocktail glasses are on the table, filled with some type of clear alcohol. In the pantheon of alcohols, I think clear alcohol is especially dangerous.

I sigh. Here is evidence that no one, not even his brother or fiancée, seemed to really know Kevin. He is drinking a cocktail and cuddling with a woman he'd just met. This woman wouldn't seem to be his type, not even in the same area code. But one thing I've learned about people is that you can't count on them to be who you think they are.

"Could you send that to me? That should be enough for my client." I realize Nicole doesn't care about my client so I offer up something better. "I'll be done with the case. I won't bother you again."

"You don't know my name. We've never met."

I nod.

"Wait here." She turns and walks back into the gym, disappearing into one of the offices beyond the reception counter. Several minutes later, she emerges with a piece of white paper in her hand, which she offers to me.

She has printed out the photo of Kevin and the Gaga lookalike. I study the image, wondering where it was taken. I don't recognize the bar.

"Thank you," I say. "This is a huge help. Do you know when they left town?"

She gives me a menacing smile. "I'd like you to think about something and think hard."

"Okay."

"The only reason you're still alive is because someone screwed up." She studies my face, as if waiting for the words to register in my expression.

I don't respond. I don't present my alternative theory that Mr. Neighborhood Watch let me get away.

She continues, "I'll put this into words even you can understand. Do you know the meaning of dumb luck?"

I nod.

"How far do you think that's going to take you?"

12

*A*t home, I take a shower, letting water pour over me as I recover from my first spinning class. As the bathroom steams up, I consider the comment from Nicole Gaga about my dumb luck. Mostly, I prefer to believe that I've benefited from skill and intelligence. Then again, by its very nature, the person experiencing dumb luck is the last to know it. I decide I'll take any kind of luck that I can get. Nicole can be fussy about the type of luck she accepts.

After the restorative cleansing, I pat myself dry and treat myself to some French lotion that's supposed to smell like a garden on the Nile River. It smells so divine that I feel no actual need to go to the Nile River, or any of its gardens. It was a gift from Dr. Fantastic, and I think of him every time I slather it behind my elbows, and I suppose I won't be completely over him until the lotion runs out. Yet, I keep it. It is too precious and lovely to waste on something as petty as my mental health.

With a towel wrapped around me, I return to my bedroom and grab my cell phone. After our recent separation, I can't stand to be apart from it too long. Separation anxiety, I suppose.

Monalisa has written with surprising news: "Charise says continue with case."

I can't help but take a deep, painful breath. Charise has absorbed the blow of learning that Kevin has been calling his mom during his so-called disappearance. I suppose you can forgive your fiancé for his love of his mother. My latest discovery, that he is with one of the Lady Gaga lookalikes, may be harder to stomach. In fact, I am certain it will mark the end of the road for Charise, which means the end of my job.

With some effort, I tend to appearances, pulling on black stretchy pants and a t-shirt. It will happen someday, I tell myself: I will get and keep a paying job. Idiots manage to do this all the time.

After the pep talk, I grit my teeth and write to Monalisa about my discovery that Kevin is with one of the Lady Gaga lookalikes.

She responds, "Do you believe that?"

It would be easy to say that I don't believe it, especially having heard other fairy tales about Kevin's whereabouts. It would be easy to say Nicole Gaga speaks with a forked tongue. It would be easy to continue working the case and making money.

I fight the impulse to put the phone down, to painstakingly blow dry and iron my hair, to try on different outfits to see if I can fit into my skinny clothes after all my biking. In other words, to wait until the impulse to do the right thing passes.

Before I lose resolve, I text: "Yes, I believe it. I have a copy of a photo of them together."

Monalisa writes, "You'd better tell Charise."

Thanks, Monalisa. I'd love to tell Charise. There is nothing I'd rather be doing on a late Saturday afternoon than to give Charise this wrenching, heart-breaking news. If possible, this may even be worse than informing frequent frowners they have been injected with bootleg Botox, stuff probably concocted in some desolate backwater by a moonlighting meth cook.

I am the consummate professional. Perhaps I've mentioned that before.

"No way, no how," Charise is saying, studying the image of Kevin and the Lady Gaga lookalike. She shakes her head. "I don't believe it."

"I'm sorry," I say.

"They're only sitting together," Charise says. "This doesn't mean they're intimate."

This is not going as I would have expected. I didn't expect disbelief, especially not at this point, when Kevin has been gone for more than a week. Love is both blind and stubborn.

"His arm is around her," I say.

"Only for the photo." Her eyes flash angrily. "When was this taken? And where?"

I explain that I don't know, that Nicole is a hostile individual, not inclined to answer questions. Charise mumbles something about how a sharp investigator should get the goods.

I am glad we are meeting in a public place, a donut shop in the civilized and sedate Arcadia neighborhood, where Charise won't scream at me. The cafe has at least twenty different types of donuts. When I suggested this meeting place, I had hoped the smell of sugar and fat would have an anesthetic effect on Charise. Of course I should have known that not a donut in the world, not even one with maple frosting flecked with bits of bacon, is consolation for losing your fiancé to another woman.

She is angry. I can't help but wonder why she wouldn't have been expecting this sort of news ever since Kevin walked out of American Egg with two half-naked women. But I do not say this, knowing better than to offer up myself as kindling to her free-wheeling, burning rage. I know all about wildfires. She is ready to consume everything in her path.

I am on my best frequent frowner behavior. "I realize this is difficult news, Charise."

As she comes at me at different speeds and angles—crackling and snapping and roaring—I keep telling her I'm sorry. Sorry, sorry, sorry. I am a machine, cranking the word out in a range of tones and speeds.

Eventually, the rage starts to fizzle out, and I say, "I wish I had different news for you."

Charise looks like someone staring down an empty well. After she takes a long drink of tea, she says, "He's made things so much worse by not telling me. That's unforgivable. Is he afraid I'd hunt his cheating ass down?

I opt for some tact. "The secrecy may be because of the woman he's with. Apparently, she's in some kind of serious financial trouble."

Charise makes a gagging noise. "A damsel in distress. You're joking."

I shake my head.

The injustice of it all makes me consider eating another jelly donut. Sitting in front of me is a loving, responsible, intelligent woman who has lost her fiancé to a Lady Gaga lookalike who distributes heroin for a living. This is not an ending condoned by the official makers of fairy tales.

"I can't see this pair lasting, if that's any consolation," I say.

I don't trust any new infatuation of less than six months. My suspicion is that Kevin is having a pre-marital, post-residency crisis.

"It doesn't matter if it lasts or not." Charise sighs. "It's over between us."

Seeing her lip quiver, I offer Charise a napkin. Luckily, there is a dispenser on our table. Donuts and breakups are messy business.

She waves the napkin away. "I'm good." She drinks more tea.

I take another gander at the donut case.

Charise says, "Why do they always want needy? Why does that appeal to men?"

I wrest my gaze from the donut case. "You're asking the wrong person."

"He wants needy he gets needy." She sniffles and takes a napkin. "He can have her." She gives me a pleading look. "But we could have gotten a pet. He didn't have to run off with this pathetic, needy woman."

"You could get a pit bull," I say. "Look how happy Monalisa is."

No sale. Charise says, "I'm not needy, never will be. I'm not a woman looking for a man to save me or pay my bills. I have my own car, my own education, my own life, my own friends. All I want is a decent guy. Is that too much to ask?"

"No," I say on cue, but I have my doubts.

Charise's litany makes me realize that I am a needy woman. I have no money or car or college degree or security deposit for an apartment. I can't afford a Milano gimlet. So where's my anesthesiologist?

Charise sniffs a few times in succession. I fight the impulse to suggest that inanimate objects don't make bad companions. I've found a great deal of satisfaction from my iPhone and Hedgie and the Kia Soul. At Iona's house, I always enjoyed seeing the stone lions, the Afghan hound, and her other lawn ornaments.

"You can't force someone to love you," Charise says, her face noticeably wet. "They either do or they don't. Maybe Kevin really thought he loved me. But he didn't."

I would call Kevin's current state temporary insanity, but I won't say this to Charise. It wouldn't be helpful. Even a little air bubble of hope might block her recovery, potentially erupting into a chandelier-lit room that blazes light powered by delusion.

Charise is blotting her face with the sleeve of her shirt. I stare down at the sugar bits that remain of my jelly donut. "A good man is right around the corner," I say.

She gazes at me with swollen, pink-rimmed eyes. "Which corner, Angela? You got an address for me?"

"I wish I knew. Ask Siri."

"A lot of help you are," she says, smiling. "You can make it up to me."

"How?" I peer at the donut case. There are still many donuts in the case, quite a few likely to grow stale and be tossed out. It seems a shame to let that happen.

"I need you to tell me about that ex-boyfriend who tried to send you to the big house. The felon."

I sink into my chair and groan. "I already told you about him."

"I'm not tired of that story yet."

Although I'm doing my best *to move on*, which are three of the sweetest, most optimistic words in the English language, I agree to regale her again with my tale of woe. Besides, who else am I going to entertain with tales of Dr. Fantastic and my financial and emotional ruin? My grandkids? Ha.

I start, "Once upon a time, there was a young lady named Angela with long dark hair and impeccable nails...."

As I leave the donut shop, I get a text from Monalisa. She is having some car trouble and would like a ride to the dojo. I write back that I would be happy to take her to the dojo, then I Google "dojo" to learn what I have gotten myself into. Apparently a dojo is a place where one practices a martial art. Despite being on the downward slope from a jelly donut high, not to mention drained of emotional juice after empathizing with Charise, I am curious about what one does at a dojo on a Saturday night.

A depressing thought occurs to me. Maybe a swanky new bar called Dojo has opened, a place I've never even heard about since my retreat from the wonderful world of Milano gimlets. I'm officially off the island of cool.

On the bright side, maybe Monalisa will buy me a drink to celebrate the end of the case. Actually, I'm struggling with finding a bright side. I am over losing jobs. The experience used to be good for some great laughs with my girlfriends. But job loss is no longer met with a hearty clink of martini glasses. For starters, I can't afford martinis anymore. I can't afford my friends anymore, either. Since I lost all my money, I hardly ever see them. Coincidence? I think not.

When I arrive, Monalisa is standing on her front steps. She is the poster girl for serious ninja glamour. She is wearing a white judo top with fierce samurai-looking black culottes on the bottom. In her hand is the wooden sword. When she sees me, she waves and puts the wooden sword in a long black nylon bag. It appears this bag was made specifically to hold the sword.

Somehow I realize that dojo is not a new bar. Drinking and swords, just like drinking and unemployment, do not go together.

Monalisa gets in the car, stowing the sword case in the back.

"What are you wearing?" I ask.

"A gi and hakama," she says in a matter-of-fact voice.

She gives me directions to the dojo. After that, I update her on the visit to the donut shop. She tells me that Charise texted her, formally ending the case.

"You'll need to draft a final report, Angela."

"I'll get that to you tomorrow."

"Great."

Great. Is that all? This has the ring of finality. I never thought I would miss the string of lawyerly questions from her. But I do.

We pass a succession of big box stores on the way to the dojo. We have no client. I want a drink. I heft an imaginary Milano gimlet. Here's to never keeping a job.

Now I have to figure out what's next. What do I want to be when I'm grown up? Not a grown-up, that's for sure. Does anyone want to be a grown up when they've actually grown up?

I think of a question for Monalisa. "Is there another case on the horizon?"

She shrugs. "Nothing has turned up."

"What about that award you mentioned. For whistleblowers?"

She stretches her neck to the left then the right. "The Salvador Foundation. That's a huge long-shot, Angela. You can't rely on that."

"Maybe someone will call you soon with another missing person case."

"You should look for another job." Her voice is flat.

I give her a sideways glance. Her face betrays no sympathy. She is right, of course, I should find a job.

The dojo is in a small strip mall off the main road, squeezed between a big box craft store and a big box discount furniture store. I pull up to the entrance and ask if she'll need a ride home, but she says that no, she'll have one of the other Aikidoka take her back after class.

We stare into the dojo for a moment.

A large glass window offers a view into a spacious room with a white mat covering the floor. A man in billowing black culottes, the same funky garb Monalisa wears, appears at the edge of the space. He kneels and bows, nose to the floor. He gets on the mat in his bare feet. I shudder, imagining the foot funk as people start sweating.

"Angela, you've got to be practical. Don't you want a full-time position that pays you benefits? That offers you professional growth?"

"Someday."

"Someday?" she asks, the question dripping with disbelief.

I clarify, "Someday soon or thereabouts."

"Angela, don't you want the best for yourself?"

I nod, even though I haven't been looking at my situation in quite this way.

"I don't want you to settle for anything than the best. And I can't offer you that with these occasional cases."

I feel a pang coming from my pelvic cradle. Staring out the windshield, I realize I am sad to see this case end. Despite all the bother and inconvenience and skin chafing, this line of work seems to suit me.

Monalisa is staring at me, probably awaiting an answer.

"You're right," I say. "I need a career with a future."

She gathers her sword bag. Seconds later, she disappears into the dojo.

THAT NIGHT, tucked into my power cocoon, I ponder my job options. I need to be practical, but practicality, like rice cakes, is a depressing invention perpetrated by grownups. I remind myself that grownups have also created useful inventions, such as strawberry lemonade, Pedialyte and iPhones.

Mid-treatment, I dismantle the power cocoon, and assume a more professional posture in bed. On a Saturday night, practical means opening my laptop and getting to work. I visit the website of the dog spa, the one that rejected me as a groomer, and draft a quick e-mail thanking the manager for her time and reminding her of my passion for dog grooming. Next, I scan Craig's List and the online classifieds. No openings are available for a spa employee within biking radius of the house. I apply for a job at Trader Joe's. They have a wonderful selection of affordable wines.

After this bit of business, I write the final report on the investigation. One nice thing about being auto-free is that I don't have to calculate mileage or gas charges for the invoice. Still, it takes a while to write. I send it to Monalisa.

Done.

I should probably search for beauty schools. Before I realize what's happening, I find myself Googling "Salvador Prize." I learn that people who report government fraud can apply for a prize of fifty thousand dollars, plus legal expenses. The Salvador Foundation, which issues the prizes, accepts applications through their website.

Visions of apartments and Kia Souls dance through my head. With that kind of money I could also have a zen room/walk-in closet.

The Salvador Prize is named for Danny Salvador, a billionaire who made his fortune with airport duty-free stores. After more clicking, I learn that Mr. Salvador resides in Paradise Valley. This is more or less local, and I'm the home team. Be still my phantom heart.

It gets better. After scrolling through many Google items about Mr. Salvador, I find a small news item from a year ago. Mr. Salvador, who drives a Ferrari Berlinetta, got a five hundred and seventy-five dollar speeding ticket.

Safe to assume Mr. Salvador is not a fan of traffic cameras.

Now all I have to do is demonstrate fraud perpetrated by a government official in connection with the traffic camera deal.

13

*O*n Sunday morning I am thrilled to discover some fresh walnut-raisin bread in the kitchen, a refreshing sign of spring detente in Moorea's New Year's war against bread. Moorea and Roy are not home, probably taking a brisk walk to get their heart rates into the fat-burning range before attending church. After making toast and sugar coffee, I sit in the living room with my laptop, enjoying a change of scenery from my bedroom.

"Haley," calls a boy's voice.

Outside, three brothers from down the block race by, chasing after their dog, a scrappy white terrier. Haley, I presume. The smallest brother, whose name I don't remember, rushes toward Haley with a large cardboard box, presumably trying to catch the poor animal. The dog easily skips away. The boy, uneven on his feet, swings the box around like a butterfly net. He's not even close to catching Haley, who prances from side to side, apparently enjoying the game.

I smile until it occurs to me that I've got my own quarry to catch. How is one well-dressed and impeccably groomed young woman going to successfully blow the whistle on a senior city official? I rub my chin and wait. Nothing. More sugar coffee. I scratch at my scalp. Still nothing. I visit the bathroom and apply makeup to my forehead bruise, which makes me feel better.

I sit on the couch and engage in some positive visualization. My eyes shut. At a gala for the Salvador Prize awards, Danny Salvador tells the black-tie audience that I demonstrated massive fraud in a government traffic camera contract. Even lawyers and accountants failed to detect this breach in the public trust. When he finishes, I walk onto the stage, where I accept the award. Moorea sits in the front row, watching me with teary eyes. I thank her for her support. I say, "I couldn't have done it without you."

After the ceremony ends, I am doing a quick interview with a TV reporter, who asks, "How did you discover the fraud?"

I open my mouth, and nothing comes out.

This is as good a time as any to open my eyes and get back to business. I return to the Sons of Liberty website, where I confirm that they don't make any specific accusations of fraud related to the traffic camera deal. Even Errol, who is cray-cray on the topic of traffic cameras, doesn't claim any illegal wrongdoing has taken place.

I push the doubts away, and take to the web, searching for stories about the traffic camera deal. As it turns out, the traffic camera deal has received a lot of media attention. How is it I've missed all this? After thirty minutes of speed-reading, I learn the following:

- The traffic camera contract with the city is worth two hundred million dollars;
- Uncle Dave leads the committee making the final decision about the award; and
- The decision will be made in two days, on Tuesday.

One of Moorea's sayings pops into my head. *Where there's money there's trouble.* Usually she utters these dark words when discussing lawyers and malpractice suits. Translated for my situation, the message is, follow the money. I wonder who stands to gain from this contract. If I don't end up proving fraud, maybe someone will hire me. I amend Moorea's saying: *Where there's money there may be career opportunity.* The company that wins the contract will surely need a few more good people to implement this life-saving work.

Of course, if I did end up in the traffic camera business, Errol would never speak to me again. This would mean never becoming a member of the New Sons of Liberty. After "constipating" over it for a moment, I decide I could live with that.

The city website has information about pending contract awards and procurement processes. There, I learn that, after soliciting concept papers for the traffic camera project, the city selected two companies to submit full proposals, including detailed budgets. The finalist companies are Vibernium and Traftech Safety Systems.

On Vibernium's website, I learn that the company, founded in 1953, is a massive enterprise with multiple divisions, including food service, traffic safety, waste management and education. The CEO looks like the love child of Frankenstein and Justin Timberlake. He is dressed well, wearing a navy suit with an immaculate white shirt and a red tie. He says the company values are quality, excellence, service, value and persistence. I could live with that.

As I read on, I decide this company may not be a good fit for me after all. For starters, I am having some trouble understanding their promotional text. About the future, the CEO is quoted saying, "We're architecting our new divisions out under an integrated umbrella." Still, I press on, learning more about the target of my fraud investigation or, alternatively, my new employer. Unfortunately, I discover that Vibernium is headquartered in North Scottsdale, which is well outside my cycling range.

The other company, Traftech Safety Systems, is smaller and more specialized. Their website indicates they do traffic cameras. Period. Their corporate values? Quality, excellence, service and value. They are only eight years old so perhaps haven't needed persistence as much as Vibernium.

The small upstart seems to be on a roll. Their news page highlights recent wins for contracts in Chicago, Kansas City and Philadelphia. Their CEO looks like Vibernium's CEO, even down to the navy suit, red tie and winning smile. His name is Clay Bowden III. I wonder if there's some CEO factory somewhere pumping out these tall guys with navy suits and chipper smiles. And who came up with the name Clay? The CEO factory must have a CEO name generator. Personally, I don't need a generator. My CEO name has already popped into my head: Whitney. I can see the door plaque, Whitney Cray.

The website indicates that Traftech Safety Systems is based in Phoenix. Most importantly, it is within biking distance. I press on, eager to learn more. Luckily, I don't spot any nonsense about architecting anything out from under an umbrella. Their media section has a photo gallery, which bodes well. I like pictures.

Sadly, most of the shots are tedious and provoke a low-level anxiety within me. They depict bored-looking people attending meetings or people in suits shaking hands with other people in suits. There isn't even a single glamour shot of a traffic light camera.

My eye snags on one of the photos. It depicts the CEO shaking hands with a woman identified as the president of Moms for Safe Streets. The two stand on a stage, smiling at each other. The photo was taken at an event held in Kansas City, an official launch for a traffic safety campaign.

I stare at the photo, unsure why I seem to be stuck on this image. The CEO is in a navy suit, and the president of Moms for Safe Streets is wearing a tasteful beige shirt-dress. They look perfectly respectable, if a little dull. I wouldn't be psyched to sit across from either one of them at a dinner party.

Eventually, I realize there is someone to the side of the stage whose face I recognize. This can't be right. I zoom in on the image, then zoom in again.

The face is a little fuzzy. I've enlarged the photo beyond its intended resolution. Still, I recognize the face. It is Mr. Neighborhood Watch.

Dazed, I stand up from the couch, shaking my head. This can't be. It is. I would jump up and down if my ribcage could withstand the stress. The dots are connecting. Finally. In my mental diagram, I can now draw a line between Mr. Neighborhood Watch, traffic cameras, and Uncle Dave. Thank you, dear goddess. She is laughing with me.

I lower myself slowly back onto the couch and study the photo again. Mr. Neighborhood Watch is staring at the audience, not the stage. This is why I can see his face. Everyone else is focused on the couple shaking hands on the dais. Mr. Neighborhood Watch is not posing for the camera so that's not the reason he's facing the audience.

Who watches crowds? Bouncers. But they work at bars. Security personnel watch crowds at concerts or other events. Could Mr. Neighborhood Watch be providing security for Traftech? In thinking about it, I realize this makes some sense. It's possible that Clay the CEO has received threats. Moms for Safe Streets may appreciate Traftech, but, if the internet is to be believed, other people passionately hate this company, which focuses exclusively on traffic cameras. This would explain why Mr. Neighborhood Watch is attending a press event in Kansas City, watching the crowd.

On the company's website, I search to see if it lists security personnel. A name would be a nice touch for my whistleblowing case. After a crazy number of clicks, I am forced to conclude they don't list staff other than the CEO and department heads. On Monday, I could call the company and see if they'd give me a name. Even if their rules allowed it, I can't imagine them disclosing his name to me without a fuss. I'd probably have to send the photo, and then they'd tell him I was looking for him.

I slowly pace around the living room, wondering if there's such a thing as ribcage replacement surgery. Nicole, aka Dolly Gaga, knows his name. My stroll reaffirms my suspicion that I would not survive another spinning class. Anyway, Nicole won't tell me his name. Plus, there's the minor detail of having promised to leave her alone for all of eternity.

My ramblings take me into the kitchen, in search of some delicious, celebratory food, perhaps leftover chocolate cake. I am hoping the walnut raisin bread has been the gateway food for other, more wonderful transgressions. My search turns up stalks of leathery kale, some goat cheese and two red peppers. The freezer offers up chicken breasts and spinach and peas. None of these items are potential cake substitutes.

I return to the living room, dissatisfied, and sit back down on the couch. Why does Nicole always seem to be the answer to my questions of late? Of course there are other unpleasant options for learning Mr. Neighborhood Watch's name. Presumably, Uncle Dave would know the name. Unfortunately, speaking to Uncle Dave directly about this is probably not consistent with me living a long, healthy life.

Uncle Dave.

This brings to mind what Nicole said when I asked who hired her to pick up Kevin. *I don't remember... Maybe it was friend or a relative or something.*

A relative. How about Uncle Dave?

It makes perfect sense. I high five with Iona's ghostly palm and take a twirl on the dance floor with my dad who art in heaven.

Uncle Dave thought a visit from two sexy ladies would be some good pre-wedding fun for Kevin. Mr. Neighborhood Watch, keen to influence Uncle Dave on the traffic camera contract, made it happen. I suspect it was a mere token of Traftech's appreciation, which would also be expressed through a pile of cold, hard cash.

But where does heroin come into all this? Traftech seems to be doing fine without a heroin trafficking division. It's hard to imagine such a legitimate-seeming business involved with celebrity lookalikes and Obamacare heroin. I also can't imagine Uncle Dave, with his serious day job, dabbling in heroin trafficking on the side.

I cast my eyes upward. Great goddess of the sun, moon, and sea, any ideas? Iona? My dad in who art in heaven? I wait thirty minutes, open to transmission, and nothing comes to mind. The heroin angle remains unclear.

What is clear is that my whistleblowing involves Mr. Neighborhood Watch. Although I hate to admit it, I am out of my depth against an armed drug trafficker. Good grooming only gets you so far in life. Ditto on dressing for success. I am not eager to get reacquainted with the trunk of a Mercedes Benz. I am also not eager to join my dad who art in heaven or Iona, much as I think of them often and with deep affection.

On the other hand, I must win the Salvador prize. To do so, I can't have a mere suggestion of fraud, an acrid whiff of the devil. For fifty thousand dollars I need to present a solid case, with actual facts.

This means I need help. My boss at the gift basket company always said that it's important to know when you can't go it alone. Luckily, I know just the person to provide assistance.

"WHAT KIND OF TURDFEST IS THIS?" Errol says, looking at the photo from Traftech's website. "I can't make out anyone's face."

"I'll expand the image," I say.

We are sitting on a bench outside a tax-free cigarette store on the Salt River Indian community. When Errol said he wanted to meet here, I figured he was interested in privacy, which is one of the two major advantages of Salt River, the other being cheap, tax-free cigarettes. Apparently, he was after the cigarettes. He has bought two large cartons.

He narrows his eyes at my iPhone screen, as though it might bite him.

"Are you sure that's a person?" he asks.

"Yes."

The photo on my iPhone is of the Traftech CEO shaking hands with the president of Moms for Safe Streets. I showed him the image of Mr. Neighborhood Watch, in an effort to convince him about the link between Traftech and Dave Newman. I told him about seeing Mr. Neighborhood Watch at Dave Newman's house. And now, how Mr. Neighborhood Watch may work for Traftech, one of the companies vying for the two hundred million dollar traffic camera contract.

Errol gazes at me with concern. "This crap has gotten to you. You've eaten too many shit sandwiches. I've seen it more times than I can count. You're so fed up that you start seeing things. Imagining things. You need a break."

I thought Errol and the New Sons of Liberty would be easy recruits for a fraud investigation into the traffic camera procurement process. Hah. This fringe New Son of Liberty, whose website rages with capital letters, thinks I'm a wingnut.

A man in a light blue Buick station wagon pulls into the parking lot. He nods to us on his way into the store. His craggy lined face, a virtual topographic map of Death Valley, belies a taste for cheap cigarettes. Smoking does horrific things to the skin.

"I appreciate your concern, Errol, but I'm not imagining things. This traffic camera deal is crooked. I think Traftech is paying off Dave Newman for the contract."

Errol frowns at his fossilized pick-up truck. He looks like he'd rather be somewhere else. This is probably cutting into his doomsday prepping time.

"Seriously, you don't think this is worth looking into?" I am looking for the man with all the flaming words about waging WAR against Dave Newman. Where did he go?

Errol's gaze sweeps across the desolate lunar landscape that is Salt River. It is an area unspoiled by day spas. It is an area where you could conduct a long, painful inquisition on someone with little chance of interruption.

"You ever think about where you really want to live?" he asks.

"Sure," I say. "In my own apartment."

My needs are increasingly simple. I have let go of my desire for a glamorous noir kitchen and a serene walk-in closet/zen room.

"If money were no object?" he asks.

"In a swanky condo with a rooftop infinity pool. Where would you live?"

"On top of a mountain. Alone."

A deserted mountaintop would pretty much be my definition of hell. "Why so high up?"

He grins. "All the better to spot the predators and parasites coming."

"That doesn't sound very convenient. What would you do for food?"

"Hunt," he says. "That's the natural way. Kill or be killed."

I imagine a rack of dead squirrels hanging in his garage. "Harsh, Errol."

I stare at my iPhone screen. The photo is small, even for my eyes. The only faces I can see well are Traftech's CEO and the president of Moms for Safe Streets.

"What's that photo of anyway?" Errol asks, nodding at my iPhone.

I tell him, and he makes a hissing noise.

"Moms for Safe Streets. I hate those moms. And I hate the idiots who believe them."

Who is against moms? "Why?"

"They're lying scum. They're a bunch of frauds. They're—" His face squishes with effort. I brace myself for him to say something truly foul. "Astroturf."

I'm not familiar with this particular insult. "Fake grass?"

"The traffic camera companies fund fake grassroots organizations to support their criminal enterprises. Moms for Safe Streets are a figment of Traftech. Once the cities issue the contracts, poof, those concerned moms go back to laying eggs."

I fan the flames for fun, which I figure I'm due for driving all the way to Salt River. "You have to admit, Errol, it's not a bad idea. Moms for traffic cameras. Companies are always using moms to sell soups, spaghetti sauce, cookbooks, baked goods."

Personally, I wouldn't purchase any baked good with Moorea's name on it. Maybe a scalpel or bandage but nothing you'd want to eat. I'd buy a tire iron she endorsed.

"Moms for stupidity. Moms for nuclear water. Moms for hemorrhoids. Moms for repealing the constitution." Errol's face is turning pink. "Moms for saving the voles."

I toss more kindling on the fire. "Come on Errol. Wanting the streets to be safe is not unreasonable." Not like saving voles. Now that's unreasonable.

"Angela, there is no such thing as safety. It's an illusion. No street is ever truly safe. But people are willing to give up their rights for an illusion of safety."

I smile. "Yes, they're giving up their right to speed or blow through red lights."

He shakes his head. "It's the classic tradeoff citizens make under authoritarian regimes. They trade their freedom for a false guarantee of safety."

As a female who has wheedled her way out of many a speeding ticket, cameras are not to my advantage. At the same time, as a fifty percent member of an ethnic minority group that may be unfairly targeted by police, I recognize some benefits. Cameras dispense justice or, depending on your view, injustice, the same way with everyone.

Nevertheless, I try to steer the conversation in a less philosophical and inflammatory direction. "Do you think Dave Newman would strike an under-the-table deal with Traftech for the contract?"

His thick eyebrow hairs quiver, as though they're about to take flight. "Dave Newman is a lifer, a guy who has blow-jobbed his way to the top. He'd never take the risk. We've looked into this for years. We've had accountants and lawyers and every dick-licker in between looking into it. We've never been able to prove a thing."

"You don't think it's worth trying this time?"

"Insanity is doing the same thing over and over and expecting a different result."

Errol is turning out to be a buzz kill. I would have expected some enthusiasm. "I know there's a connection," I say.

He scratches his elbow. "You've got it bad. This happens. You want to change things too quickly. But you've got to be patient. We'll triumph in the end."

"You think so?"

"I know so," he says, a sour grin appearing beneath a curtain of whiskers. "Right now you need a break. Doctor Errol says so."

"If you say so."

"Keep the faith, Angie," he says. "But give it a rest."

BACK HOME, I ponder the concept of Astroturf. Soon my thinking has taken me into the back yard, where I walk crop circles amidst thundercloud sage and Bougainvillea. Soon I have a plan.

At Target, I pick up a fifteen-dollar cell-phone and a calling card. Back in my beautiful Kia Soul rental, I open a new e-mail account under the name of Claire Stillman. I love this name. I fell in love with it in the seventh grade. Instead of decorating my notebooks with the names of male love interests, I wrote "Claire Stillman" inside the front cover, making the letters as upright and sophisticated as I could.

Claire Stillman was not a real person. My imagination conjured her up to torture me. Claire got perfect grades, had two loving parents and a brother, and was an excellent tennis player. She had reddish-blond hair and a tasteful sprinkling of freckles across her nose. She wore lovely diamond studs in both ears. Every winter she and her family went skiing in Vail. In the summers, she visited her grandparents in Connecticut. She is mainland American back to the 18th century.

Apparently, other people also like the idea of Claire Stillman. With so many other women with this name, I am Claire222. Claire would not be caught dead lying to strangers. This is where Claire and I part ways.

Like so many brilliant, attractive women, Claire has not been fortunate in her love life. I can't decide if her husband has run off or is a gambling addict or is terrible with money. Whatever, she has a young son and is in need of more income. Otherwise, someone like Claire would not be caught dead in the Astroturf business.

Thanks to Google and ZabaSearch, I obtain the name and phone number for Theresa Kent, president of Moms for Safe Streets in Kansas City.

On the third ring, she answers, which surprises me. For a nanosecond, I freeze. I expected to be speaking to her voicemail, especially on a Sunday.

"Hi Theresa," I say. "I'm Claire Stillman from Phoenix. I apologize for calling on a Sunday but I wanted to talk to you about Moms for Safe Streets. Do you have a few minutes?"

"Of course, Claire. I'd be happy to speak to you."

Everyone is always happy to speak with Claire Stillman.

"I'm being encouraged to start a chapter of Moms for Safe Streets here in Phoenix. Everyone talks about you in such glowing terms. I'd really appreciate your advice."

In my experience, people love to give advice. Alas, most people hate to take it.

"I'd love to help you," she says.

I sigh. "Wonderful. I'm so excited about this opportunity, but I have some concerns."

She laughs. "I don't blame you. The opposition is really tough in your area. Clay has mentioned how hard it is there. I'm surprised there isn't already a chapter."

Clay. A line reels back through my brain, casting about for a vague memory. A second later, I'm remembering where I've heard that name. The line shakes, a hook drags across the white matter, and I recall that Clay is the name of Traftech's CEO.

"Have you seen the New Sons of Liberty website?" I say, trying to sound like a usually calm person who is ruffled. "This group is calling for war by any means necessary. They've held lots of protests."

"What pests," she says. "But don't worry. Clay told me the contract in Phoenix is a sure thing. No matter what, Traftech will take care of you."

My heart flutters. *A sure thing? Traftech will take care of you?* I nearly pinch myself.

"He's sure Traftech is going to get the contract?"

"He sounded very confident. But your role is still important. Whatever happens, Traftech will take care of you."

"That's been your experience?" I ask, making an effort to keep my voice neutral.

"They gave me everything I needed. You'll find them very generous. We're quiet right now but Clay and the company still support me. I do media interviews on road safety. I've written articles for the paper and various websites. In a few years, when the city contract opens up again, we'll go back into the active phase."

"That's reassuring," I say. "We've talked about doing a press event to launch the new Moms for Safe Streets chapter. Naturally, I'm hesitant, given the aggressive opposition here."

"I was concerned as well. But our event came off without a hitch. It also helped establish me as a go-to person for reporters covering road safety."

I gaze out my windshield. A woman wheels a cart full of Target bags by my car. The cart clatters loudly, and I hope Theresa Kent doesn't find this sound odd. At least I'm not calling her from a restroom.

"You're a media spokesperson?" I ask, seasoning the question with a dash of awe.

"Yes, that's what I've become. They even gave me some media training. It's always been part of our long-term strategy."

Our long-term strategy. I love that.

"This is sounding better and better," I respond. "The company has offered me a security person to help out. I can't remember the name they mentioned." I give it a beat. She doesn't say anything. I continue, "Silly how I can't remember."

"It could be Alexander Zakan. He handled security when Clay came to Kansas City for our press conference. He's a consultant. Traftech seems to use him quite a bit."

"He did a good job?"

"Terrific. He's a little scary on the outside, but a total sweetie inside."

A total sweetie. I wonder how I missed that side of him. "Really?"

"Absolutely," she says, drawing out the word. "He's a cat lover. And you should have seen him with my son Michael. Within minutes, they were thick as thieves. Both of them are obsessed with muscle cars."

"How wonderful," I say, pouring on the sugar substitute. "It sounds like he was also great with security."

"Absolutely. I even wrote about all the careful preparations that went into the press conference."

"Really? Is it on your website?"

"No, it was a blog post. It's no longer live. If you'd like I could send it to you."

"Great," I say and give her the brand spanking new e-mail address for Claire Stillman.

"Theresa," I say. "I can't thank you enough. This seems like such a great opportunity. But, as you can imagine, my family's safety comes first."

"Absolutely," she says. "You know what I've loved the most about this experience?"

"What?"

"Being able to do good and to do well at the same time."

Claire Stillman agrees. "That's a dream come true."

I AM DRIVING home in the Kia Soul after my productive conversation with Theresa Kent. A number of thoughts jostle through my mind. I can guess why Clay, Traftech's CEO, is so confident about securing the traffic camera contract in Phoenix. This is probably also why he hasn't bothered to set up a local chapter of Moms for Safe Streets. Traftech is paying off Uncle Dave Newman.

Part of me is amazed that Errol was right, that Moms for Safe Streets is Astroturf funded by Traftech. After all his huffing and puffing, I thought he was making it up or exaggerating. Admittedly, I am uninformed on this subject, never having given much thought to grassroots activist organizations.

The evidence is starting to come together. If I get the blog piece from Theresa Kent, I will have some proof that Alexander Zakan works with Traftech. The other big news is that I have a name: Mr. Neighborhood Watch is Alexander Zakan. What's more, I am delighted to learn he is a real sweetie. Until now, I have only been a *victim* of his particular charms.

My next task at hand is to gather evidence on Zakan's connection with Uncle Dave. A paper trail would be nice, but I have my doubts about unearthing that kind of proof. My best guess is that any money from Traftech to Uncle Dave would be channeled through numbered accounts of various shell corporations in multiple countries.

When I get home, I grab a Vitamin Water Zero from the fridge and go into the backyard and walk more crop circles. How can I prove a connection between Dave Newman and Alexander Zakan? I haven't seen them together even though Zakan appears to be loitering outside Uncle Dave's house. Doing what, exactly? Smoking. Stopping intruders like me. Providing security?

Yes. I bet he was handling security for Uncle Dave, courtesy of Traftech. From the company's perspective, it would make sense to assign their go-to security freelancer to Uncle Dave. The protest movement in Arizona seems aggressive. WAR. Theresa Kent mentioned it, noting the CEO of Traftech complained about the opposition here. The opposition would heighten Uncle Dave's risk, and Traftech would want to, in Theresa Kent's words, take care of him. No one seems to realize Errol is such a softy.

This gets me thinking about the logistics of an illegal deal between Traftech and Uncle Dave. How would they communicate with each other? Neither party would want to leave any kind of trail, be it electronic, cellular, or paper. Given the risks, I would think some of this deal would be handled the old fashioned way: in person. But no one employed by the company, especially from the executive suite, would want to take this chance. The company would need a trusted intermediary.

Enter Alexander Zakan, who could be the middleman between the company and Uncle Dave. He could protect Uncle Dave from the frothing enemies of traffic cameras. He also could be the pal who arranges for the Gaga lookalikes to sweep Kevin, Uncle Dave's nephew, off his hospital-weary feet.

And the heroin? I can't see Uncle Dave or Traftech involved. Since Zakan is a consultant, it could be a separate endeavor altogether from the traffic camera contract. It could be yet another income stream for the enterprising security professional/cat lover/sweetie.

I am no longer walking crop circles in the back yard. I am walking to Monalisa's house.

At the door, Boo gives me his usual frothy greeting.

Monalisa does not invite me inside. Instead, we sit on two new lime green patio chairs on her front porch. The eyeless stone lions, guardians of Iona's empire, have disappeared from the front steps. I feel a pang from my phantom heart.

After a moment of silence for the lions, I tell Monalisa the news about Alexander Zakan (aka Mr. Neighborhood Watch) and his link to Traftech and Uncle Dave. As she listens, a small divot appears between her eyebrows. When I'm finished, she does not comment on my top-notch detecting. My exceptional prospects as a whistleblower. My persistence.

Instead, she asks, "How did you find out his name?"

I tell her about calling Theresa Kent, the president of Moms for Safe Streets. As I regale her with this tale, the divot between her brows deepens. Small ripples fan out from the corners of her almond-shaped eyes.

"You misrepresented yourself to get information. That's called pretexting."

"Good to know," I say, thinking I can add "pretexting" to my skills list on job applications. Still, Monalisa does not look pleased. I wonder if I should warn her about becoming a frequent frowner.

"Pretexting can be highly illegal."

No wonder I enjoyed it so much! "All I did was get a name from Theresa Kent."

Monalisa is massaging her wrist, as if it's sore from punching someone.

"We need to be careful," she says, catching my eye. "How you get evidence is important, especially if the case will end up in court. You want admissible evidence. You don't want to end up in legal trouble because of how you got your evidence."

For lack of anything better to say, I agree. "You're right."

"What are you going to do now that you know Alexander Zakan's name?"

Given her picky, by-the-book attitude, I realize she will not like the plan I have hatched. I lie and say, "I'll give it to the police."

"I'm relieved to hear you say that." The divot between her brows disappears. "He's dangerous. I know you haven't told me everything about what happened in Prescott. I suspect it was frightening." She gives me a look. "You've probably got enough information to trigger an official investigation."

"I hope so," I say. "I would have liked the Salvador Award but—"

"You've taken this as far as you could go. You should be proud."

I nod, knowing I am being dishonest with her and not feeling proud at all.

"If you need a job recommendation, Angela, I'd be happy to give you one. Any prospects?"

"Not yet."

Boo circles our chairs, then licks my leg. I swoop down, taking his face into my hands.

"You shouldn't have any problem," she says. "You're great with people."

In light of recent events, I could argue with her. But experience suggests it's not a good idea to contradict your employer when she or he offers you a compliment.

I shrug.

"Not everyone has that skill set," Monalisa says.

I smile. "Okay."

"Seriously," she responds. "I don't."

I tilt my head sympathetically, trying to avoid a response. It pays to be tactful with one's employer.

She continues, "I was born without the ability to recognize faces very well. It's called prosopagnosia. Do you know what I'd give to have your people skills?"

Proso-what? My mouth hangs open. My mind whirs, nearly derailing into the side of a building. Doesn't recognize faces very well. Could there be such a thing? Yes, I realize, there could be such a thing. This explains why she scans me like an alien gathering data whenever I turn up at her door.

I am an ungrateful worm. How often I have been *woe is me* when all this time I can recognize faces. I am lucky and blessed in ways I don't even realize. *Goddess, help me become a better, more grateful worm.*

14

*I*n my bedroom, I recline on my bed with a Diet Coke and gaze at the photo of Iona on my wall. It was taken eight months before, on her eighty-third birthday. Looking at her face, at the wary expression she reserved especially for cameras, the soft brown eyes, the red reading glasses planted crookedly off her forehead, bobbing in a shock of self-cut Einstein hair, I can almost hear her hoarse laughter. I can almost believe she'll be calling me tonight to invite me over to watch the Lucha Libre wrestlers. She's still in my contacts list on my phone. I could call her.

I can't imagine what it would be like to suffer from face blindness and not recognize Iona's face.

The face brings her back to me. If I didn't have the photo, maybe I'd remember her voice, the way she'd say "whoa, whoa, whoa" when she was excited, distressed or amazed. Smell would be the more likely portal to Iona, especially the scent of maraschino cherries and 7Up on wrestling nights.

All this time, I've been thinking of Monalisa as an alien being, never realizing she might have an impairment, never knowing there was even such a thing as prosopagnosia. Now, thanks to Google and Wikipedia, I'm an expert on the condition.

She must feel like an alien being. It boggles my mind how she navigates the course of a day, not able to recognize neighbors, friends, acquaintances, enemies, loved ones. Most people probably think she's rude or strange, like I did. Like Moorea does.

By these standards, yes, I am great with people. I am a genius with people.

I open my laptop, preparing to implement Part Two of my whistleblowing plan. Yes, more action. I'm turning into a regular dynamo. I take another slug of Diet Coke, hoping the caffeine will smooth over any hard feelings from my ribcage. I've already figured out how to get around any hard feelings from Errol, who will oppose my plan.

A wise person once said it is better to ask forgiveness than permission. This is fine career advice, which has served me well. After all, I haven't gotten to where I am by following the rules.

Claire Stillman is organizing a last-minute flash protest against traffic cameras near Uncle Dave's house. Although the proper etiquette for planning this protest would be to contact Errol first, as his group has been leading the charge on this issue, I decide he will not have a say in this matter. Besides, I already know he will hate the plan.

Admittedly, Claire is not the ideal organizer. Only this morning she contacted Theresa Kent about fronting for Moms for Safe Streets. But I am quite fond of Claire, who does everything well, and to be honest, I'm not up to concocting another character whom I have to get to know from scratch. If anyone asks, Claire can claim her e-mail accounts were hacked. This little detail ironed out, I proceed to whip up a storm.

Claire signs up for Facebook and "likes" the New Sons for Liberty page.

I craft an announcement:

FIGHT TRAFFIC CAMERAS: FLASH Protest today at 5:00 p.m.

This Tuesday, a $200 million contract will be awarded to install more speeding and red light cameras throughout our city. Not a single public hearing has been held on this issue. Hasn't the government taken enough of your hard-earned money? Stomped on your constitutional freedoms?

Join us and let the chair of the Transportation committee, David Newman, know how we feel about traffic cameras in our streets.

Tea will be served or tossed. Crumpets, hats, and clothes are optional.

For the location, I list the intersection of the pocket park near Uncle Dave's house. It is a few houses away from his place, a sliver of green at the end of his block.

In Claire's name, I drop the announcement on the Facebook page of New Sons of Liberty.

I tweet, announcing the protest. After that, I go to Connect, the social networking site, and transmit the announcement to groups of anarchists, libertarians and Republicans. On an impulse, I also disseminate the announcement to Wiccans and nudists (aka clothing-optional enthusiasts) and Atheists for Jesus. I stumble upon a group called Mad Hatters. To cast an even broader net, I post the invite on the "Rants and Raves" section of Craigslist.

Claire soon receives a warning message from Connect about spamming fellow members. She writes a quick apology, saying she thought the announcement would be of interest to these groups. Despite her sincere apology, the moderator is not swayed. Her Connect account is frozen for the next forty-eight hours, pending review.

Claire continues to disseminate the announcement elsewhere, hitting the news media and bloggers. Her fingers are burning up the keys on my laptop. A local blogger writes Claire that he's planning to attend the protest. Claire also returns to the New Sons of Liberty Facebook page and, fibbing boldly, posts a message that she got a call from TV2 news about the protest. Media interest is bound to inspire attendance among the New Sons.

Within a half-hour, Claire receives an irate message from Errol. "Who is organizing this so-called protest? Why weren't we informed about it earlier? As the major opponents of traffic cameras, we should have been consulted."

Claire responds, "Only passing along the message I received. No idea who is organizing. Guerrilla activists? Anyway, should be fun!"

ABOUT A HALF-HOUR before the protest starts, I park a block from Uncle Dave's house and walk the rest of the way, sticking to the opposite side of the street. The pocket park, the official location for the protest, is still empty. In Uncle Dave's front yard, a solidly built blond woman holds a hand mirror and applies lipstick. She is wearing a black skirt suit and sensible pumps.

This is odd. If anyone should be in the front yard, it should be Uncle Dave, ideally accompanied by his security guard, Alexander Zakan. They should be standing together, talking, so I could get a few photos of them from a civilized distance. Instead, a person dressed like an office forewoman is planted on the lawn.

Where is Uncle Dave? He appears to be home. His luscious convertible is parked under his carport. I sigh. No one involved in this case ever seems to cooperate with my brilliant plans.

I huddle deeper into the shadow cast by the tree. Of course, this is the blond woman's cue to look up and stare at me. I study my phone messages, trying to ignore her. She takes this as an invitation to walk across the street and talk to me.

"Are you a reporter?" she asks.

"I'm a bystander." Not the innocent kind, either. "Are you a reporter?"

"I'm a spokesperson for the Department of Transportation."

This is great, a sign Uncle Dave is taking the protest seriously. "Great."

She heads to the pocket park. I keep watch on Uncle Dave's house, and a minute later, catch sight of a man in the backyard. He's on a ladder propped against the front of the pool cabana and appears to be tinkering with a security camera. A black baseball cap prevents me from seeing much of his face. I don't think it's Uncle Dave, but it's hard to tell for sure. I take a photo with my iPhone. Checking the image, I realize I am too far away to get a decent shot.

A real camera with a telephoto lens would be perfect. Why didn't I bring one? Oh, yeah, I don't have one. Drat. This means I will have to get closer.

I slowly cross the street, heart thumping, and pause at the base of Uncle Dave's driveway. The man in the backyard promptly carries the ladder away and disappears from view. I wait for a moment, hoping he'll reappear, but he doesn't. Not wanting to call any further attention to myself by loitering in front of the house, I continue down the sidewalk toward the pocket park.

If it's Alexander Zakan, aka Mr. Neighborhood Watch, he can't very well murder me with a spokeswoman for the Department of Transportation in the vicinity. This doesn't do much to calm me. He can always pay me a visit at my house later.

Moorea is such an interesting name.

Empty words, I tell myself. He was only trying to frighten me that night.

This is my last chance to establish a link between Zakan and Dave Newman. A quick photo will make my case. Fifty thousand dollars. Moorea's eyes welling up when the Salvador Foundation announces that I've won the whistleblowing award.

I walk past Uncle Dave's house and stop, pretending to admire his neighbor's darling stone cottage. Up ahead, in the pocket park, the blond spokeswoman is talking to a TV news cameraman. On the other side of the tiny park, a plain white utility van pulls up to the curb, and a gaggle of tall men dressed in heels, pastel hats, and frilly church office dresses spill out. Their signs identify them as the Ladies for Safe Streets, who are definitely not to be confused with the Moms for Safe Streets. I smile, imagining Errol's sputtering fury when he encounters the Ladies for Safe Streets.

Four of the ladies pitch their signs in the grass and heft a folding metal table out of the back of the van. As they set up the table, other ladies bring out red thermoses and tins of Danish butter cookies. They appear to be setting up a tea stand.

Unbelievable. My announcement brought out supporters of traffic cameras. Perhaps my future is not in Astroturf.

At Uncle Dave's house, Alexander Zakan appears on the right side of the front yard. He's wearing a black baseball cap and staring at his phone. I grab my phone and manage to get several photos of him with Uncle Dave's house in the background.

When he spots me, his head turtles slightly forward, as though he can't quite believe his eyes. My legs suggest that I run. Even my ribcage chimes in, expressing its support for a speedy departure. I shuffle toward the pocket park on trembling doe legs.

"Angela?"

I walk right into the center of action, where the Ladies for Safe Streets have their tea stand. One is stacking cups for tea. Another pours sugar cubes into a bowl. The tin of butter cookies is open.

I glance behind me. Zakan grins. I quickly see the escape routes are limited. The pocket park is small, and not enough people are around for me to get lost in the crowd. The surrounding streets are quiet and residential. I can't outrun Zakan. I can't hope to make it back to my car.

"Darling?" A towering lady behind the tea stand leans toward me. I've never seen anyone above the age of twelve wear quite so much sparkly blue eye shadow. "Would you care for some tea?"

Boiling hot water. Not a bad weapon. "Thank you so much."

I receive a cup of lukewarm tea. Not weapon caliber temperature.

Stalling for time, I spoon a few squares of sugar into the tea. Meanwhile, three prematurely middle-aged men arrive at the tea stand, decked out in poorly fitting jeans and pristine white gym shoes. They look lost, like they took a wrong turn from a science fiction conference and somehow landed here.

To my right, Uncle Dave speeds by in his Thunderbird convertible, escaping the protest and protesters.

I wobble, as though I've stood up too quickly. No! I stare at the convertible until it disappears at the next intersection, turning left.

There goes today's brilliant plan to score a photo of Zakan and Uncle Dave together.

"Still looking for your envelope?" Zakan asks.

For some reason, Claire pops into my head. She is blessed with courage. What would she do right now? One of Iona's purple unicorns protests, *Claire is only your imaginary friend. She cannot help you.*

"Alexander Zakan." My voice sounds tinny to me, perhaps because my lungs are congested with bits of squelched scream.

"Call me Alex," he says, gently taking my elbow and steering me away from the tea stand hubbub. My right hand trembles, spilling lukewarm tea onto my wrist.

I get a disassociated feeling in my legs. They are seceding from the union. *Claire, I need you.*

"How about we don't call each other anything at all?" Claire says. "How about we pretend we've never met?"

Zakan smiles, and something odd happens. My panic subsides; I feel good, almost giddy. I've reached this state in the past after a few Milano gimlets. This must be the state beyond fear.

"Are you still looking for Kevin?" he asks.

"No."

He rubs his chin. "If you're not looking for Kevin, what are you doing here?"

This will remain my little secret for the moment. "I'm a member of the New Sons of Liberty."

His eyes pinch in apparent disbelief. "These losers?"

He laughs. And laughs. And laughs some more. This is hilarious. I would join him except my ribcage is not in the mood.

When his laughter dies down, I say, "You should join us. It would give you something to do instead of assaulting people and trafficking heroin."

Did I just say that? No, it must be that sassy Claire again. Claire is perfect except that she lacks a strong sense of self-preservation. I never knew that about her until now.

Zakan shakes his head slowly, waggling a finger at me, as though I'm being horribly unfair. "Be nice."

Goddess forbid I'm not nice to this cretin. He grins, and I realize he is baiting me.

"Thank you for not killing me the other night. That was kind of you."

"I hope you weren't too uncomfortable under the vehicle."

He just admitted he was only trying to scare me. Now that I've supposedly shown I don't scare easily, what will he try next? I tighten the screws that keep my head on my neck.

"Yes, I can't think of a better way to spend my evening." Claire is speaking now, having taken over again for Angela, who is cowering in a small, tastefully appointed dressing room in my imagination.

"You're upset." He steps closer. "Tell me, how can I make it up to you?"

Oh. My. God. Angela peeks her head out of the dressing

room. He is flirting. That is what is happening here. Claire gestures for Angela to go back inside the dressing room.

Claire says, "How about no more attempts on my life?"

A car horn honks, and Zakan waves. A vintage gold Pontiac Firebird pulls up to the curb.

"Bye, Angela," he says. "Don't take any envelopes from strangers."

I nod, my tongue temporarily stuck to the roof of my mouth.

ALL AROUND ME, the world moves in a blur. Voices from the pocket park become increasingly louder, but I don't process the words. I stand facing the street, staring into the space the gold Firebird recently occupied.

Eventually, I find my feet and take a few photos of the protest. The Ladies for Safe Streets are busy giving away tea and cookies. By my rough estimate, around thirty people total have turned up. Arguably, the Ladies for Safe Streets have won the afternoon, turning the so-called protest into a party in support of traffic cameras.

This makes me feel a little better for having lied to Theresa Kent. I'm surprised how much I enjoyed the deceit. Maybe, deep down, I am a bad person. That's probably why I didn't succeed in the nursing program. I lack the necessary good character.

Errol waves to me. I walk toward him, navigating around a few skinny young guys on bicycles. Errol's t-shirt reads: ANY SOCIETY THAT WOULD GIVE UP A LITTLE LIBERTY TO GAIN A LITTLE SECURITY WILL DESERVE NEITHER AND LOSE BOTH—BEN FRANKLIN.

Errol says, "You're supposed to be taking a break. I guess you couldn't resist coming. You want to see Dave Newman's dick in a wringer, right?"

"Not literally."

He points to the tea stand. "They've got crumpets." He holds up what looks like a thicker, rounder form of English muffin. I can't help but notice the large purple-black bruise on his thumbnail.

Beyond Errol, I spot a tall, skinny man wearing a top hat. Could this be one of the Mad Hatters I invited? Errol tracks my gaze.

"Have you met someone named Claire Stillman?" he asks.

I shake my head and study his face, wondering if knows about my secret life. But he looks genuinely curious, with no suspicion festering below the surface.

"She says she didn't organize this to-do. But all the announcements seem to lead back to her."

"A woman spoke to the crowd earlier," I lie. "She didn't say her name."

"What's she look like?"

"Blond," I say, quickly realizing how one lie leads to many more. "She's wearing black jeans and a striped top with a slight boat neck. Gold metallic flats. Her hair is up in a chignon."

"How old is she?" He is scanning the crowd, searching for this woman.

"Probably somewhere in her forties."

I describe Claire this way to divert Errol. As he takes off into the crowd, looking for this blond woman, I realize I may have provoked his personal interest in her. I should stop him, let him know Claire is not his type. This is what a person of fine character and high principle would do. Today, however, I'm just not feeling it.

At the Ladies for Safe Streets tea stand, I get a refill of tea and grab a cookie. I find a shady spot under a Mesquite tree to enjoy my tea break.

I am biting into a butter cookie when a voice says, "Nice protest, isn't it?"

A gangly, dark-haired man smiles at me. He is tall but looks intelligent, and, thank the goddess, does not appear to be overly impressed with his tallness. He wears jeans, a t-shirt that announces JUST PASSING THROUGH and vile flip-flops.

Determined to enjoy one truthful moment this afternoon, I introduce myself as Angela. His name is Jim.

His just passing through shirt wouldn't seem to bode well for his prospects as a romantic partner.

We sip our tea and gaze out at the protest, which seems to be winding down.

"Are traffic cameras a big issue for you?" I ask.

This is a question with an agenda. I am wondering if he will turn into Errol later in life. His flip-flops are highly questionable.

He seems to realize this may be a loaded question. "A friend invited me. He's tight with Errol and said we'd stop by. After this, we're heading to the Le Grande Orange."

The goddess smiles upon the Le Grande Orange, a center of heavenly deliciousness in Phoenix. I decide that Jim will not turn into Errol in time, that even the young Errol would not be caught dead at a place like Le Grande Orange.

"How about you?" he asks.

I tell him about meeting Errol while looking for a missing person.

"Seriously?" he asks. "You're a detective."

I get all shucks on him and admit that I've been doing some detective work, but that I am not a licensed private detective. Not yet, I say.

He asks more questions, appearing to be sincerely interested in my work. No man ever responded this way when I mentioned my job at a day spa. Occasionally, under the influence of alcohol, some men would ask shy questions about Brazilian waxes. Occasionally, I'd get rid of a pest by offering him a great discount on eyebrow shaping.

Twenty minutes whip by in a minute. Jim is an engineer who

enjoys flying planes in his spare time. He's also interested in my professional opinion about guarding personal privacy.

"No Facebook or Twitter, for starters." He is gazing into my eyes, appearing to soak up every word. This spurs me on to think of other measures to protect privacy. "Use prepaid credit cards. You probably don't want to use your real name or address for any online accounts or e-mail. Get a Post Office Box for your mail."

About ten feet from us, a guy in baggy jeans waves at him. Jim nods back.

"Looks like we're heading to dinner," he says.

Dinner, I think. What a lovely concept. "It was nice meeting you."

"Would you like to go out sometime?"

Yes, thank you. "That would be fun."

As I give him my digits, I imagine the two of us in a plane, flying over treetops to Sedona, where we enjoy dinner.

"Hey Angie," Errol says, appearing out of nowhere. He's got crumpet crumbs in his beard. "Did you hear about another protest tomorrow at the ass crack of dawn?"

"No."

My new friend, Jim, smiles.

Errol gives Jim a thorough once-over. "Not bad, Angie." Heat rushes up and over my scalp then back to my toes. Errol leans into the discomfort and says, "If you could point me to Claire Stillman, I'll leave you two kids alone to bump uglies."

15

On Monday morning, I must bid adieu to my Kia Soul rental. We've had such sweet times together. I tell myself not to be sad. After all, we will meet again someday.

After I return the car, I walk a mile and a half back to the house and take shelter on the patio, enjoying a glass of ice water and a view of the magenta Bougainvillea. I check Claire Stillman's e-mail account. Claire is popular, maybe even trending, after spamming everyone on earth about the traffic camera protest. She has received plenty of spam in return. The spam looks suspiciously like the single gal spam I've been getting recently in my own accounts, with offers from express lenders, LASEK, knitting daily, ADT, and burial insurance.

Holding my nose, I wade through a flood of e-mails until I find one from Theresa Kent. True to her word, Theresa has sent me her blog post and—bonus!—some photos.

Standing Up For Our Freedom to Enjoy Safer Roads

As executive director of Moms for Safe Streets, I have been blessed to meet so many inspiring, caring people. Tragically, many of these people have lost loved ones to car accidents. In this job, I have also had my share of surprises. When I took this position, little did I know that there are actually people against road safety!

There are people who believe that accurate, cost-effective devices proven to prevent road accidents infringe upon our rights as Americans.

Luckily, the majority of voters fully support road safety. Our opponents belong to a tiny, fringe group. But some of our opponents are highly vocal and even potentially dangerous. Believe it or not, threats have been made against people like us, who support safety measures such as traffic cameras to help police patrol our streets.

Recently, we held an event with Traftech Safety Systems to announce an exciting new safety initiative for Kansas City, "Safe Streets are Secure Streets." I was proud to welcome Traftech CEO Clay Bowden to our fine city. Traftech is a leader in traffic safety technology.

Clay was accompanied by Traftech's security consultant, Alex Zakan, who made sure the event went smoothly. He also paid a visit to my house to advise us on how we could personally protect ourselves. He and my son turned out to share an interest that bonds boys of all ages. Muscle cars!

I want to thank Clay, Alex, and Traftech personally. The event was a huge success!

Two photos accompany the blog. One shows Theresa Kent shaking hands with Clay Bowden, the CEO. The other photo depicts Theresa Kent and Zakan, sharing a laugh under a towering Oak tree. That Alex, what a sweetie.

This is perfect, another piece of evidence for my collection, which is starting to come together nicely. Maybe I won't even need the photo of Zakan and Uncle Dave together. I've got Zakan at Uncle Dave's house.

I am humming as I craft an e-mail thanking Theresa for the

terrific blog and photos. At the same time, I feel the slightest twinge of guilt deep down, maybe a little itch around my right ankle, for having deceived Theresa. I draft Theresa an effusive thank you note and send.

A moment later, Claire receives a new e-mail. It is addressed to me, the real me, as in Angela. My heart thumps.

The e-mail reads: "Angela (my darling grey dove), When are we going to make beautiful babies together? They will enjoy safe streets thanks to your efforts. We need to talk. Warmly, Alex."

Oh goddess, help me. If I were queen, I would ban the use of the phrase, "We need to talk." It is particularly terrifying when it comes from the heroin kingpin who abducted me. How did he discover I'm Claire? All I know is that I may have to adjust my prejudice against tall men. Some of them are sharp, much sharper than I would have thought possible. I rake my nails through my hair. He's a professional security consultant. I have to stop underestimating him.

I burrow into my power cocoon for a quick treatment. Sadly, it is of little comfort, and I make the brave decision to get back out of bed. Then I make the even braver decision to seek the help of an expert.

"I THOUGHT I might see you today," Monalisa says as she leads me into her office.

Boo dances around us. If there is a heaven, it will be full of dogs. Boo and I enjoy a quick embrace. He gives my legs a few affectionate head butts.

"Why?" I ask, wondering if she's seen news about the traffic camera protest.

She sits behind her desk. "You heard about the police raid on NB Entertainment?"

"No." This startling news item blew right past me, maybe

because I have been so busy with my own fake news event. "When did that happen?"

"This past weekend. I only saw the news on it this morning."

My face heats up. The time for lies is over.

"About NB Entertainment, I was going to tell you—"

Monalisa flips both palms in the air. "Don't. I don't want to know the details. I figured this wouldn't be a surprise to you. The raid wasn't successful. I spoke with my contact at the police department. He said it looked like the drug operation shut down a few days ago."

"Wow."

"They probably closed shop soon after your field trip to Prescott."

I nod, deciding that words are not my friends at the moment.

Did my actions botch the police drug raid on NB Entertainment? I rub my temples. I did interrupt the heroin supply chain, albeit inadvertently. This could have led to Zakan discontinuing distribution activities, which resulted to the police turning up nothing during their raid.

Monalisa reaches across her desk and hands me a business card. "This is the detective leading the investigation. You might want to give him a call and tell him what you know."

She studies me with her blue-green eyes, displeasure written in the grim set of her mouth. My stomach lurches as the thought of what I'm about to do. Confessing the truth doesn't come naturally to me.

"I'm afraid to talk to the police," I say. "One of the NB Entertainment people threatened Moorea."

She pulls at her chin. "They threatened you as well?"

"Yes," I say, my voice small.

"The raid wasn't successful but the police aren't giving up. If anything they're going to intensify pressure. The NB Entertainment people are on the run. They're going to be desperate."

"Desperate," I repeat, not liking the sound of that.

"Did you witness them engaging in any criminal behavior?"

I nod.

Her eyebrows rise in tandem. "Major criminal activity?"

I nod again.

"You're a witness to major criminal activity," she says. "And at least one person involved in a major drug operation knows your name and where you live."

Zakan also knows Moorea's name. I swallow hard. "Correct."

"Where's your mom?"

"At work."

Monalisa opens a drawer in her desk and grabs her car keys. "Let's go."

AT THE HOSPITAL, Monalisa drops me off at the main entrance with the instruction to stay put until I hear from her. She suggests I find a hotel for the evening. No one should stay at the house tonight. Monalisa is adamant on that point.

I follow the signs to the emergency room, wondering how I am going to tell Moorea we need to stay in a hotel. How I am going to explain all the lies I told her? Oh, goddess, help me.

At the emergency room counter, I learn that Moorea is busy with a patient. She and her colleagues are probably working feverishly on a typical emergency, breaking ribs trying to resuscitate someone, or in some other kind of mortal combat with the Grim Reaper. As if she doesn't have enough stress in her life, now she needs to hide out in a hotel because I'm a witness against a heroin distribution ring.

I leave a message for Moorea that I'm in the hospital and will see her at six p.m., when she gets off.

Behind me, there's loud clatter as two orderlies wheel a bed down the hallway. The patient is barely visible beneath a network of tubes and rods. My gut twinges at the sight of this person. I want to take her bruised hand and give it a comforting squeeze. I also want to run as fast as I can to the nearest exit.

I hate hospitals, which is another reason I dropped out of nursing. They are inhospitable places, full of blood and needles and the sound of people sobbing. Who wouldn't prefer to be in a spa, listening to the sound of water cascading through a streambed?

In the cafeteria, I purchase a small green salad, yogurt and orange juice, mostly to have something to do. In the far right corner, I sit down and watch the entryway. A woman passes by with a large slice of chocolate cake. I don't even blink.

Instead, I lift a spoon, take a bit of yogurt, and force it into my mouth, where it coats my tongue. I look at the yogurt, wondering what flavor I bought. The carton indicates it's plain yogurt.

Zakan can't get to Moorea in the emergency room. Even people coming in with a bleeding hand wrapped in a kitchen towel can't get to her. Take a number.

If anything happens to Moorea, I'll die.

How could I have been so thoughtless and reckless?

A woman stares at me, curiosity in her grey eyes. Apparently I have spoken out loud to myself. She offers up a game smile. I wrench my expression into something resembling normal.

I should find Zakan and give myself up. This way he and the others won't track down Moorea and hurt her.

Zakan. My mind goes back to the protest. He didn't seem concerned about the police on Sunday. If anything, he seemed relaxed. He smiled. He even flirted. This doesn't strike me as the proper attitude after a police raid on your center of operations.

I take another drink of orange juice then temper the sugar rush with a spoonful of plain yogurt. The salad remains virgin territory.

The remarkable thing about this past weekend was that Zakan didn't warn me off or threaten me.

I rake my fork through the salad. No dressing. I take a

mouthful of lettuce. I may as well get some fiber if there's a chance I'll survive.

Then again, if I were him, I would want to eliminate me. I am an eyewitness who saw a gym bag full of Obamacare heroin. Well, technically, I stole the gym bag of heroin. I am also a witness he abducted. The abduction alone would have to be good for some time behind bars.

I check my messages. He has written me a text: "What's wrong? Don't you want to talk to me? I hope I didn't do anything to offend you. Are you concerned that your mom won't approve of us? Don't worry, little dove. Moms love me!"

Cortisone floods my system. A wave of fear hits me, and my vision blurs for a moment. I spring up from the cafeteria table and rush to the bathroom.

AT FIVE P.M., with an hour still to go before Moorea is off work, I leave the cafeteria and take a stroll through the hospital. I find myself peering at a stuffed giraffe in the window of the gift shop. It has impossibly long eyelashes.

"Angela." Zakan is behind me, a few feet away. "I've been looking everywhere for you."

For a moment, my bones seem to dissolve. I stumble and lurch to the side, bracing myself against the window of the gift shop.

Zakan frowns and reaches for my arm.

I hold up a palm. "No. Leave me alone."

Run. I must run. I make it across the hall into a waiting area, where I collapse into an armchair. My throat burns, and I taste the acid from the orange juice burbling up.

Claire, where are you?

Zakan smiles at me. "I come in peace, little dove."

I shake my head as he goes to the water dispenser and fills a cup with cold water. He hands me the cup, and I gulp. Zakan looks around the waiting room, his expression bemused.

He sits in the chair next to me. "Are you feeling better?"

I make an indeterminate noise.

"Good," he says. "Let's find an empty room and play doctor and nurse."

"No."

He laughs. "You're not that type, I can see that now. I'll get us a room at the Phoenician."

I shake my head.

"You fear falling in love. You fear intimacy."

"Why are you here?"

"Angela, I'm here for love." He takes my hand. "Let's go. This is not an appealing spot. I bet they don't even have a liquor license. The lighting is harsh. Sick people everywhere. And the food—"

"The food is actually better than it used to be."

His gaze sweeps my body. "On the other hand, I bet you are wearing your best underwear. Isn't that what you're supposed to do in case you go to the hospital?"

"Stop," I say. "This is about me talking to the authorities, isn't it?"

"The authorities aren't our friends, Angela. You should know that by now."

"Personally, I count them as friends. But I can see why you wouldn't."

"You're so innocent?" His lolls back in his chair, eyes wide with disbelief. "Or is it all a misunderstanding that your ex-lover is in prison?"

"I had nothing to do with that. Nothing."

He sways back and forth, as if to music. "Do you hear that?"

"Hear what?"

"A violin is playing your sad song of innocence. You're innocent the same way I am innocent."

"There's a reason he's in prison and I'm not. I had no idea what he was doing."

"You were always giving him ideas for how to improve the business. Making changes. Always pushing, pushing, pushing. Like a good American, striving for more and more."

"I loved that job." I also loved him, or thought I did.

"You planted the idea in his head."

"No."

He is staring intently at me. My face is burning up.

"Yes," he says.

"I made a joke. It was a joke. I had no idea he'd actually do it."

"See." He points at me. "I know you. You were angry with him. What was it? He wouldn't marry you?" His eyes narrow. "He was seeing another woman."

My mouth is open. The denials are stumbling to get out my mouth, falling over each other, getting confused. Nothing is coming out. I stare down at the tile floor. When I glance back up, I see he looks pleased. He is toying with me, poking and prodding the tender parts, trying for an explosion.

"Don't be afraid of yourself, Angela. Don't be afraid of your ambition. Come home with me tonight."

He is trying to keep a straight face, but I can see the twitch at the side of his lips.

"I'm not going anywhere with you tonight."

He smiles. "Truthfully, Angela, I have a favor to ask. You are correct that I am not in love with you. I think we could grow to love each other, with time. But right now my heart belongs to Pepper."

"Pepper."

"She's a delightful creature." He shows me a photo on his phone, a black cat lounging on a tan leather couch. "The minute you see her, your heart will be gone. You'll be her slave, exactly like I am."

"What's the favor?" Maybe Pepper is ill, needing regularly

administered shots that don't suit a heroin kingpin's busy schedule.

"I'm leaving the country tomorrow. As of yesterday, I've retired. Going back to Russia. Sadly, my plans have been made in haste and I can't take Pepper with me."

"A cat." A cat is probably the last thing I need right now.

"Please, she prefers to be called Pepper." He leans over and whispers. "She doesn't know she's a cat."

"You want me to have your cat."

Both hands shoot up. "No, she's not yours to keep. When I become settled, I will make arrangements to be reunited with her. You'll be kitty mamma for several months, that's it."

"Alex," I say, "I have no job. I have no car. My mom and her boyfriend are moving out of the house together soon, and I have no money for an apartment. I can't give Pepper a proper life."

He frowns. "You're working all the time. You must be making money. I don't understand."

I start talking and can't seem to stop. You could set much of what I say to violin music. I have no savings because all my money went to the lawyer who saved me from going to prison. The case with Charise has ended. I blather on about the fraudulent traffic camera deal and the whistleblower award for fifty thousand dollars.

He sits back in his chair and tilts his head back. A second later his body shudders with laughter. This is not nervous, tittering laughter. This is the real thing.

A passing nurse glances over at us. This kind of amusement is rare in the waiting area of the hospital. More typically, the place is full of anxious people chewing their nails raw and downing pills so their stomach linings and intestines don't spring leaks.

"Angela, crime is what pays. I thought all Americans knew that." He angles his head at me. "Crime-fighting, on the other hand, does not."

Somehow I know he is not going to be swayed by the intrinsic rewards of fighting crime or its social value. Instead, I say, "It doesn't matter. I'm done. I'm done with the Salvador Award."

This is the truth. Just like I know I will never be president of the United States or an emergency room nurse, I know I will not win the Salvador Award for whistleblowing.

"Americans never give up their dreams. It's against the law."

"I have other dreams."

"Yes," he says. "I know. You dream about me."

"I'm sorry I can't take care of Pepper."

"Yes, you can," he says. "I don't trust anyone else with her." He shrugs. "Plus, there is no one else. I have no friends. Even the postman doesn't know who I am. I hate my neighbors. They're barbaric." He gazes at me. "I'll give you money. For everything you need."

A cat. I have a history with dogs. And scientific research shows that owning a dog does wonders for reducing cortisol levels.

"I don't know."

"Please," he says, squeezing my hand. "I'll give you what you need to create a comfortable, happy home for Pepper."

His eyes turn glassy. I find myself saying, "Okay."

He takes my hand and kisses it. "I could love you if you gave us a chance."

"When do you want to drop off the cat?"

"Drop off Pepper?" He shakes his head emphatically. "We'll be together until the last moment. You can pick her up tomorrow morning at my house. I'll leave everything for you there."

I'm thinking my lack of a car is a problem. But then I realize I'm not going to his house tomorrow alone to pick up Pepper. Someone will have to accompany me.

He pulls a small key ring out of his pocket and hands it to me. It has two keys on it. I put the key ring in the small front zippered compartment of my backpack.

"What's your address?"

"I'll give that to you later. Much as I adore you, I don't need to see the police before I leave the country."

I smile. "You don't trust me."

"I trust you to come home with me tonight, where I can keep you busy with more interesting matters than the authorities or the crime-fighting award. After, we can have a romantic breakfast together, just the three of us: you, me and Pepper."

"Not going to happen."

He smiles. "I'll text you the address when I'm ready. I don't want to give you the opportunity to betray me. As my mama says, everyone is a better person without temptation."

Doubts creep into my mind. "You threatened my life a few days ago."

He shrugs. "Now that I'm retired, all that's behind us." He leans closer to me, and I can smell cigarettes on his skin. "You see, Angela, it's no longer only about me and my career. I have Pepper to consider now. If Pepper can't be with me, the next best thing is a single woman. There's almost nothing better for a cat than a lonely, single woman."

"Sure," I say, feeling light-headed, wondering if a stereotype about single women and cats may have saved my life.

It is a few minutes before six p.m., when Moorea is due to finish work. In the hallway outside the ER, I sit on a molded plastic chair and check my messages. Jim, the man I met at the flash protest, has written. He asks if I'd care to join him for drinks sometime this week. He enjoyed meeting me. For a second, I levitate off the plastic chair, going higher and higher until I'm in the clouds. No, I'm in an airplane. Jim is the pilot. We're going to have champagne together somewhere in northern Arizona.

Back on earth, my finger hovers over my phone screen. Of course romance strikes while I'm busy with work. I suspect it might be too forward to suggest we go out this very evening and, if he wouldn't mind, I'd like to spend the night on his couch. Tempting, but no.

I draft: "YAY!!! I'd love to get together. Later in the week would be better for me. Looking forward to it!"

I delete "YAY!!!" and send.

Errol has written, saying he hopes I'm taking his advice to sit out the shit war for a while. He's all ears if I need to talk. It's good for people to blow smoke out their ass every so often.

When I check Claire's e-mails, I find Errol has also been in touch with her. He would like to grab a cold one with her. He suggests they have much in common. They should join forces.

"Angela?" Moorea's head is jutting forward, her mouth slightly open. Her hand has gone to her heart.

Apparently she didn't receive the message I left for her earlier.

"I'm okay," I say, smiling. "I was in the area so I decided to stop by."

Yes, I just happened to be in the hospital, hiding out from a heroin distribution gang. This would be the juncture where I should tell my mother that we need to talk. I need to tell her about drugs, lies, and armed men.

"You need a ride home?" she says.

I nod, realizing this doesn't quite cover it.

"I'm going to Roy's tonight. We need to buy some moving supplies." She glances at her watch. "He's picking me up soon. But we can drop you off at the house first."

Perfect. Moorea won't be at home tonight so there's no need to discuss a hotel room. As kitty mamma, I seem to have protected status, at least with Zakan. Even so, I probably shouldn't spend the night alone at the house. But the problem with a hotel is that it costs money.

"I'd love a ride to the house if it isn't too much trouble."

"Of course it isn't a problem." She searches my face. "How did you end up down here?"

Good question. I rack my brain for a story. "I met someone nearby."

"Someone I should know about?" A twinkle lights her eyes.

"Absolutely not."

She puts her arm around my shoulder, and we walk out the sliding doors that lead to the circular drive.

"Angela, I'm so happy you're finally getting back out and meeting people. You're going to kiss some frogs. But you've got to get out there again. I've been worried about how isolated you've become."

Perhaps I could use a little more isolation these days.

Roy pulls into the drive in his Outback, an excellent post-heart attack vehicle. Moorea gets into the front, and I slide into the back seat. He's prepared a chilled bottle of water with chunks of pineapple and bits of mint in it for Moorea. He apologizes for not having one for me as well, but he didn't realize I'd be there.

Moorea insists I have a sip, passing me the perspiring bottle. It is delicious. This is the taste of love.

At home, I enter through the garage, grabbing the U-lock from the bike. After searching the place, heavy lock in hand, I discover no one is there. I eat some leftover stir-fry, washing it down with one of Roy's light beers.

As the light starts to fade outside, I decide I should not be in the house tonight in case the drug dealers come calling. Who knows, maybe Zakan will change his mind, or find another single woman to serve as kitty mamma. I will camp outside, in a shadowy cove next to the shed. It is a reasonable hiding place, near the back gate if a quick escape proves necessary but not far from a flush toilet and other forms of civilization.

While I'm assembling my camping gear, Monalisa calls.

"I haven't been able to speak with the detective yet," she says. "But I did have one more question for you."

From the cautious tone of her voice, I know this is going to be a good question. "Yes?" I ask, bracing myself.

"You mentioned that you witnessed illegal activity in connection with NB Entertainment."

"Yes."

"How did you end up witnessing this activity?"

This seems like a trick question. "I saw it."

Monalisa clears her throat. "Did you do anything illegal in the process of witnessing their criminal activity?"

I stole a gym bag full of heroin from the back of Nicole's car. Before that I snuck into her car without a formal invitation. Yep, I can safely conclude that some laws were broken.

One thing my spotty professional record has taught me is to frame a mistake in a positive light. "I'm afraid my enthusiasm to find Kevin got the better of me."

"You broke the law."

"Probably more than one law."

I fight the impulse to go into defense mode. Dolly Gaga broke the law first. People break the law on TV shows all the time, and it's no big deal. I mean, there are laws and then there are Laws, right?

Monalisa sighs. I can imagine her eyes going into laser mode, burning through the walls, torching the withered tomato vines in the side yard.

Eventually, she says, "Angela."

In her voice I hear disappointment, weariness, annoyance. Others have said my name this way before. Generally, I would let it wash over me, figuring their disappointment was their problem. But coming from Monalisa it hurts. After all, she and Iona appear to be among the few people who actually think highly of me. And Iona is no longer among the living.

"I'm sorry," I say. And I can honestly say that is the truth. I am sorry my reckless behavior has endangered Moorea and Roy and maybe Monalisa as well. I am so sorry I can barely stand it. I hope there is more light beer in the fridge.

She makes a humming noise. "Just how illegal was your behavior?"

"I wasn't helping them distribute heroin if that's what you're asking."

"Okay," she says, drawing out the word.

"I stole their drugs. But I didn't mean to."

"Good lord."

"Not all of their heroin," I say. "I took a gym bag. I didn't know what it contained."

"Why would you take a gym bag that didn't belong to you?"

"I borrowed it, really. I was hoping to exchange it for information on Kevin's whereabouts."

"And how did that work out for you?"

"Hindsight is 20-20," I say, aiming for some humor.

"This was supposed to be a straightforward case. We agreed to look into Kevin's disappearance. Maybe we'd locate him, maybe not. We made no promises. You were supposed to ask his family some questions and go to the restaurant where he was last seen."

"I did all those things."

"And much, much more," she says. "You've broken the law and risked your life to find a loser who dumped his fiancée."

"It was my job to find him. That's what Charise wanted. I gave it my best."

"You outdid yourself," Monalisa says. "Where are you right now?"

At home, where you told me not to be.

"Better that you don't know."

"Good thinking," she says. "You're right, better I don't know. I'll be in touch when I've worked something out with the police."

"Thank you."

"You may have to find a lawyer."

On that chilling note, she clicks off the phone. Oh dad who art in heaven. Not another lawyer. Please no.

16

I wake up on a chaise lounge in the back yard. It is early. How early I don't know but a hazy blue-gray glaze covers the sky. I wonder if it is going to be hazy today or if this is how it actually looks this early in the morning. On another note, I wonder if today is the day I, or someone I love dearly, will die.

Don't be ridiculous, I tell myself. I might have said it out loud.

In a few minutes, I gather up my camping gear, including my phone, hedgehog, sheets, comforter, pillow and empty cans of light beer. I put the sheets in the wash. The comforter, which is so fluffy it can't fit into our washing machine, feels damp, so I drape it over an armchair in the living room, where it can air out. Hedgie is the sole occupant on my bed, looking marooned on the mattress top.

In the kitchen, I stretch my neck and back. Surprisingly, nothing hurts except my ribcage. This was my first camping experience ever, and I have to admit it wasn't that bad. I didn't have to fend off any bugs or snakes or drug traffickers. Even my noisy pigeon neighbors, flapping about in the disreputable pineapple palm tree, a bunkhouse with five-minute rentals, eventually went from a coo to a whisper.

I pour myself a glass of cucumber and mint-infused water (thank you, Roy!) and check my messages.

Zakan has sent me a text with his address. He also wishes me a wonderful life, which doesn't suggest he'll be back in touch for his cat. I suspect distance will not make his heart grow fonder for Pepper.

Errol has also written. He wants to know how I'm doing and, by the way, have I heard from Claire again? I wonder if I should nip this in the bud and confess.

I roll some water around my palate, considering. Fruity. Sweet on the palate. Nice finish.

No, I won't fess up just yet. I may need to use Claire again. Anyway, next week I'll have the energy to be a more genuine and considerate person. Today is not the day for honesty, not with Pepper to pick up.

I write to Errol, knowing I'm about to make a deal with the devil, and ask if he could drive me over to pick up a cat. As I wait to hear from him, I put some walnut raisin bread in the toaster oven. The fridge contains actual butter because I bought it and put it there. Toast with a slab of butter is one of my culinary specialties.

I sip my water and scroll through job listings. Lo and behold, a burst of heavenly light streams through the back window. A chorus of angelic voices hits a high note. A new yoga spa is opening. It's called Shades of Blue. It offers services for the "inner and outer you." They are looking for someone fit, upbeat, and organized to be their receptionist or, in their lingo, "client welcome associate."

I am all about warm welcomes and, with the angry purple bruise fading on my forehead, I am looking more upbeat with every passing day. This is the perfect job. Everyone serene, wearing a healthy yoga glow, speaking softly and kindly, mindfully replenishing and restoring their mind-body connections. No frequent frowners club. No Lady Gaga lookalikes or heroin distributors. I fill out an electronic application form and send. Yes, it will be perfect, I reassure myself. Even if it's the slightest bit too serene, maybe even a little dull, that is exactly what I need.

My cell alerts me to a new e-mail. It is from Jim, my fetching new pilot/engineer friend. He has sent me a photo of some roses, taken during his run early this morning. He's an early riser; we have that in common (hah).

He wants to know if I'd like to join me for a drink on Thursday evening. Let me think about that for a nanosecond.

Yes, please.

He also hopes my investigation is going well. Isn't that lovely of him? Perfect, dare I say it. The angelic chorus chimes in, *He is perfect.* Part of me walks on air.

About an hour later, Errol checks in, agreeing to drive me to pick up the cat. I know his ulterior motive is to discuss Claire. I suggest we meet at Grove coffee shop so I can buy him a coffee and treat. It's the least I can do given the circumstances.

Getting out of the house takes longer than I anticipate. No one outfit can take me from an industrial chic coffee shop into Errol's pick-up truck and on to Zakan's house, where I will meet Pepper for the first time. In the end, I settle for chino Capri pants and a grey t-shirt.

Thus equipped, I walk to the coffee shop and splurge on a soy latte with extra froth while I wait for Errol. I have finished lapping up the froth when I hear the grumbling sounds of Errol's pick-up truck. When he cuts the engine, the vehicle shudders with the relief of being put out of its misery. Oh, how I miss the Kia Soul.

He lurches inside. The barista greets him with a cheery "Good morning" and Errol grunts in response. It's probably not the most hostile grunt in his repertoire, but it's not exactly cordial either. The barista grins at me, and I smile back, both of us acknowledging how adorable Errol is in the morning.

Errol walks over to me, looking shaggy and rumpled. Between

the two of us, no one would ever guess who actually slept outside last night. He smells feral.

"Ready?" he asks.

"Can I buy you a coffee? Some breakfast? My treat."

He glances around like it's some dump instead of a place that roasts its own shade-grown beans from organic farms in Latin America.

"Too rich for my blood," he says.

Inside his pick-up truck, my seat is gloriously clear. Unfortunately, it appears as though he's swept all the junk that was on my seat into the foot well. Good thing I am wearing gym shoes. The day clearly called for closed-toe footwear.

He starts the engine. I direct him to take a right out of the lot then a left onto Center Street, which will take us toward Zakan's house.

"What is it about women and cats?" he asks.

"I'm not a cat person," I say.

He glances over at me. "You sure?"

I tell him about how Zakan, the go-between for Traftech and Dave Newman, is leaving me his cat. As I tell him about Zakan retiring and returning to Russia, Errol leans forward and frowns, as though I'm speaking with a heavy accent. The pick-up slows to a crawl. He can't seem to process information and drive at a normal speed at the same time.

"You're out of your sprocket," he says.

I wonder what he'd think if I told him about the heroin. He'd probably take me to the nearest mental hospital.

"Pot calling the kettle black," I say.

"But at least now I can see why he's giving you a cat."

"He's leaving the country and had no one else to give it to."

Errol grunts skeptically. "Cats are piss bags with fur. He's punishing you for harassing him."

"Can't you drive any faster?"

When we reach Zakan's address, a ranch-style house, Errol

pulls to the curb and cuts the engine. We walk up the driveway and to the door together.

"I don't see any cat." His head swivels around nervously.

I pull out the key chain. "Pepper is probably inside."

"You got his keys?" Errol squints suspiciously at me. "Did you bang this guy?"

I fumble with the key, trying to get it into the lock. "Of course not."

He makes a *pffft* sound. "That's your reward. A cat. You know what cats think people are?"

I open the door. "No, what?"

"Oversized can openers."

"Practical creatures."

We enter a narrow hallway with a set of empty coat hooks along the wall. The hallway opens up to a large living and kitchen space on our right and, to our left, a corridor, which probably leads to the bedrooms.

"Every time you clean up cat turds you can think of this guy. Talk about a hit and run. Did he tell you he loved you?"

"We weren't dating."

"You were just banging each other."

Beside me, I hear the sound of gravel shaking in a tin cup. Errol is laughing.

The living room has sliding doors leading onto a back patio. The sliding door is cracked open, allowing the air into the room. Still, the air has a rotten, metallic tinge to it.

Errol takes a dramatically deep breath. "Ah, the fine smell of ripe kitty litter."

I scan the room and don't see any sign of the cat. "Could you see if Pepper is in the back yard?"

"Here little piss bag," Errol calls, heading to the sliding doors. He walks out the patio doors. "Piss bag!"

"The name is Pepper."

On the kitchen counter is a brown cat carrier along with a

plastic bag full of cat food. On the front of a white envelope, Zakan wrote: ENVELOPE FOR ANGELA. I smile and wince at the same time, remembering my pathetic lie about the envelope awaiting me at Uncle Dave's house. Oddly, the envelope is empty. A note written on the back of the envelope says, "Dearest Angela, Pepper will be your loyal, loving companion so long as you feed her regularly. Yours, A."

Errol comes back inside. "The little beast isn't back there."

"She goes by Pepper."

He thumps down the corridor, calling, "Here, douchebag. Come to Uncle Errol."

The carrier has mesh windows and a thick pad inside. Thankfully, it doesn't smell. The pad seems a little off center so I try to straighten it out. As I fiddle with it, I spot a manila envelope underneath. It's a small clasped envelope, with no name or note on it.

I open the envelope, thinking it will contain a check. Zakan did agree to help cover Pepper's care. But inside are two pages. The first page is a printout from a bank account showing a transfer of $1,500,000 to AZ Security Inc. The second page shows a transfer of $1,500,000 to Samui Development Inc. In black pen, someone has written David Newman in parentheses next to Samui Development.

My mind flashes back to Uncle Dave's vacation photos on Facebook. Coconut groves and glorious beaches and water a blue-green shade that brings me to my knees. Those photos were from Koh Samui in Thailand. Koh Samui is on my bucket list.

My hands tremble. This is the money trail. This is the evidence that demonstrates fraud.

"Errol," I call out, enunciating carefully, keeping the quiver out of my voice. "You won't believe this. He's left me a paper trail. Traftech paid off David Newman."

No response.

I slip the papers into the envelope, which I tuck into my back pack. I grab my own cell and walk past a bedroom and a bathroom.

"Errol? The traffic camera contract is history. Zakan left me proof."

Still nothing. "Errol?"

At the end of the hall is another bedroom, and I peek through the door.

Errol is inside the room. He is staring at Zakan, who is slumped against the wall. The front of Zakan's shirt is a stiffened mass of blood. His hands, brushing against the tan carpet, are reddish-purple. His face is parchment white. A black roller bag is propped next to him.

No. My stomach drops to the floor. I scream.

"You retired," I say, the words slurring. "You were leaving."

Errol puts a finger to his lips, as if I'm making too much noise, as if I'm going to wake up Zakan.

"We need to call for help," I say, wiping my face, which is wet.

"I did."

His voice is monotone.

"I don't hear any sirens," I say. "Maybe there's still hope."

"He's gone," Errol says. "Worm food."

My stomach rises and twists. I cover my mouth and turn, heading to the hallway. Bathroom, I need a bathroom. Errol grabs my arm, holding me in place.

"You spent the night with him."

"No, I didn't," I say, my words muffled behind my hand. Errol is losing it, and I need cold water. A toilet.

"Yes, you did."

He's pulling me into the room. I'm pushing away, trying to escape. But Errol is strong. He pitches me toward Zakan. A searing pain pulses through my ribs.

"No!" I scream, my voice hoarse and frayed. I stumble forward, falling onto my knees, before wheeling back and upward, spinning away from Zakan's blank staring eyes.

Errol is pointing a gun at me.

"You were here when he was shot." He motions the gun toward the wall, toward Zakan. "It's a shame, but it's me or you, kid. And I've got the gun."

My eyes search Errol's face. His eyes register outrage, as if to say: *How dare you?*

How dare I what?

Theresa Kent's words come back to me: *The opposition is so tough in your area. Clay has mentioned how hard it is there.*

"It's you," I say, realization dawning.

"Go on," Errol says. "Sit down with your boyfriend. We may as well take advantage of the opportunity.

The opposition isn't tough. It's only manufactured to look tough. Engineered to get the most money out of Traftech. WAR. Errol talks big on the website but doesn't deliver. He's Astroturf.

Errol made it seem like the politics around traffic cameras were radioactive. Errol made it seem like Dave Newman would need security to protect him from traffic camera protesters. Errol helped make it seem like Dave Newman was taking a huge risk.

"You and Dave Newman are working together. You made it seem like he needed security to protect him from traffic camera protesters. Given the supposed risks, Dave Newman could ask for more money from Traftech. And he's giving you some of it."

"Good thing you found the paper trail. Would hate to see the deal fail, not when we're so close. I've already got my mountaintop picked out." He pointed to Zakan. "Go on, Angela, get closer to your boy toy."

I take a slow step toward Zakan. A fly buzzes past, landing on his mauled chest. A sickly sweet stench permeates the room. It coats my mouth.

"I won't tell anyone," I say. "You can have your mountaintop place."

"You won't give up." He laughs. "It's funny how you think you can wrap me around your little finger. You can flip your hair and bat your lashes all you want. Survival is survival. Eat or be eaten."

"I promise."

"Go ahead and sit. You'll be worm food together."

I slowly lower myself. Somewhere in the house a door opens and shuts.

"Help!" I scream. "Fire! There's a fire!"

Footsteps pound down the hallway.

17

"*H*elp!" I back up against the bedroom wall.

Errol smiles. "Shut up."

The footsteps seem to stop. *Please, rescuer, don't disappear. Please call for help.*

Errol points the gun at my head. I collapse onto the carpet, my weight dropping like I'm in a plummeting elevator. A gunshot blasts through the air, thudding into the wall.

I scream. The gun aims downward. I burrow behind Zakan. I'm still screaming, sounding like a broken teakettle. His cold, wet mass covers me. I pull the roller bag over, providing another barrier.

"Where is this so-called evidence?" a voice asks.

David Newman appears in the doorway. A horrible realization hits me. Errol didn't call the police; he called Uncle Dave.

My heart goes into overdrive. Slow down, I tell myself. Slow way down. I inhale for four long seconds and I exhale for four long seconds.

"I was just finishing up," Errol says. "Thanks for interrupting."

"Don't you have a suppressor? My ears are ringing. Someone's going to call the police any minute now."

Long inhale. Curled on my side, I tap the screen of my phone until I've got video. *Long exhale.* I telescope my arm around the roller bag and aim the phone toward the two men. *Long inhale.*

"I didn't think I'd need it," Errol says. "We were picking up a cat."

"Is that corpse happy to see us or is that a woman crawling around beneath him?"

"Balls," Errol says.

"Why don't we just set a fire?" Uncle Dave asks. I hear the flicking of a lighter.

"If we set a fire we need to tie her up," Errol says. "Won't that seem suspicious?"

"Fine, shoot her. But the police will discover that two different guns shot our star-crossed lovers."

Errol's knees click as he walks. Above me, I hear his labored breathing. He kicks away the roller bag.

"Busted," I yell, holding up my phone. "You're on live video. Streaming to my blog."

Behind him, Uncle Dave whips around like a vampire exposed to light and disappears, leaving the door to bang the wall. I push up from my forearms and scramble onto my feet.

Errol rocks from side to side. "You lying turd."

"Everyone can see you," I lie, waving the phone, waving to a charging bull.

He lurches forward. "Give me that."

"Too late," I say, stepping out of his reach. "It's out there. You and Dave Newman. Trying to kill me."

I extend the phone in front of him. He comes at me again. As he lurches for the phone, I lower my hand and claw the side of his face with my nails.

"Mother..." he says, tripping into Zakan's crumpled mass.

I sprint into the hallway, my feet sliding over laminate.

"I'm going to kill you," Errol yells.

The front door is open, and I fly through it. I run until my lungs are on fire and my legs give out. At that point, collapsed on someone's lawn, I call for help.

18

*S*eventeen days after defying death, I am packing up my belongings, preparing for my move out of the house. This is the less glamorous side of life as a famous crime fighter. Sadly, fame has not changed me. I thought rich and famous went together, but apparently not. Monalisa spotted me a loan to cover my moving expenses and the security deposit for my new apartment.

Even if it hasn't led to riches, the press coverage has been entertaining. My favorite internet headline: PARTY GIRL NABS HEROIN KINGPIN. Party girl? Seriously, moi? I suppose I should be grateful that desperate, former day spa professional doesn't make for a catchy headline. Plus, the idea that I nabbed anything is a joke. I can almost hear Zakan's laughter. Occasionally, I look at the photos I took of him with my phone.

The police have not caught his murderer but believe a rival drug gang may be to blame.

After I fled, the police came to Zakan's house and found a stash of heroin hidden in one of the toilets. Apparently, he also left behind some records about the heroin distribution operation through NB Entertainment. This is surprising as it seems careless of Zakan. Maybe he was shot before he had a chance to tidy up.

The news about the traffic camera corruption got a lot of local play but not much national attention. Admittedly, corruption in city procurement processes is not as compelling as heroin and celebrity lookalikes. Still, the police did a great job of tracking down Errol, arresting him on Route 60 near Globe, Arizona. In the video of his arrest, he looks like something dug out of a potato.

Errol hasn't said anything publicly about the traffic camera deal. He did release a statement saying that he'd never met Zakan and had no knowledge of heroin distribution. The news reports also suggest the traffic camera fraud and heroin distribution were separate business ventures of Zakan's. The police haven't said anything about leveling drug charges against Errol and Uncle Dave.

Dave Newman has proved harder to locate than Errol. The authorities figured he'd be fleeing to Thailand. He surprised everyone and, after a few days of searching, the police found he'd flown to Jakarta en route to Bali. Apparently, Uncle Dave had been preparing to make a getaway for at least a year. He seems to have planned well, leaving false clues about Thailand to make everyone think that would be his destination. He may have found the perfect new life in Bali, and it's unclear whether he'll be extradited as no formal treaty exists between the US and Indonesia.

Returning to my packing, I bag an armful of winter shoes and put them into a moving box. The old me would have wrapped them individually in tissue paper. But my move date is tomorrow, and I'm forced to throw caution to the wind to get everything done in time. Behind the shoe rack, I find a pair of once beloved strappy gold metallic sandals. The elegant heel speaks of flirtatious laughter and third dates. As I finger the glimmering leather, I try to remember when I last wore these shoes.

Unable to recall the last occasion in my life calling for gold sandals, I toss the shoes into a moving box. This is the new practical me, who packs efficiently and also now sports short nails. Having scratched Errol's face, the police needed to gather evidence from under my nails. As the evidence tech scraped, he told me long nails harbored a large amount of dirt and germs. They could spread pinworms. A quick internet search confirmed this terrible truth.

The following day, I cut my nails. Oddly, no one seems to have noticed this earth-shattering change in my life. I even asked Moorea if she noticed anything different about me, fluttering my hands around as if I was showing off an engagement ring. She told me the bruise on my forehead was now a light gold. Roy, bless his heart, insisted I had lost some weight.

I grab a tape gun and seal up the moving box. With a smelly black marker, I label the box: WINTER SHOES AND SPRING HEELS.

My cell-phone dings. Jim has sent me a photo of Pepper sleeping on a dining room chair. Goodness, as Iona used to say. I sit on a moving box to give the photo my full attention before I write, "Sweet!"

This is a big step for Pepper, who has mostly stayed hidden behind a stack of baskets in Jim's laundry room, only coming out to eat at night. Pepper is slowly recovering from her traumatic experiences at Zakan's house, where the police found her in the dark corner of a closet in the guest room. Jim and I are carefully monitoring Pepper's progress.

How did this happen? Jim and I were supposed to have met for drinks a little while ago. After finding Zakan and nearly getting killed, I told him we'd need to postpone drinks and, by the way, could he take care of a cat until I moved into my new place? I couldn't bring Pepper home since the landlord doesn't allow cats, plus Roy is allergic.

Jim's response? Yes of course. I'd be happy to. Is there anything else you need?

Le sigh.

He sends me photos and regular updates on Pepper. It's like we have skipped dating and entered a new phase of our relationship: co-parenting a cat. Well, maybe he's doing all the parenting. There's a lot you can tell from someone by how well they take care of someone else's animal. Maybe I should have been testing potential boyfriends this way all along.

I was telling Charise this the other day when she called to see how I was doing. She counseled me to hold out judgment on Jim. She said: "Homeboy knows he's going to be rewarded for good behavior." Trust, she added, is for suckers.

Call me a sucker.

I start gathering up tank tops to fill a large clothing box. After I load them in, I pause, taking a moment to enjoy the discomfort coming from my ribs. As if that sensation isn't sufficiently unpleasant, I survey my empire of boxes and shoes, enough to fill a small room. How much money might I have today if I'd not blown my cash on tank tops and strappy sandals in various metallic hues? My stomach knots. By my rough calculation, I'd have thousands of dollars, possibly millions if I factored in compounding until I reached the age of sixty-five.

Luckily, I am not good enough with numbers to come up with an actual estimate.

I am almost finished with the packing. After the bike gear, which Moorea is gifting me, I'll only have my weekender to fill with clothes and toiletries for the next few days.

My cell-phone dings. Monalisa has sent a text: "Can you come by now? I've got a surprise for you."

I write back, "Good surprise?"

In typical Monalisa form, she responds, "I think you'll find this interesting."

An interesting surprise. *Not my favorite kind.*

BOO IS BARKING EVEN before Monalisa opens the door. As I enter, Boo backs down the hallway, still barking. Dogs have that clever trick of appearing aggressive even while stepping away from you.

"Boo!" Monalisa says.

"Boo," I say. "It's Angela. Your friend. Remember me?"

I take a tentative step forward. He crouches down and growls. Part of me wonders if some space alien has taken the real Boo away and left this belligerent creature in his place.

"Kitchen," Monalisa says. "Now!"

Boo lets go one more throaty bark then retreats.

"Is Boo okay?" I ask.

I can hear the patter of his paws on the kitchen tiles. He seems to be pacing.

"Sure," Monalisa says, as if his behavior is perfectly normal.

No, I want to tell her, you don't understand. Boo and I have something special. We have unconditional love. This sudden, inexplicable moodiness reminds me of male human behavior, and I have higher standards than that for Boo.

Inside Monalisa's office, a man is sitting in my usual chair. Now I realize why Boo is upset. This is my chair. Who is this interloper?

He wears a tasteful light denim button down shirt, khakis, and dark brown boat shoes with no socks. I recognize this man. For many days, I walked around with his photo etched into my brain.

"Kevin, I presume."

Monalisa gazes at me with trace amounts of admiration. With her condition, she wouldn't have been able to recognize his face. Sometimes I forget to be grateful for all my powers of observation, even the ones that don't seem to be that big a deal.

Kevin gives me a tentative smile. Unlike his brother Tate, he doesn't have a beguiling gap between his front teeth. For that, I am truly grateful.

"Nice to finally meet you," he says, standing to shake my hand.

"I wouldn't have thought you'd want to meet me," I say.

He glances nervously from me to Monalisa, who gestures for him to sit down. We both sit, and he clears his throat.

"I love my uncle. I also think that if he's guilty, he should face the consequences. Give him a little time and he'll come back from Indonesia."

Monalisa's right eyebrow goes up. She won't be holding her breath for the return of Dave Newman, who has probably found a lovely luxury golf resort with breathtaking views. Since the thought of him golfing is going to spike my cortisol, I change the topic.

"You did a great job of disappearing, Kevin."

He grins and shyly looks at the floor. "One of my hidden talents."

He's not the cold, arrogant, cowardly bastard I imagined.

"Now that you've returned," I say. "How can we help you?"

Kevin looks up at Monalisa. "Do you mind if I speak with Angela privately? It's about a personal issue."

Monalisa sits back, her eyebrows up slightly. She gazes at me and asks, "Why don't you two take Boo for a walk?"

Kevin's mouth pulls to the side. "I don't know."

"We'd love to," I say.

"Boo?" Monalisa calls.

He appears in the doorway and barks. I give him a friendly wave, and he rushes toward me. We hug as he whines softly.

In the entryway, Monalisa puts some serious metal hardwear around Boo's neck and hooks a leash onto him. He is shimmying with excitement. Who knew the little matter of a walk could do such wonders for his mood? I take the leash while Monalisa hands Kevin some plastic poop bags.

Outside, Boo yanks the leash, rushing to sniff a palm tree. I pull him back, away from a brown-green splatter of something unpleasant looking.

"Don't let him eat that," Kevin says.

"Thanks for the advice," I say, increasing the pressure, tilting back like a water skier. Boo gives me a backward look and whines.

"Absolutely not," I say.

He trots on to the next palm tree, circling it slowly. I circle the tree alongside him. Kevin watches, fiddling with his hands as he shifts from one foot to the other.

About a half-minute later, we're back on the sidewalk, actually moving forward. Kevin gazes into the distance, his expression grave. This does not appear to be a man glowing with happiness from an exciting new sexual conquest.

"I take it the honeymoon with Lady Gaga is over."

His head angles to the side. "It wasn't like that."

"Where is she?"

His eyes cloud over. "Away. I'm not sure where."

I can't resist some snark. "I hope you enjoyed your visit to Italy."

He frowns at the sidewalk. "I screwed up. But I wasn't unfaithful to Charise. I know how it looks, but Joni needed help. She was in serious trouble and I could help her. She didn't have anyone else."

I could point out that Joni has a sister, Nicole, who presumably would count as someone who could help, but decide to let it slide. As Charise observed, men are suckers for needy women. There's no use arguing the point with Kevin so I decide to satisfy my curiosity.

"It was your uncle who arranged for the Lady Gaga lookalikes to sweep you off your feet?"

Kevin has the decency to wince. "Yes. And Zakan made it happen."

"Great way to end a marriage before it begins."

"My family wasn't enthusiastic about my relationship with Charise."

I feel a pang of disgust for Uncle Dave, which I try to release through a long exhale. Boo jangles his collar. I rub behind his ears, and we continue down the block.

"After you took off with Nicole and Joni, you went drinking. I'm told you never drink."

"Almost never. That night, I wanted to escape my life. I just wanted out. Have you ever felt like that?"

Uh, yes. "Occasionally."

"We went to a bar. Nicole left early because she had to teach a class the next morning. After she left, Joni told me she stole some money so she could leave the drug business. Her story freaked me out, which made me drink even more, and I'm a lightweight. She begged me to help her escape."

"Why didn't you let Charise know?"

"After we left the city, Joni was terrified she'd be found. She was convinced she'd be killed. She was a wreck. She couldn't even keep food down."

"She must have taken a boatload of money."

"Yes," he says. "She was in a cash business. Anyway, she agreed I could call my mom, as long as I didn't reveal our where-abouts. I didn't tell Joni but I also contacted my uncle. He was panicked, thinking Traftech had abducted me to pressure him."

"What made you decide to come back?"

"I needed to face my problems. It also became clear that Joni could take care of herself."

"What's going on with Charise?"

Kevin stops. I stop. Boo stops. Boo tilts his head at us.

Kevin opens his mouth then closes it. I wait. Boo barks.

"It's complicated," Kevin says.

"It's never complicated," I say. "You don't love her anymore, right?"

"I do love her. And I have these feelings for..." He squirms, and I wonder if he's going to cough up a five-inch stiletto bootie.

"For what?" I ask, wondering if I should do the Heimlich maneuver on him.

"For other..."

"You're interested in someone else?"

"I'm not a big fan of labels."

I'm not either but they can come in handy. "Are you—"

"I'm attracted to men."

"You're only figuring this out now?"

Boo tugs on the leash. We continue walking.

"I thought I loved Charise. Then I thought I didn't. Now I think I still love her."

"You're bisexual." Yes, that's me, using labels. "And you love Charise. And you disappeared with another woman, but weren't intimate with her."

He nods.

"Wow," I say, thinking: *what a mess.* Some investigator I am. I didn't see this coming, not at all.

"Charise won't speak to me. She has every right to be furious. Angela, I need to speak to her. She's my best friend."

I am beginning to understand what he wants from me.

He gives me this pleading look. I sink a few inches under its force.

"I'll talk to her," I say. "But only because I think this might make her feel better."

Boo shoots out in front of us. A quartet of Gambol's quail run for their lives, zipping across the street and into some thorn bushes. I fly forward, my feet slapping pavement.

"Boo," I say. "Back. Now."

Boo turns and wags his bottom. He rushes up to us, rubbing against my leg. I scratch his head.

Capitalizing on my weakness during this charged emotional

moment, Kevin says, "You'll tell Charise how much I care about her?"

I look up at him. "I'll get down on my knees and beg her to talk to you."

"You're not serious."

"Of course not."

AMID A ROOM full of moving boxes, Charise takes the news about Kevin as well as might be expected. "Damn," she says, sitting on a stack of book boxes and brushing her sleeves, which are flecked with cardboard bits. She has helped me move some boxes from my bedroom to the living room. Moorea said the boxes needed to be in a tight, orderly formation for the movers.

"I don't think he's been unfaithful to you," I say. "Mostly, he seems confused."

"Just what am I supposed to do with that? In relationship-speak, we both know 'confused' is a close relative of 'complicated.' And when I hear crap like 'it's complicated,' all I know is I better run."

"He said he still loves you."

She takes a deep inhale then exhales loudly. "You had to tell me that."

"I'm only the messenger," I say. "But go ahead and shoot. I'm used to it."

For a moment, we don't speak. Charise's eyes turn inward. I've given her a heaping load of craziness to sort through.

A minute later, she smiles. "What was going on between you and the smack kingpin?"

"Nothing."

"Don't you nothing me, Angela. That might work with your mom, but I know how much you like trouble. That homeboy gave you the goods. Something was going on between you two."

"There may have been some flirtation."

"Were you interested or were you just toying with him?"

"It was complicated." We both laugh. "I was confused." We laugh again. "Truthfully, he really did get to me. He also scared me to death."

"You found yourself the king of bad boys."

"On Saturday night he suggested he get us a hotel room. If I'd said yes, maybe he'd still be alive."

"Maybe. And maybe you wouldn't have survived. Didn't he kill people who got in his way?"

"He didn't seem like that kind of person."

"Did you believe your spa doctor would inject crap into patients to make a few more bucks?"

"No."

"People never believe it when they find out a neighbor is a serial killer or drug kingpin."

"You're right," I say.

She smiles. "You still don't believe your Russian was a stone-cold killah."

"Doesn't matter," I say. "Are you going to take pity on Kevin and talk to him?"

She stands up. "Eventually."

We walk to the door. "Eventually?"

She wiggles her fingers in the air. The massive rock is no longer on her engagement finger. She wears no rings whatsoever. And she looks like a little kid about to dig into a bowl of strawberry ice cream.

"I'm going to Italy tomorrow," she says. "My mom is coming with me. We've both always dreamed of going."

I gave Charise a small hug. "Congratulations."

As she skips out the door, she says, "Try not to do anything dumb while I'm away."

~

IN THE EARLY AFTERNOON, a slender business-sized envelope from the Salvador Foundation arrives in the mail. The letter inside is addressed to Mr. Angela Cray. It's from the Salvador Foundation Award Committee. I stand at the front door to the house and read the letter.

"Congratulations on your success in reducing the availability of heroin in our community and in helping root out corruption in city government. Your investigation was as impressive as it was dogged. Unfortunately, we cannot support individuals whose livelihood is connected with uncovering crime. Additionally, we cannot condone individual vigilantism, no matter how well meaning."

What? I reread the letter. *Individual vigilantism?* I suppose they'd turn down Supergirl as well. Aren't all superheroes vigilantes? I can almost hear Zakan's laughter.

I go out of the house and toss the letter into the recycling bin. Who needs them? Monalisa said we'd have plenty of business in the coming months. She's received a number of calls about potential new work. Some of the callers may even be halfway sane. If all goes well, I'll keep busy through the summer. Come fall, I'll be taking some criminal justice classes.

Take that, Salvador Foundation Award Committee!

WITH MY PACKING MOSTLY FINISHED, I exile myself onto the back patio with a Vitamin Water Zero. I sit on the back step and try not to think about how much I'll miss having a back yard. The fairy dusters are in bloom. Hummingbirds jostle each other at the feeder.

Moorea slides the patio doors open and pops her head outside. "I just stopped by to see how you're doing. You finished packing?"

Trust but verify is Moorea's motto. She and Roy have already moved their things into the new house. As usual, I'm the laggard.

"There's only the bedding I'll be sleeping on tonight. I'll box it up before the movers arrive." I laugh and sigh at the same time, my version of multitasking. "What a week."

Moorea shakes her head. "There's never a good time to move. At least we don't have to deal with the reporters any longer."

The press beach is gone, the reporters having taken off for other, more entertaining destinations. Yesterday, the police busted a house full of sex therapists. The police said it was a brothel. The sex therapists claimed otherwise.

"Fame is overrated," I say.

"There's this one persistent woman I keep spotting. Today she was near the end of the block." Moorea grins. "I had a chat with her. I don't think she'll be bothering us anymore."

I follow Moorea into the kitchen, where she pulls out her house keys and puts them on the counter. "I'll come by tomorrow morning again to check on things. But I don't want to forget to leave the keys. You can let me in tomorrow."

This reminds me of my own keys, which is probably what Moorea was trying to accomplish. I dig into my backpack and pull out a key chain with two keys, a silver house key and a small gold key. My breath catches for a moment as I finger the keys.

Moorea asks, "What are those?"

"Zakan's house keys," I say. "I should have given them to the police but I forgot."

Surprisingly, I don't get a lecture from Moorea. "They're no good to anyone now."

"True," I say, studying the gold key, which looks like it's for a suitcase or mailbox. It has a number on it, #549, and tiny print that says, "Business Inc."

Moorea says, "By the way, did we get any mail today? I put a forwarding order in for tomorrow."

Business Inc. has ads all over Phoenix. They provide mailbox services. Curiosity wells up inside me.

Moorea waves a hand in front of my face. "Earth to Angela. Did we get any mail today?"

"Yes, there was a letter for me. It's in the recycling bin."

"I'm going to do a last sweep of the rooms."

The gold key glints in the sun. If you are attempting to live in a completely private, anonymous way, you'd have your mail delivered to a postal box. That would be my advice to someone trying to protect his or her privacy.

The mailman doesn't even know who I am.

My hands tingle. I try to calm myself down. Zakan must have cleaned out everything from his postal box before he left. Wouldn't he have?

Yes. He left a paper trail for me to find. And the police found other evidence in his house, proof that he ran a heroin distribution operation.

Why would he have left that proof in his house? He was retiring. *No.* He was rushing to leave town and got sloppy. *No.* He was killed before he could wrap up his business.

I turn the key over in my palm.

Moorea stands in the doorway. "All clear."

"Do you think I could borrow your car for a little bit?"

"Sorry, Angela. I'm about to head back to the other house."

"I'll drive you there and return within an hour."

"You need to run some errands?"

"Yes." My heart rate revs.

"What kind of errands exactly?" Moorea asks.

My mind scrambles: detergent, broom, toilet paper, sponges, kitchen gloves, microfiber cloths. Unfortunately, I already bought all these items with Roy. They are in my new apartment, awaiting my arrival. And Moorea knows it.

"Forget it," I say. "I'll figure something else out."

Moorea walks over to me and arranges a hank of my hair behind my ear, the way she used to when I was seven. It bugged me then and it bugs me now.

"It's that mail key isn't it?"

Why does she have to be so smart? "Yes."

"We should give those keys to the police."

"Don't you want to take a peek first? We'll give them everything afterward. I don't think there's even anything in there."

We stare at each other for a moment.

She sighs and says, "Fine, I'll go with you."

She says this as if I've been begging her to accompany me and she's finally giving in to my pleas.

On the way to Business Inc., Moorea glances in the rear view mirror. Several times.

"What is it?" I ask.

She shakes her head. "Nothing."

Twenty minutes later we are at Business Inc., where Moorea is insisting to the counter guy that I should have access to the postal box even though it is not registered in my name. The problem is that the number stamped on the postal box key is not the actual number of the postal box. We need to get that number from the counter guy.

"The owner gave my daughter the key. He left important papers for her in there."

The counter guy looks about sixteen-years-old. He folds his stick-like arms across his concave chest. Reedy though he is, he's weathering the blast from Moorea surprisingly well.

"We have our rules," he says.

"The owner gave Angela his house keys and his cat."

I show him the other key and a photo of Pepper, which Jim took when the cat first moved into his place. Pepper is gazing out of her cat carrier, looking small and lost.

"Can't you help us?" I ask.

He glances at the photo then back at me and shakes his head.

Moorea says, "She needs instructions and prescriptions for the cat."

Nice story, Mom! I flash Pepper's photo again. As the counter guy gazes into Pepper's eyes, his face softens. His shoulders hunch.

"Don't get me fired," he says.

Moorea holds a finger against her lips. "We promise. Not a word."

He looks up the account on the computer and tells us the mail box number.

With Moorea hovering over my shoulder, I open the box and pull out two manila envelopes, one quite a bit thicker than the other. The return address is Zakan's house. It looks like he mailed both of these to his own box. My body quivers with excitement.

"You finished?" the counter guy asks.

"Yes, thanks. These should have everything we need."

BACK AT HOME, Moorea and I hover over the kitchen island, the two envelopes in front of us. The first envelope contains printouts of bank records, some of which I've already seen. A small notebook has the times and dates of meetings with Dave Newman, written in black pen.

"This was his insurance," Moorea says. "He probably expected to be betrayed."

I open the second, thicker envelope and empty it out on the island. We take in a written letter, a notebook, bank record print outs, and a flash drive. Keeping records on dead trees seems so old school. But many people wouldn't think to look for paper.

Moorea opens the folded letter and presses it flat on the counter.

> Dear Crime Fighter,
>
> In the event you are reading this, I am probably dead. Nicole Bruin is the largest distributor of heroin in the Valley. She first hired me under the pretense of providing security for her and

her other celebrity lookalikes, who appeared at clubs and events. Soon, I learned she and her team muled large amounts of heroin throughout the area.

After discovering this, I attempted to tender my resignation. Alas, Nicole does not abide by America's wonderful labor laws. She gave me two choices: continue working for her or exit the drug business feet first.

I chose life. You can see how well that worked out for me. Enclosed is documentation supporting these claims.

Happy hunting,

Alexander E. Zakan

"My goodness," Moorea says, her gaze shifting beyond me. She looks a shade paler than usual.

"This is shocking," I say.

Moorea isn't listening. Her attention is focused elsewhere.

Nicole Bruin, aka Dolly Gaga, is in our dining room. She is walking toward us, pointing a handgun at my head. It's a small gun with a long snout, which I realize is probably an apparatus for silencing noise.

NB Entertainment. Nicole Bruin. Dear lord. Joni was fleeing her sister.

"Alex told me about the mailbox," Nicole says. "It took a lot of persuasion to extract this information from him. But I'm so glad I did."

Moorea's hand flutters toward her heart. "No."

"Put it back in the envelope," Nicole says.

"Other people know about this," I say.

"Right," Nicole replies, with a sharp laugh.

Moorea is shrinking, folding into herself. This is my fault. Of course we should have given the police the keys. Of course Moorea was right.

"Take everything," I say. "But please don't hurt my mom. She hasn't been involved at all. She won't say anything."

"That's sweet." Nicole tilts her head sympathetically. "But business is business."

"No," I say, my voice cracking.

"It's a business decision. This is exactly what I told Alex before he got eliminated." Nicole grins. "Think of death as your next big mother-daughter adventure."

Moorea's chest rolls like she's going to vomit. "Please don't hurt my baby."

"Your baby." She points the gun at my forehead. "Your baby is a major pain in the ass."

Moorea is unraveling. She's shaking. Her face is cratering, and I want to die. With shaking hands, I shuffle the letter and the flash drive and the rest of the items back into the manila envelope, which I extend to Nicole.

As she reaches for it, I drop it onto the floor.

"Oh," Nicole says, drawing out the word into dangerous territory.

I catch only a glint of metal before the gun whacks the side of my face. All around me, the world shakes. I hear myself gagging. As I bob downward, Moorea flashes across my vision, a storming blur of fabric, a thrusting fist, a boulder crashing down a mountain.

Nicole yells. Moorea seems to be draped around Nicole's neck.

I reach toward them, trying to help, but I nearly fall over. Grey specks fill my vision. I shake my head, trying to clear my sightline.

"Stay put, Angela," Moorea says.

I turn, reaching for a knife from the butcher block. My hand grabs at air. The counter is empty, the knives packed and gone.

Nicole yowls. Moorea has hold of Nicole's wrist, which is bending in on itself. Nicole's mouth is one gaping, agonized circle. Moorea is hunched over, pressing hard into that wrist joint. With a long groan, Nicole lets go of the gun, and it clatters onto the floor. I swoop down and pick it up. I point the gun at Nicole, bracing myself against the kitchen island for balance.

"I've got the gun," I say.

"It's okay, honey," Moorea says. "Put the gun somewhere safe right now."

Nicole, on her tiptoes, howls. With Moorea still cranking the wrist joint, Nicole is contorting into herself. It looks like she's being suspended from the ceiling by the crook of her elbow.

Moorea gazes at me and does the most amazing thing. She smiles. I smile back and almost lose my balance.

With one hand on Nicole's wrist, Moorea uses her other hand to press her fingers against Nicole's neck, right below her ear.

"You think my daughter is a pain in the ass?" she asks. "Try me for size."

I look down. I'm still holding the handgun.

"Call 911," Moorea says.

I put the gun down and call 911. The operator has many questions. I tell her we're busy trying to subdue a woman who attacked us with a firearm. I tell the operator my mom is holding her own against the psychopath but we need reinforcements. After that, I yell out our address in one burst of breath.

A moment later, Nicole's head bobs onto her chest. Moorea steps away, letting Nicole crumple onto the floor.

"Gun," Moorea says.

I give her the gun.

Moorea aims the gun at Nicole. Moorea isn't even sweating. Her eyebrows are knit together with a look of steady concentration. She could be reading a low-fat cookbook in dim light.

I open my mouth. A strange sound comes out. A Martian language.

"What?" Moorea laughs. "You think I've never taken a gun away from a crazy person? I've taken away guns, bats, knives, screwdrivers, golf clubs, you name it."

My badass mother. I'm shaking my head, saying, "Of course."

"How do you think I paid for nursing school? I was the front-line person at a mental health clinic. Five years of that and you learn something."

Nicole groans, and I leap about a foot straight up in the air. She is stirring, her feet pedaling.

"Get down there," Moorea says.

"Down where?" I ask.

"Secure her," Moorea says. "Get on her back. She's going to fight, and I don't want to have to use this gun today."

I kneel down and push Nicole over onto her stomach. I straddle her back.

"What the hell?" Nicole says, twisting upward. She starts to writhe. My knees and thighs tense, trying to keep her in place.

"Pin that skinny girl's arms," Moorea says. "Use your weight to press down."

I clasp her arms and press hard.

"You," Nicole says, rolling back and forth, "are going to die."

"Keep pressing," Moorea says. "I'm a nurse and a Christian. You know I don't want to have to shoot this woman."

I push so hard my arms shake. My teeth clamp together. My thighs quiver. Nicole is fish flopping. I can't hold on for too much longer.

I gasp, "I don't think—"

"Remember to breathe."

I inhale and expel a roomful of air. *Ouch.*

"Hold her there," Moorea says. "That's a good girl."

The sound of a siren fills the air. Soon I hear several sirens. A tangle of them.

"We got her," Moorea says. "Don't loosen your grip, sweetheart." Moorea laughs. "I love you so much, honey. Just smash that woman into the floor with all your might. You can do it. You're my daughter. This is how I raised you."

"I love you."

"Of course you do. But don't make me shoot this woman. I could lose my nursing license."

Several minutes later, our living room bursts with armed police personnel. Two strapping young men airlift me off Nicole. My legs are like noodles when they set me back on the ground. I am shaking all over.

Moorea tells the police who Nicole is and why she broke into our house. She hands an officer Zakan's letter. The police surround Nicole.

A moment later, Moorea walks over and wraps an arm around my shoulders. She gives me a squeeze. "You okay?"

I manage to make a positive-sounding noise. Of course, the woman who actually engaged in hand-to-hand combat is comforting me.

As the police take Nicole away, I say a silent little prayer of gratitude.

Thank you to the spirit who gave me life and to Moorea, my mother who art on earth, healing the sick and fighting evildoers. Thank you, oh dad who art in heaven, for giving me strength. Iona, who also art in heaven, I am so lucky to count you as my best friend. I promise to write again soon. Roy, I am deeply grateful for your kindness and the stir-fry that has sustained my body. Monalisa, wise elder and provider of employment opportunities, thank you for setting a high bar. I owe you. I will pay you back soon, I swear. Boo, thank you for your unconditional love. Charise and Kevin, I wish you great happiness, whether you find it together or apart. Thank you, oh goddess, mother of the sky, moon, and sea, for I have been truly blessed.

Amen.

Now pass me a freaking Milano gimlet before I faint.

THE END

ACKNOWLEDGMENTS

Although crime writers traffic in tales of mischief and mayhem, they are among the most supportive people you'll meet. Many thanks to Virginia Caggiano and Marta Tanrikulu for their editorial guidance. Denise Dietz did a terrific job editing the manuscript, saving me from my worse impulses. Well, at least she tried to do that.

Wendy Grant, dear friend and ace writer and editor, provided invaluable assistance in reviewing draft text and helping compress this novel into a few snappy paragraphs.

A big thank you to the judges of the 2016 Freddie Awards for Writing Excellence, a contest sponsored by the Florida Chapter of the Mystery Writers of America. Becoming a finalist gave me the nudge I needed to finish the novel and release it into the world.

A shout out to the dynamic duo, Andrew and Rebecca Brown from Design for Writers, for the cover.

Special thanks to supporters, tastemakers, and fellow travelers: Sarah Anderson, Renae Ask, Debbie Barker, Samantha Bennett, Amy Berg, Daniel del Castillo, Tish Hicks, Gabrielle

Karras, Giulietta Karras, Renee Moore, Cheryl Owen, Rhonda Smith, Sarah Sullivan, and Margaret Weber.

None of this nonsense would have been possible without my family, including my parents and rabble-rousing brothers, Andrew Carr, Chuck Carr, and Richard Carr.

ABOUT THE AUTHOR

Dara Carr lives in Mount Rainier, Maryland. Her short stories have appeared in *Alfred Hitchcock's Mystery Magazine, Ellery Queen's Mystery Magazine,* and *Shotgun Honey. Angela Cray Gets Real* was a finalist for a Freddie Award for Writing Excellence.

If you'd like to get an email when Dara's next novel or short story is released, visit her mailing list sign-up page. You will only be contacted when she releases something new. Your address will never be shared.

Thank you for reading this book. Reviews are critical for any author to succeed. If you have the time and inclination, please consider leaving a review. A few quick sentences would be greatly appreciated.

www.daracarr.com